A *Note* OF CHANGE

TIMELESS
Victorian
COLLECTION

A *Note* OF
CHANGE

ESTHER HATCH • NICOLE VAN • ANNETTE LYON

Interior Design by Cora Johnson
Edited by Joanne Lui and Lisa Shepherd
Cover design by Rachael Anderson and Nichole Van
Cover Photo Credit: Arcangel, photographer: Ildiko Neer

Published by Mirror Press, LLC
Timeless Romance Anthology® is a registered trademark of Mirror Press, LLC

ISBN-13: 978-1-947152-93-9

TABLE OF CONTENTS

Waiting for the Post

-ESTHER HATCH-

"Love is begun by time . . . time qualifies the spark
and fire of it."

—William Shakespeare

One

PROGRESS, AT TIMES, can demand a step backward. Surely, Harrison Chase had heard that somewhere before.

Harrison eyed his minute office. Mrs. Ryan had finished unpacking and organizing his desk, but boxes of books still littered what was left of the floor space. This office had only one small bookcase, whereas his last office had walls of shelves.

His old ambitions had sloughed off like a layer of heavy clothing. He still had plans—plans that would require as much work as his former desires to make a wealthy man of himself. But he wasn't working alone now, and he wasn't doing all of this for personal gain.

It was time to burn the one last relic of his old life that remained.

There was no fire going in the fireplace, but there were two candles on the mantle that should do the job just as well.

It only took two steps to reach his desk from the doorway. He marched around it, sat on his oak chair, and pulled out the two middle drawers centered along the topside of his desk. Those two drawers were the reason he purchased this desk. He lay each of the drawers on top of his desk and pulled on the wooden divider that separated the two empty slots the drawers had left behind. The divider slid out of the desk and with it came a secret drawer attached to the back. It was long and thin—the perfect place to hide a letter.

He slipped his hand into the narrow opening, expecting the softened envelope of a well-worn letter. All he felt was the smooth wooden sides of the drawer.

Harrison pushed the two other drawers aside and flipped the secret drawer upside down.

Nothing.

He dumped out the contents of his desk drawer and scattered about the papers, pens, and mementos from the last six years of his life, but it wasn't there. He opened a few of the boxes of books—nothing.

He slammed one fist down on the desk, causing pens to roll and a solitary paper to flutter to the floor. The Christine letter didn't matter. He had been about to burn the deuced thing. It didn't represent anything—not like it used to. He couldn't even remember the last time he had looked at it.

Nothing was more useless than that letter.

He closed his eyes and went through the move in his head. Mrs. Ryan and a maid they had hired for the day had boxed up each item in his desk at Matlock Nail and Co. Mrs. Ryan had done the unpacking herself.

He stormed out of the small, cramped study, half the size of his last one. Mrs. Ryan must have thrown out some of the useless garbage he had managed to keep with him during his years working at the nail factory.

"Mrs. Ryan," he called up the stairs. She was busy putting linens on the bed, and had been overworked ever since he had decided to move. He hated to add more to her plate, but he wouldn't be able to relax until that letter was found. Harrison took the stairs two at a time and met his housekeeper as she was leaving his bedroom.

"Yes, Mr. Chase?"

"I seem to have misplaced a letter."

Mrs. Ryan nodded, but didn't answer.

"It was addressed to a Miss Stone," Harrison said. "Have you seen it?"

Mrs. Ryan smiled. "Oh *that* letter. No need to worry about it."

A small pit at the bottom of his stomach twisted with the thought of never looking at the letter again, but he pushed it down. For years, it had driven him, encouraged him to work later and harder than anyone else. But he was a different man than he had been six years ago. His choices over the last few months had proven that. "You threw it out?"

"Threw it out?" Mrs. Ryan's face scrunched together. "I would never throw out any of your papers. I posted it for you."

Harrison reached for the banister behind him. He dug his fingers into the hard, dark wood. "You posted it?"

"Yes," she nodded, the cap on her head bouncing in a nonchalant way, as if its owner hadn't just been the orchestrator of what was certain to become the most deeply embarrassing moment of his life. Her eyes widened, and her hand went to her chest. "Wasn't I supposed to? It was sealed and ready. I dropped it off this morning."

This morning? It would already be on its way out of London by now. Mrs. Ryan was the only servant he had dared keep, and she had offered to come at her rate from two years ago. She was the only person who believed in him enough to stake her living on it. He let go of the banister and smiled. "It is fine," he said. I was worried I had lost it, was all. How did you even find it?"

"Oh, that was easy; it was on the top of all the other things Nancy had removed from the desk while I'd been busy boxing up your books. They aren't all going to fit here, you know. You may have to get rid of some."

"There are other rooms besides my study. We will find a place for them." There was a hard edge to his voice he couldn't control, despite his pretended calm. Mrs. Ryan was a close friend—much more than a servant. But how could she have mailed that letter without contacting him first?

"Where? In the kitchen?"

"If need be."

Mrs. Ryan laughed. "There isn't a cook in London who would put up with that. Even if you do become a Member of Parliament. It is fortunate you've only got me to do the cooking." She leaned forward with interest. "Who is this Miss Stone? Are you thinking of hiring a maid? I know some fine ones right here in London, so no need to uproot someone from Dorset. Nancy likes her new employer, but I'm certain she would return and work for you if you asked."

"No, she isn't a maid."

"A wealthy spinster who would like to support your candidacy?"

"No. She isn't anyone important. Someone I knew while growing up."

That made her eyes light up like hot iron. "An old flame?"

Harrison gritted his teeth. "No."

Mrs. Ryan laughed. "Of course it isn't. I know you better than that. I've never seen your head turned by a young lady. You've got your ambition."

"Quite right." Harrison turned to go back down the stairs, but glanced back at Mrs. Ryan before he reached them. She was headed back into the bedroom. "Mrs. Ryan, would you please pack my trunk and have it sent to Dorset? I believe I will visit my parents before I get too busy with the Anti-Corn Law League."

"What a wonderful idea. The League can't fault you for spending some of your money on a trip home. You will still have plenty if they need it come an election. I'm certain your family will be so pleased to see you."

They would be. He hadn't been home once in the six years since he had left, although they came to visit him fairly regularly. But his first order of business wouldn't be a visit with his parents. He had a letter to intercept. If Christine Stone—or, even worse, her brother Gerald—managed to read that letter, his humiliation would be unbearable. It was bad enough he was about to embark on a campaign that would fight the very laws set up to protect a wealthy land owner like Gerald's father. If his good friend read the letter Harrison had written his sister, he would never allow himself to set foot in Dorset again.

Two

MEMORIES WASHED PAST Harrison's eyes. He tightened his hands around the reins of his rented horse while it crossed over onto the Stone Property. He hadn't visited in over six years. The train ride to Dorset was only a few hours long. He should have come back to visit his parents, at least. But Harrison had promised himself he wouldn't return until he had made his fortune and could approach Gerald Stone—not as a poor neighbor and one time friend—but as an equal. One qualified to ask to court his younger sister.

That promise had caused him to work harder than most of the young men at the nail factory where he had found employment. Even his work ethic wouldn't have been enough, though. He had seen many poor young men work as hard as he did, yet they didn't get the chances he had.

Even all the way in London, the influence from the Stone family had helped him. He spoke better than most of the boys, and his handwriting was legible and clear. After a year of shaping nails, he moved up to the position of scribe, then office manager. Four years after starting at Matlock Nail, the company owner found himself in trouble after a late night of piquet. In desperation, he sold a fourth of the company to Harrison.

Two years of scrimping later, Harrison bought the rest of it.

Luck had brought him to the one nail company whose owner was more interested in ready money than income.

He was owner for six months before the first strike hit. There was never enough money to go around in the nail business, and it was always the workers that took the brunt of the burden. He navigated that strike as best he could, pleading with the other factory owners to raise their wages.

Two months into the strike was the first time a factory worker had brought a starving child to his door. It wouldn't be the last.

Harrison clicked his tongue and nudged his horse forward with his heel. He just needed to get this over with so he could return to London.

He hadn't heard of Christine marrying. For the first few years, his hands would shake with worry every time he opened a letter from his parents, certain she would have been snatched up by some gentleman. In the last year, he had stopped listening for news of her. She was twenty-one. Her future was most likely sorted out by now. And his plans had changed. Saving money to court a leisurely lady while children were starving because of the high cost of grain was no longer something he allowed himself to do.

Besides, Christine's eyes wouldn't light up at the sight of him like they had when they were young. She probably wouldn't even recognize him. She was kind, and had probably thought about the poor steward's son a time or two after he had left, but if he had to wager money on it, he would bet she hadn't thought of him for the past four or five years.

Which was just as well, since Christine must have changed as much as he had. She wouldn't wade in streams anymore or leave her hair down in a long braid. She wouldn't hold a tenant's wee baby in her arms, making him ache to become a parent with her. The person to whom he had written that letter no longer existed.

The young, idealistic man who wrote that letter, filled with hopes and dreams, no longer existed, either.

Stonehouse came into view on his next turn. He had always felt astonished that one family could live on such an enormous estate, but after seeing some of the magnificent homes of London, he was oddly let down. It was as if Stonehouse had been replaced by a smaller, less inspiring version of itself. Large, grey stones still made up the walls, and windows still lined the first and second stories. But surely, there had been more of them when he was a boy.

He truly had outgrown this place.

A yelp to his left turned his attention to the stream that followed his path.

He pulled on the reins and drew his horse to a standstill.

Another yelp—this one followed by a groan—came from the stream that was mostly hidden by trees. The noises were feminine and frustrated.

He dropped from his horse and ran to the side of the path. Looping the reins to a tree branch that wouldn't hold the horse if he really wanted to get away, Harrison navigated the dense underbrush that led to the stream.

A young lady with her back to him was halfway across the stream, her voluminous skirts pulled up nearly to her knees. She slipped on a rock, but managed to right herself, only to have her skirt drop into the water and pull her once again off-balance.

Her hair hung in a long, dark braid down her back.

Christine. She held something in a bundle in her arms, but he couldn't see it from this angle. If it was a baby, though, he would eat his hat.

Her boots were on this side of the river, stockings laid out next to them.

He should most definitely leave.

But he couldn't. Not quite yet. Harrison stood in the dark shade from the trees lining the stream. Had she received his letter? It was nearly impossible to beat the mail coach anywhere. If she had, what would she think of him?

Christine waded in the sunlight, flashes of light seeming to bounce off of her. She jerked to one side, stepping on a stone that must not have been steady, but righted herself almost immediately with a peal of laughter.

Christine's laughter.

It hadn't changed. It still sounded like a string of bells hung up by the seashore, the wind pulling music from them in waves. He inhaled deeply, closed his eyes, and simply listened. While Harrison had been out slaving over a hot iron, or meticulously copying number after number on his boss's expense sheets and order books, Christine had been here, growing older, but staying the same.

Her skirts caught once again in the current of the stream, and even though it wasn't swift, her skirts must have weighed upwards of twenty pounds when wet. Her feet stumbled about, trying to find a firm stepping place. Without thinking, Harrison pushed away from the tree he was leaning against and stomped through the calf-deep water, catching her by the waist as she was about to fall in.

Christine screamed but grabbed his lapel with her one free hand. Her earlier thrashing about had splashed water on her face, and her eyes were closed. Her bundle was much too small to be a child. So at least his hat was safe.

He shouldn't have his heavy, work-ridden hand on her person, but if he were to let go, she would still fall. She still hadn't been able to find her equilibrium. Her feet slipped about on the rocks.

"Gerald, I told you not to follow me," she said as she wiped her eyes on the shoulder of her dress.

When her thick, water-splashed eyelashes raised and her eyes opened, so did her mouth, forming a perfect O. She pushed away from Harrison, as she should have when he had first taken hold of her. He loosened his grip, and she tumbled into the water.

She sat half-submerged in the clean water of the stream. Her nose scrunched up, and she let out a frustrated groan.

Harrison pulled his lips together. It was his first time seeing Christine again. He would not laugh at her. She didn't even seem to remember who he was, which meant she must not have received the letter. He had somehow managed to beat it here.

She slapped a hand down on the water and struggled to rise, her bundle making the task difficult.

He held his hand out to her.

"Oh, no," Christine said, still trying to find a way to stand with the yard of wet fabric weighing her down. "You don't get to help me now—not when you have so callously dumped me here."

A deep chuckle rose from his chest. Even if she had forgotten him, she was the same.

"And now you're laughing?" Her head spun, and for the second time, he caught sight of the amber eyes that had haunted his dreams for years. "Fine, you can help me." She lifted her hand out of the water and reached up in his direction.

He narrowed his eyes at her. In their youth, she had pulled him into the water more times than he could count. Gerald, too.

"You won't pull me down?" he asked.

"What kind of person do you think I am?"

She definitely didn't remember him. Harrison Chase knew almost everything there was to know about Christine

Stone. He deepened his stance in the water, just in case, and reached out to her.

Her bare hand tightened around his gloved one. She didn't pull, but instead used him to help get her feet under herself. She must have matured, after all. He relaxed his posture.

She dropped her bundle into the stream, reached up to him with her other hand, and pulled down with all her might.

Harrison tried to keep his balance, but to do so, he would have had to step forward onto her skirts. His foot shot out to the side, but it wasn't enough to save him. He landed in a heap sitting next to her. Whatever had been in her hands had dropped to the bottom of the stream, and the cloth she had wrapped around it floated away on the current. She placed a hand on his shoulder and stood up in the most gracious manner a soaking-wet woman could do.

Once she was standing, she looked down at him and gestured toward his shoulder with her defiant chin. "Thank you for the help."

It would have been a grand departure had her skirts not been wet. She could barely lift them as she gingerly placed one foot in front of the other.

Harrison jumped to his feet. He wasn't about to have her fall and pull him in again. She may not remember him, but she was his childhood friend. He came up behind her, dipped his hand to her knees, and swept her up into his arms. Every part of him that hadn't gotten wet in his fall was now soaking from her dripping skirts, but he didn't care. He just needed to get Christine out of the stream so he could make it to Stonehouse in one piece. If the letter came today, he would still have time to see his parents. Then he could be on his way back to London in the morning.

Christine was stiff in his arms, but she didn't scream or

hit him. He stepped carefully, not wanting to end up in the stream again. Each step was slow and calculated. He tested each rock before he stepped on it to ensure its sturdiness— never mind that it meant he could keep Christine in his arms a few seconds longer. He was breathing heavily by the time he placed her on the side of the stream, while she hadn't seemed to breathe at all.

Without knowing what else to do, he gave her a tip of his hat, which had somehow miraculously stayed on his head. She could find her own way back to Stonehouse. It was, after all, her home. Even though he had grown up here, it had never been his.

He had taken three steps toward his horse when he heard the rustling of the underbrush behind him. She reached for his arm and spun him around. Her feet were still bare, although he could no longer see them.

"Harry Chase," she said, her amber eyes on fire. "You come here after six years with no word from you, push me into the stream, make me drop the herring I snatched from Cook, and then tip your hat and walk away?"

Her hand was still on his arm, one delicate drop of water sliding from her temple, down her face, until it caught in a hollow under her cheekbone that hadn't been there before. His fingers ached to brush it away. *Harry.* He hadn't been called that in six years. Even his parents didn't call him Harry. Gerald and Christine were the only people in the world who called him that.

"Christine." The named formed on his lips like a caress, although he hadn't meant it to. Her eyes widened, but it was too late. He couldn't take it back now. At any rate, she had called him by his name first.

"It has been so many years—I have forgotten," he said. "What is the proper way to leave you after pushing you into a stream?"

"The proper way," Christine brought her other hand up to his elbow so she now held him by both arms and looked up into his eyes, "is to not leave at all."

The birds in the trees quieted, and even the stream seemed to still. He shouldn't have come back. He left too much behind in London for one moment with Christine to have him calculating what it would mean for his future if he simply stayed. But that wasn't what she meant. "Are you asking me to stay here while you put on your stockings?"

"I suppose I am. At any rate, you don't get to leave just yet." She jutted her chin out. "You may look the other way."

"I need to go to Stonehouse."

"Well, I happen to be going there as well. If you would be so kind as to wait for me, we can go together. After all, some-one needs to explain to Cook what happened to her herring."

"I thought you just said you stole it."

"Well, yes, I did. But thanks to you, it ended up in the stream."

"Were you planning on returning it, then?"

Christine's eyes fell, but then lifted half a moment later. Her face scrunched, and a hand went to one hip. If she weren't soaking wet and barefooted, she might have looked intimidating. "I might have. Now we will never know, will we?"

The corners of his lips threatened to raise. Christine would never admit to being wrong about anything. He pushed them back down though. He wasn't going to be taken in by her again. "Are you going to tell me what you were doing?"

"No." She spun and gingerly walked to where her shoes and stockings lay haphazardly on the ground. She reached down and picked up one of her shoes. Looking back at him, she sighed and scooped up a stocking. "I was looking for an otters' den. I had heard there was one near here."

"And the herring was . . ."

"For the otters. A welcome gift."

Not knowing a better way to respond, Harrison nodded. He didn't know what else to do. It had been too long since he had been in a world where leisure existed. Two days ago, he had met with Richard Cobden in a sunless London office, discussing the economic and moral injustice of the Corn Laws. Now, he stood near a bubbling stream surrounded by shrubbery, speaking to Christine, who had spent her afternoon searching for otters. How could two such different worlds exist?

"I'll turn my back while you put your shoes on."

Harrison rubbed his temples and looked at the ground. He simply needed to intercept that letter and return to London. He didn't belong here, not anymore. The less time he spent in the fresh air and sunshine, the better. There were children in London who had never had a day like this in their lives, and the sooner he returned to fight for them, the better.

Three

CHRISTINE SAT ON Harry's horse while he led them to the house, her dripping dress leaving trails of moisture down the side of her mount. In all her dreams of Harry returning home, being wet, clumsy, and tongue-tied had never been a part of them.

It was bad enough that she smelled like herring and was completely soaked. Why hadn't she thought to bring a pin for her hair? She must still look like a child.

Harry, on the other hand, had nothing of the young man she had known left in him. She could only see his back, with his arm hanging behind him as he held the reins. His hair had darkened from a sun streaked blond to a dusty brown. The width of his shoulders must have doubled in the time he was away. Even in her soaked dress, he had picked her up as if she had been a young girl. Lifting her onto his horse had been the same.

"What have you been doing since you left Stonehouse?" she asked him, no longer comfortable with the silence that had surrounded them since she put on her stockings. "Breaking boulders to clear a path for the railroad?"

His step faltered, but he didn't turn around or stop. "No."

One-word answers would get her nowhere. She could cross Navy off the list of possible types of employment, but there were thousands of other things he could have done.

"Are you married?"

This time, his step didn't falter. "No."

"Every time I asked Gerald or your father about you, all they ever said was, 'He is working hard and doing well.'" It had been so infuriating. After receiving similar answers from Gerald several times, she had resorted to asking Mr. Chase, their steward. No one felt the need to give her any specifics, and after a while, she stopped asking. Harry became a memory of a better time, when she had a friend to spend time with nearly every day.

The slow clops of the horse's hooves were as infuriating as Harry's one-word answers. Riding sidesaddle in a man's saddle was nearly impossible. She tried to reach forward to grip the bridle, but it threw her off balance. Without reaching the bridle, she couldn't make the horse come to a stop, but at the pace they were going, she hardly needed it to.

She slid down the side of the horse and landed—thankfully—on both feet.

Harry spun, finally looking at her. "What are you doing?" he asked. "We are nearly there."

"I know we are nearly there. That is why I dismounted."

"You don't want Gerald to see us together?"

Why would he think that? She didn't care what Gerald thought of the two of them talking together, although they were both wet and quite a mess. If he were any other man, she would perhaps be more circumspect, but Harry? He was practically family, and she needed some answers.

"I don't care who sees us together. But if you are going to be as taciturn as you have been up to this point, I will never hear what has occurred in your life since you left. If it wasn't the railroad that filled out your arms and chest, just what sort of work have you been doing?"

Harry's face went blank, and he blinked several times. He

pulled at his coat as if he was embarrassed by her mentioning his physical transformation. She had seen him swim in the creek with Gerald plenty of times, sometimes without their shirts. He couldn't be embarrassed by her mentioning his arms. What else could be making him uncomfortable? Perhaps, she shouldn't have asked about his line of work. What if he had been involved in businesses of ill repute? Would that have been cause for both his father's and her brother's silence on the matter? Harry wouldn't, though. He couldn't. He was one of the most upstanding men she knew.

He shook his head and marched up to her. "Nails," he finally answered, before crouching down and locking his fingers together. Oh, no. She wasn't ready to mount yet. She stood her ground.

"I haven't seen you for years, and that is the explanation you give as to what you have been doing? *Nails?*"

He uncupped his hands and straightened. Only a few inches apart, she was reminded again that this was not the young boy she had practically been raised with. Harry was a man. She shouldn't even be thinking of him as Harry. In front of her stood Mr. Harrison Chase, with dark stubble on his chin that she never would have seen on him when he left at 17. The muscles in his neck corded, making promises of what his arms would look like if he rolled up his sleeves. But the most striking change was his countenance. He hadn't smiled at her—not once. He had laughed at her when she fell in the stream, but laughing at her was very different from smiling. Behind his eyes was a dark storm of emotions that belied the carefree young man she had once known.

"Nails is the only answer I can give you." He leaned forward, and her stomach tightened. She shuffled one step back. "I have lived only for nails since leaving. I have spent days and nights making them. I have poured over accounts and ledgers full of them. I have slept and lived and breathed nails. If I could have, I would have eaten nails. So you see, Miss Stone, there is no other answer I can give. Nails. For six years, that is the only thing I have thought of. If it isn't an interesting enough topic for you, then I suggest we continue to ride in silence."

He crouched down once more, and this time, she carefully placed her foot in his hands. Once again, he lifted her into his saddle. The house wasn't far. She could have easily walked beside him, but it seemed as though Harry preferred distance between them.

"How long will you be here?" she asked. Harry suddenly showing up shouldn't change her plans. But if he were here to stay . . . ?

Harry pulled his horse forward. "A day. Perhaps two or three."

Christine lowered her head. Only a few days at most. No matter. Her plans would remain the same, then. Not that she would have changed them just because Harry came home. But now she didn't need to worry about it. She straightened. "Three days—that should be enough."

He took three steps before asking. "Enough for what?"

"To make you smile at me again, before you have to go back to living your life for nails."

If Christine had thought that would be enough to make him turn around and smile at her, she was wrong. Instead, he shook his head and groaned.

Four

HARRISON STOPPED HIS horse and its frustratingly inquisitive burden outside the front of Stonehouse. Growing up, he was certain there could be no place more grand than Gerald and Christine's home. It was still large, but not the massive, unforgiving place he had made it in his mind. Two stories tall, rectangular, with four large windows on each level, it was almost inviting and pleasant. He had been in much larger homes in London and felt no reason to question his place there. He kept his face forward as he waited for the sound of Christine sliding down from his horse.

"Won't you help me dismount?"

He turned. She was sitting atop his horse with her arms folded across her chest. He knew that look. She had given him that same look just before she had talked him into practicing her dance instructions with her. He held out as long as he could, but thanks to her, he was probably the only young man at the nail factory that could waltz as well as the owners.

Once he had become an owner, it had come in handy once or twice.

"You can dismount perfectly on your own. You did so only a moment ago."

"I did, but I noticed my ankle was a bit sore." He raised an eyebrow. She hadn't limped earlier. "It is—those rocks in the stream were quite slippery."

19

"Which is why most young ladies don't wade out in them."

"You could hardly call it wading. The water didn't even reach my knees."

"And yet, you managed to injure your ankle."

"Would you kindly help me down? Or should I yell in hopes of a footman hearing?"

And she had done it. Won again. He didn't trust her not to call out for a footman, and while it was one thing for her to return home half-drowned, it was quite another for them to be seen together in such a state.

The reins were soft in his hands as he strode over to her side. He would help her, then leave as quickly as possible. Women generally dismounted on their own. He had no idea what exactly she expected him to do. He reached an arm up, expecting her to take his hand and then dismount by sliding down the horse as she normally would. She wasn't in a riding habit, so once again, he turned his attention to Stonehouse.

Taking his eyes off of Christine was always a mistake.

Instead of taking his hand and sliding forward, she used it to pull him closer to the horse. Dropping his hand, she looped hers together and threw them around his neck. Her forward momentum propelled her off of the horse, crashing her into his chest. He stepped backward and, for the second time since returning, lost his footing. His feet fumbled, and his arms came about her waist as he tried to steady them both.

Her feet touched the ground, but she didn't release his neck.

Nor did he release her waist.

She smiled up at him with complete confidence. Her mouth always smiled, even when resting, but when she meant to smile, her light eyes brightened and her chin jutted out. People didn't smile like that in London—with every part of their faces. He had held women nearly this close as he danced with them, but none of them were Christine. Her face showed no signs of concern. It was as open and friendly as it had been when she was a child. His fingers bent into her back and he breathed in her scent, stream bed and sunshine. The damp smell of her clothing mixed with the floral scent of Dorset. Even wet, nothing in London smelled as fresh as she did.

A crunch of dirt announced the arrival of someone from the house. "Christine! What are you doing?" The voice was low and growling, but he would know it anywhere.

Gerald.

Harrison dropped Christine's waist. He was a cad. What had he been doing, exactly? Smelling Christine? He closed his eyes and waited for Gerald's fist to connect to his face. But it never came. "Harry?"

There it was again. That name. *Harry.*

Christine was pushed aside, and he was crushed instead into Gerald's embrace. "Harry! What the devil? I thought you were up to your neck in selling your nail company."

"*His* nail company?" Christine's soft voice floated to him from somewhere to his left. Gerald was making it hard to breathe, but the sensation wasn't unpleasant. Unlike Christine, he must have followed what Harrison had been doing, if he knew, and was still willing to hug him. Harrison pulled his friend tightly to him. The six years they had been apart seemed to melt away.

Gerald pushed away from him after a moment, and instead held Harrison by the shoulders. They examined each other. Gerald wasn't taller, or at least if he was, Harrison didn't notice it. But he was thicker—he had filled out. His formerly wild hair was parted to one side and tamed. He had become a man while Harrison was gone. Gerald was probably thinking the same thing about him.

Gerald narrowed his eyes and glanced back and forth between Harrison and Christine. "Why are the two of you wet?" His fingers dug firmly into Harrison's shoulders. "Did she push you into the stream for not visiting?" Gerald's dark eyes slid to his sister. She stood with her hands on her hips, neither apologetic nor worried about how her brother had found them. "I don't blame her. I have half a mind to do the same."

"One dousing in the stream is quite enough for me today. You will have to wait until tomorrow at least."

"How long will you be staying? This must be a busy time for you."

"Not as busy as it will be in a few weeks. I should be here for a day or two. It depends on a few things." Once he had that letter, he would return home as quickly as he could. It didn't do him well to see Dorset, so clean and welcoming, when he had plans to potentially break apart the economy here.

"Well, we will take you as long as we can. I hope you will dine with us this evening. Our parents are spending a few weeks visiting our aunt in Surrey. It would be just the three of us."

Dine with them? Even though he had spent the whole of his childhood here, he had never dined with the family. He was the steward's son. "That depends."

"Depends on what?"

"Will Miss Stone be planning on any more stunts, like pulling me into the stream?"

Christine snorted, throwing her head back in a manner that would have looked much more regal had she not been dripping wet, with a muddied hem.

"*Miss Stone*," Gerald said, looking to the sky. "Are you going to call me Mr. Stone? For heaven's sake, Harry, you are family. I'm sorry if you have been away so long you've forgotten that."

"I don't think I can call a young woman of her age by her Christian name."

"Why not?" Christine said. "I don't mind calling you Harry, and you are two years my senior."

Of course she didn't mind calling him by name. She thought of him like Gerald did. Almost as if they were siblings. There had been a time when he had felt the same. But that had been a long time ago.

Harrison cleared his throat. After a full day of travel, he didn't feel any desire to argue over the matter. "What time does the post usually arrive?"

Gerald wrinkled his brow. "Around two o'clock most days, unless there is a letter or invitation that seems of particular importance, and then it could be delivered anytime."

"So it already arrived today?"

"We didn't receive any correspondences today," Gerald said. "Most days, we do not. But if you are expecting a letter, I assume it would go to your father's home. All of his letters get delivered there."

Harrison nodded. If only it were that simple. He was going to have to intercept the mail carrier, and somehow convince him to hand over that letter. An unlikely prospect. It might be simpler to bribe the housekeeper to keep a lookout for the letter. He would come to dinner and pay attention to the servants. If they still employed Mrs. Nash, he might have a chance to return to London without Christine or Gerald ever finding out what a foolish youth he had been.

Five

PHOEBE TUCKED A final pin into Christine's hair. Even though she would only be going on a walk, she didn't want to risk Harry seeing her with her hair down again. Last night at dinner, he had barely talked to her, let alone smiled. In all the years she had hoped to see him again, she hadn't imagined him so changed.

Christine thanked her maid and pulled her shawl tighter around her shoulders. Phoebe saw the thanks for what it was: a polite dismissal. Her maid understood her desire to spend her afternoon walks alone. The sky was overcast, and the wind was picking up, making it cold for a June day. But Phoebe knew well there wasn't anything—short of a full-scale storm— that would stop Christine from spending time outside.

Especially the past few weeks.

Christine spent a few moments idly walking around the back garden. Carnations and sweet peas were in full bloom, casting a delicate scent about as her skirt brushed past them. When she was certain enough time had passed to defer suspicion, she cut across the backyard and followed the trail that led to the front of the home.

Her eyes went up the lane as soon as it came into view. No horse and rider yet. Perhaps there would be no post today, either. It had been two weeks since she had written to Mr. Wilstead. If he was going to reply to her, the reply should come soon. It wouldn't be the end of the world if Gerald saw the letter first. Not like if Mama or Papa had been home and seen it. They wouldn't understand. She couldn't sit back and watch the estate fall into ruin. Leaving her dowry behind seemed to be the only thing tangible she could do to help.

With no sign of a letter being delivered, her eyes cast toward the path that led to the Chase cottage. Her hand flew to her chest. Harry was making his way toward their home. After spending dinner with her and Gerald last night, she had thought he would spend all of today with his family. She had been half-tempted to visit them this morning, but she knew she shouldn't monopolize all of Harry's time. If he was only to be here a few days, he would want to spend at least some of that with his parents.

"Harry," she called out to him, waving her hand. If the mail came and he was here, she would have to tell him her plans. Could she trust him to not tell Gerald?

She would have trusted the old Harry. But she needed to escape this new, serious one.

Harry marched the rest of the way toward her. His jacket was well-tailored and as fine as any her brother owned. Perhaps finer, none of the Stones had ordered new clothing for over a year. Although he hadn't said more than one or two words to her last night, his conversation with Gerald had finally brought to light how well he had done for himself in London. And he had done very well indeed.

Harry came to a stop in front of her. His face still felt foreign to her. Without his characteristic smile, it was as if he wasn't the same person.

If the corners of his mouth would turn up . . . just a little . . .

There was no sign of a rider coming. Serious or no, with only a few days to enjoy his company, she couldn't make herself find an excuse to send him away, no matter how much she should have.

"You really should call me Mr. Chase," he said with a frown.

Christine cocked her head to one side. "Mr. Chase is our steward."

"And your steward's son."

He may have lost his desire to smile, but he hadn't lost his stubborn streak. Thank goodness. She could work with that. To see something of her old friend was better than seeing a complete stranger. There was no point in arguing with Harry. She wouldn't change his mind. Of course, that didn't mean she needed to actually follow his edict. Not while they were alone. She just wouldn't argue.

"Are you walking into Dorset?" Harry asked. "It is quite a distance."

"No, are you?"

"No."

It was quiet as they both eyed the other. She couldn't exactly ask him where he was walking, or he might do the same. If Harry discovered she was waiting for a letter, he would hound her until he discovered just what the letter was. If he was here when it came, she would tell him, but otherwise, it was easier not to.

"Will you be here long?"

"I already mentioned I was planning on leaving in the next day or two."

"I meant here, on our front path."

"Oh." He glanced about their property. "I don't know exactly. It is a beautiful day."

Christine eyed the dark clouds above them. This new Harry had strange ideas about beauty. The last thing she wanted was for him to see her intercept the mail. She never knew exactly when or if the courier would arrive. Hopefully today, if he came at all, it would be later rather than sooner.

They couldn't stand here all day. "Would you join me in a walk to the stream?"

"So you can push me in it again?"

"Push you? I never pushed you into the stream. Not in years, anyway."

"Then how would you explain my clothing hanging out to dry all night?"

"Oh, you mean yesterday? I didn't push you in; I pulled you in." She smiled. "Two very different things."

A corner of Harry's lips turned up. She leaned forward, but it quickly turned back down. No smile for her just yet.

"Ah, yes," Harry said. "Very different, indeed. And will you be pulling me into the stream today?"

"No."

"Good."

"Not unless you give me cause."

He shook his head and looked to the ever-darkening skies. "Heaven help me, Christine, if you make up some reason that I deserve to be thrown into the stream . . ."

"Me?" she asked innocently, not missing the fact that despite his protests, he still called her by her Christian name. "I would never. Now, will you walk with me?" The sooner they completed the walk, the sooner he would go back to his parents' house.

He looked up the lane, then back at her. "Yes," he said, starting up the path without holding an arm out for her. "Perhaps, we will find that otters' den while we are there."

Christine jumped into motion, her strides long and quick to catch up to him. "I believe it is on the other side of the stream, so unless we are willing to risk getting wet a second time, I'm not certain we shall."

"Are you certain it is there?"

"Gerald told me it was just yesterday."

Harry pursed his lips together.

"What?"

"Gerald told you of it?"

"Yes."

"And he told you it was at the other side of the stream?"

"Not exactly. He said it was at the bend where the oak tree grows near the water's edge. But I didn't see it on the near side, so I figured it must be on the other side."

Harry narrowed his eyes. "Have you been bothering him in any way lately?"

"No."

Well, she had been asking to see the accounts of late. And asking about her dowry. It was ridiculous that her family still kept so much money tied up in her dowry when she knew the estate could use it. But Gerald never listened to her.

"Are you trying to say my brother was working to get rid of me, and there is, in fact, no otters' den?"

Harry tipped his head to one side and raised a shoulder with a squint. His feet didn't slow. Perhaps, he wanted this walk to be over as soon as she did. "He once told me he spotted a wolf on the east edge of your property. I *knew* there were no longer wolves in England, but he assured me they had crossed the border from France."

"Are there wolves in France?"

"Certainly," Harry said. "But they don't swim."

Christine laughed. That was just like Gerald. "But there *are* otters nearby. I've seen them several times in the past."

"Would you like to look for the den, then?"

She thought back to the first time Gerald had mentioned it. He had been quite vague on where it was located. It was only after she had pressed him that he brought up the old oak tree. It was one of the best-known landmarks near the stream. Quite convenient for his story. She sighed, "No."

Harry once again glanced up the road. His eyes narrowed as he searched the horizon.

"Are you waiting for someone?" she asked.

"No," he replied, snatching his eyes off the road and returning them to her.

"You keep glancing up the road."

"I'm not waiting for anyone. Almost no one knows I'm here." He quickened his step. His legs were quite long, and he didn't have the burden of a multitude of petticoats. Christine hastened to stay with him. This walk was turning out to be much less leisurely than any she had been on of late. Any faster, and she would have to pick up her skirts and run.

"Then someone knows you are here."

He didn't answer. Harry was more quiet than he should be. If he was only here for a few days, she would have a conversation with him at least. She needed to get a rise out of him.

"Have you quarreled with a lady?"

He scoffed. "I would have to have spoken to one for that to happen."

"Ah, yes. Nails. No time for things like speaking to young women. Now I understand why you have hardly strung a few sentences together when we have conversed."

Harry didn't slow as she spoke to him. If anything, he marched even faster. "I've spoken with you sufficiently. More than I had planned."

More than he had planned? He came to Stonehouse with a plan *not* to speak much to her? What exactly had she done to receive such treatment? First, he left so long ago without saying so much as a goodbye. Now, he came back hoping not to say much more than hello. This from the man she had practically grown up with.

Did he even understand the hole he left once he was gone? He was the only other person close to her and Gerald's age in miles. His leaving had been the end of an era. She and Gerald went to bed one evening children who played outside, explored the stream, and chased dragonflies, only to wake up as grown-ups. Playing together—just the two of them—was just not the same. The day Harry left was the day her childhood died.

She stretched her legs to match his pace, then shoved him slightly to the side. "Whatever your plans on conversing with me might have been," she said, "they are about to change."

"I had no plans on conversing with you."

"Exactly. Every day you are here, you will speak with Gerald and me as much as we like. You left us here alone, and now you have six years of conversation to make up for."

"Did you expect me to stay here forever?"

"Yes."

"Well then, you were a fool."

She stopped. They were nearly to the oak, but she wasn't going to keep up with his furious walking anymore. Her arms were stiff at her side, and her hands curled into tight fists. Turning around, she marched off at a pace not much slower than they had been going. Harry wasn't going to smile at her. He wasn't even going to speak with her more than he absolutely had to. A large drop of water landed in front of her skirts. She wasn't crying, was she? She rubbed her eye, but it was dry. Another drop, then another landed on the pathway. The dark skies had given up on holding in their water.

Rain.

She marched even faster. Phoebe wasn't going to be happy about two soaked gowns in as many days.

"Christine, wait," Harry called out from behind her, but she didn't stop.

He said an oath under his breath that she didn't quite catch. A moment later, a shadow fell over her head, and the warmth of Harry's jacket enveloped her as he threw it over her damp head and shoulders. He ducked his head low and held the material over both of them. His sudden nearness made her lose her footing, and she nearly tripped. His arm around her shoulder tightened, keeping her upright.

Under the canopy of his jacket, the world had gone even more shadowed. Rain splashed Harry's cheeks and eyelashes, making him look younger. He still held her firm by her one shoulder, his face only inches from her own. "I'm sorry," he said. "You are not a fool. Far from it."

Her lips wanted to quiver at his words, but she refused to let them. *I'm sorry.* How long had she waited to hear those words from him? She had long since given up on it.

"It was hard when you left. Of course, I knew you wouldn't stay here forever. Although, at times, I know Father had hoped you would stay on as a steward for Gerald. But you left so suddenly. It was hard on all of us. Your parents, Gerald." She looked down. "Me."

"I didn't think anyone would really miss the steward's son."

"Gerald and I didn't miss the steward's son. We missed our friend. I still miss you at times." He stiffened. She shouldn't have said that. Harry wasn't a boy anymore. But he wasn't exactly like any of the men she knew, either. He knew her too well to keep her heart from him. "Things were never the same after you left. We all had to grow up. Even you, it seems."

"True."

"I would have liked a few more years to be a child with you."

"Oh, Christine." In his eyes was a deep sadness. "I was growing up whether we liked it or not. I'm sorry I didn't say goodbye. I think I was afraid of what I might have said or done if I had."

"It couldn't have been any worse than when you put frogs in my hair."

"It could have been." He was already only inches from her face, but leaned forward ever so slightly. "It could have been much worse."

"Spiders?"

That same corner of his mouth that had risen earlier lifted again. "I would never put spiders in your hair."

She scoffed. "Just frogs."

And there it was. Harry's smile. Both corners raised. His teeth showing through the part in his lips. She forgot the coldness of the rain and Harry's earlier comments. At last, her friend had come home. Her right hand lifted, her thumb aching to stroke the side of his mouth. She pulled her hand behind her back. What was she thinking? She couldn't touch Harry on the face. Even as close a friend as he was, she had no right to inspect his stubble. No matter how curious she was about its texture. Now that she had him smiling, she would keep him thus.

"Now what should we do to Gerald, since he sent me on a wild otter chase?"

"So you agree, there was no otters' den?"

"I've come to see the light."

"I'll think on it."

"It will have to be something marvelous to make up for the years I've had to deal with Gerald on my own."

Their heads were mostly dry under Harry's jacket, but the sound of the rain changed from soft patters on the ground to a sudden, deeper roar. His jacket directly above them bowed with water and started to drip. Harry ignored it. "Was it that unbearable, dealing with Gerald on your own?"

"Unbearable?" Christine shook her head, averting her eyes from the rain that had managed to settle on Harry's lashes. "No, it wasn't unbearable. It was simply dull and predictable."

"Well, I'm not certain how having me around is going to help rectify that situation. I've become quite dull and predictable myself."

Nothing about being this close to Harry felt dull. Her chest was on fire, her feet ready to dance. If he could ignore the sudden downpour, so would she. "It sounds as though we all need each other. Even if it is only for a day or two. Now, what should we do to Gerald? Something shocking."

"I could tell him I am hoping to return as steward and expect him to give my father the boot."

Her heart stilled. If he actually returned to stay, would that change her plans to leave? "But it would break his heart when he found it to be untrue. We need something less likely to damage him."

"Frogs in his hair?"

"Spiders at the very least." Christine smiled. And then she had a very terrible idea. "We could tell him we are betrothed. Just for an afternoon. Make him nervous."

She regretted the words as soon as she saw his reaction. His face recoiled in horror, and he stepped out from under their shelter, leaving her alone under his wet jacket. With his arms no longer holding it up, it flopped down onto her face. She frantically pulled the fabric off of her face and gasped when the torrential rain hit her. Harry was three feet away, bent over with his hands on his knees.

"I was in jest," she called out to him through the rain. "Forget I mentioned it."

He wiped the rain from his brow. "We need to get you back to the house. I didn't pack enough clothing to get soaked every day. I assume you have had enough of your walk."

There was no trace of a carriage or horse and rider. No mail would be delivered in this downpour.

"You will still be here tomorrow?" she asked.

He looked down the lane just as she just had. "It looks as though I will be."

"What are you waiting for?"

Harry pursed his lips together, then wiped the rain from his forehead once again. She still held his jacket, and the white sleeves of his shirt were starting to stick to his corded arms. She swallowed and held his jacket out to him. He took it but didn't put it on. What was the point, when everything was already wet? She wished there was some sensible way to mention that his arms were making it hard for her to focus.

He held his jacket in front of him and, without answering, started walking toward her house. "I'm waiting for a letter," he said in a low, rumbling voice.

"*You* are waiting for a letter?" She almost said "too" but stopped herself before the word came. "As in, you are going to stand outside my home each afternoon waiting for a letter?"

"Yes."

"We can deliver it to you, should it arrive."

He cleared his throat and kept his eyes on the path before them. "I will wait for it."

'You don't want us to see it?" She understood that sentiment. She had her own letter coming any day now—or at least, she hoped—and she wasn't ready to let anyone know about her letter, either. But Harry couldn't be waiting for an offer of employment. If he was, there would be no reason to hide it, and he would have received the letter in London. What would have possessed him to have it delivered here? Who would send him a letter he wanted no one to see?

A woman.

"I thought you said you didn't even speak to women. Why is one sending you a letter here?"

"It isn't from a woman."

"Is it a letter of business, then?"

"Not exactly."

"And it has nothing to do with romance? Nothing at all?"

The sound of their feet squelching through the mud filled her ears. His silence made a small pit in her stomach open up. So it was from a lady, or at least had something to do with a lady.

"I'm sorry I brought it up," Harry said, and he looked it. "But if the post arrives, and I am not there to meet it, I want you to promise to come get me before you look at it."

She slipped on a particularly muddy spot on the path and, in an instant, Harry's arms were around her. His hair was plastered to the side of his head, his cravat a complete wreck, but having him near made her breath hitch. Harry. This was Harry. This strong, warm, and vexing man was her childhood friend. She shouldn't be distracted by his arms around her, or notice the way his eyes softened as he scanned her person. "Are you all right? I had forgotten about your sore ankle."

Her ankle?

Ah, yes, her ankle.

"It is feeling much better today. I must not have hurt it much."

Harry's arm was still on her own, and his eyes locked onto hers. "Will you promise to tell me if the mail arrives? I would ask the servants, but they are all new since I have been here, and I know they wouldn't trust me."

How could she promise him that? She had her own letter to look for. If Harry saw it, what would he think of her?

"Please?"

Oh, bother. It had always been particularly hard to say no to Harry. No matter how strange his ideas. What were the chances that his letter, due to arrive in the next day or two, would arrive before a letter she wasn't certain was coming at all? Most likely her letter, which she had been expecting for over a week, wouldn't arrive until after he left.

"All right."

"And you won't look at any of the letters that come?"

"Not until you have scanned them yourself."

He slid his hand from her elbow to her wrist. It must have been the cold rain on her arm that made his touch feel like fire. He reached her hand and enveloped it in his own. "Thank you, my dear friend."

"Christine," she said.

"Thank you, Christine." He had called her Christine all afternoon. She didn't know why she felt the need to make him say it then. But *friend* no longer felt right. Not like her name did on his lips.

They both turned back to the house. Her hand was still in his, and she wondered if he noticed. Every one of her senses only pointed to that contact, as if she had cut a small hole in a card and was experiencing life through it. She no longer felt the rain splashing on her face or heard it pounding on the path. The world became their hands intertwined. His cupped hers softly. It would only take the slightest pull, and her hand would be her own again. She would feel the rain again, and her breathing would return to normal.

For the first time since writing to Mr. Wilstead and hatching her plan to become a governess, she wondered if she had made a mistake. Perhaps, she wasn't quite ready to set aside the idea of marriage after all. Would the estate survive even if she could convince her parents to put her dowry into it? She had hoped so, she'd risked her future on it, but if Harry showed interest in her, would she change her mind?

They reached the path that stood in front of her home and led toward the Chase cottage. They both stopped, as if on command. Harry's thumb stroked her own in a touch so light she wasn't certain she felt it, and then he dropped her hand.

"Can you make it to your door without slipping again?"

She frowned and whipped her head around. That was why he had not let her go? Because he felt she was clumsy?

"I'm perfectly capable of making it to my door."

He smiled. It was his old smile, that one he gave her when he knew he was indulging Gerald's little sister. It was good to see it, and also oddly discomforting after realizing her heart no longer thought of him as simply a childhood friend.

"I know you are, but it is wet, and you are injured."

She pushed away her indignation and leaned toward him, testing this new feeling between them. "And there are stairs. I could fall."

She didn't know if it was her imagination, but he seemed to lean into her as well. They were close enough that it was hard to tell whether he had moved or she had. A raindrop managed to run down his temple, and this time, she didn't resist. She reached up and wiped it away, her thumb sliding across the smooth skin of his face just above his cheekbone, while her fingers grazed the rough skin of his cheek.

Harry froze. His eyes closed slowly. His chest rose, and she pulled her hand away.

She ran up the stairs before he could open his eyes. She wasn't ready to see what was in them.

Did Harry see her as a woman, or still as a child? In all of their previous interactions, she had been a girl, and a girl didn't have to worry about whether a man was holding her hand to help her, or if he merely didn't want to let go. A girl could wipe a raindrop from her friend's cheek with no worry about what he might think.

But she was no longer a girl. And Harry was most definitely a man.

If he opened those eyes and looked at her as if she was still a friend to tease and torment, she wasn't sure what her reaction would have been. She was still processing her own shift in feelings toward him.

Much better to run away.

Six

"WHY IS IT that Miss Stone hasn't married?" Harrison had no subtle way to ask his father, so he just asked.

His father set his pipe on the small wooden kitchen table. It was the same table he had eaten at every day as a child. Mother was outside in the vegetable garden gathering peas for their breakfast. Their cottage only had the two bedrooms and this kitchen. Gerald and Christine had never been inside. There was no sitting room for guests.

"I don't suppose she has had much of an opportunity to meet any upstanding gentlemen." Father rubbed the skin on the sides of his cheeks, and Harrison mentally blocked out the image of another's hand on his own cheek.

He had slept fitfully, wondering if he should have come here at all. It felt wrong to sleep in the bed he had slept in as a young man. He could have simply written another letter to explain the first, and tried never to see the Stone family again.

"Most young ladies of her standing would go to London for a season," Harrison said.

Father cleared his throat and lifted his pipe once again. "I have no doubt that had she been born twenty years earlier, that is exactly what she would have done. But things are getting harder for families like the Stones.

A deep scoff rose in Harrison's throat. The Stones didn't

know what true hardship was. Not going to London for the Season? That didn't classify as hard.

Father ran his thumb along the corner of the table. He found a knot and worked his way back and forth, smoothing it. "Don't you scoff at the Stones' struggles. If they lose this land, there are plenty of people who will be out of work. Your father included. Would you have us all looking for work in London? Would there be a place for us in one of those nail factories of yours?"

His father in the blistering heat of the nail factory? Harrison shuddered.

"It can't be as bad as that."

The Stones had everything: a beautiful home, servants that worked for them, land, clothing, food. So much food. He had seen the waste there before he had ever realized what lack of food was.

"I cannot believe the Stones are in any danger," Harrison said.

"Then why didn't they send Miss Stone to London?" his father asked.

"Perhaps, she didn't want to go."

"You forget that I am the land steward here. I know precisely why she didn't. The cost of a season in London would mean letting several servants go. Perhaps, it would push them to start selling off land. Miss Stone's dowry is about the only money left in the family's coffers. They are one bad year of crops or one sickness in the lambs away from selling the whole place."

That couldn't be true. But Father's frown and the deep wrinkles of worry around his eyes told Harrison otherwise.

Harrison grabbed the edge of the table. When he had given up on returning and decided to devote himself to fighting the Corn Laws, he hadn't once thought about how that would affect Father and the Stone tenants. If the Anti-Corn Law League had its way—and he prayed they did—the Stones wouldn't need a bad year of crops to lose their land. Once less expensive imported grain was available, the low price of grain would finish them off just as easily.

The back door opened, and Mother stepped in, carrying a bundle of sweet peas. She dropped them on the table and sat down. Father reached for a pod and snapped it open. He slid his finger along the inside and popped out each individual pea before scooping them into his mouth. Mother handed Harrison a bunch and opened a pod for herself.

"It is so good to have you home, son," she said.

He knew what she meant. She wanted him to come more often. With three experiences under his belt with Christine, he knew the fallacy in that. He would never be able to be near her and not be affected by her. He had thought six years would be enough time to get over his silly infatuation, but he had jumped right back into his younger self.

He opened his own sweet pea and plopped the peas into his mouth just as his parents had taught him when he was a boy. Some things were never forgotten. He knew exactly how to press on a pod to pop it open, and he knew how to love Christine. Neither of those were things he could change. They were ingrained into his being.

Unfortunately, opening pea pods was the much more useful knowledge. Loving Christine could do him no good. The money he got from the sale of Matlock Nail he had already pledged to donate to the League or use for campaign funds. He had nothing to offer her, and the very thing he fought for now would very likely send her family into ruin.

It was the same circle he had run around for months. But always the memory of a baby lying much too still in his arms would lead him back to the path he had chosen.

"What are your plans for work today, Father?" It was still too early for the post, but Harrison was anxious to move about. He wasn't used to the slow country life anymore. He was accustomed to working long, hard days.

"I was going to ride over to the east side of the Stone property and inspect the cows and pastures there. The rain yesterday may have caused some damage."

"Would you like some company?"

Father nodded. He wasn't one to use words when actions would suffice. Father stood from the table and kissed Mother on the top of her head. It was all the thanks she would receive for the peas.

The smile on Mother's face told him it was enough.

Christine fidgeted as she walked up the lane away from Stonehouse. It was her typical time to walk about, keeping her eye on the road and looking for a rider. Her eyes snaked over to the path that led to the Chase cottage. She smoothed down the front of her full skirts for the hundredth time. Thankfully, the skies were mostly clear today. No threatening clouds promising rain. She apparently couldn't be trusted with a wet Harry Chase. Today, she would stay dry and proper. Harry was her friend. A good friend—one she didn't want to scare away by touching his cheek at uncalled-for moments. Would it have hurt him to have the raindrop run down his cheek? Hundreds of them had run down his cheek earlier in their conversation. Why had she felt the need to interfere with that one?

Christine picked at her fingernail. What would she do if her letter came first? She wouldn't know until she had shown Harry the letters. Taking a deep breath, she checked down the path to Harry's home once again. She would tell him. Harry would understand her reasons, or at the very least, would respect her wishes. She dropped her hands to her sides. Where was Harry, anyway? She thought for certain he would be here by now.

The muted clomping of hooves on the still-damp ground made her spin around. Harry was atop one of the estate's horses and trotting toward her. He had traded in his black suit coat from London for a brown jacket like his father wore when he was out among the fields.

He reined in his horse as he came up beside her. "Any sign of mail today?"

"No," she managed. Why was her voice breathless? She cleared her throat and jutted out her chin. "Not yet."

Harry nodded. "I'll be right back." He turned his horse toward the stables.

He'll be right back. She flattened her hands against her stomach. *He'll be right back.* She paced back and forth. Removing her hands from her stomach, she shook them at her sides. It was just Harry. She would be able to think of a word or two to say to the man she had practically grown up with. Wouldn't she?

Too soon, the crunch of boots upon rocks announced his return. Her hands returned once more to her stomach. Taking a deep breath, she turned around.

He wore no cravat. His shirt made a deep V where it opened, showing his neck and collarbones. His cheeks must have been clean-shaven in the morning, but they were already starting to show dark stubble.

She swallowed. This dark, serious man was not the boy she had grown up with.

"You've changed your jacket," she said. His eyebrows furrowed, and he pulled at the breast of his jacket. That was

43

the wrong thing to say. What else could she say? "How is your family?"

"They are doing well, thank you." He looked down the path that led to Dorset. "No mail today?"

Hadn't he asked her that already? "No, not yet."

He nodded his head just as he had before. He kicked a stone near his feet, and a patch of hair fell forward onto his face. It was the same movement he had done a thousand times when they were growing up. Whenever the three of them were trying to think of something to do, he would kick at the ground near his feet. His coarse jacket and unkempt hair brought him back. Her Harry.

"What have you been doing?" she asked.

"Checking the cows out in the east pasture." He looked up, his intense eyes, more green than grey in the afternoon sun, meeting hers. "It seems as though they are all healthy."

"And what would you have done if they weren't?"

"I may have bought a few."

She laughed. "From us? You would buy our unhealthy cows?"

"For you," he said. "I would buy unhealthy cows *for* you."

Her stomach made a silly little flop. She didn't know what to do with it, so instead she laughed again. It sounded forced even to her ears.

"I'm very capable of buying livestock," he said.

"I know. That isn't why I laughed," she replied.

"Why did you laugh, then?"

"I don't know. When I don't know what to say, sometimes I laugh."

"You laugh when you are nervous."

"That, too." She glanced at Harry quickly and then brought her attention back to her hands.

"And you laugh when you are excited," he continued.

"Yes, I do that as well." Harry made her all of those things. Even now as he questioned her, she didn't know if she should step away or step forward to him.

"It makes it hard to know exactly what you are feeling."

"Well, thank the heavens for that."

He raised an eyebrow. It was time to change the subject before he had a chance to question her any further.

"There is to be a social in Dorset tonight. Would you like to attend?" she asked.

"That would depend on the post."

"You will leave as soon as the letter comes?"

"Yes. I must." His eyes flashed outward to the road. Was he so anxious to leave?

"Then if it doesn't come today, will you join us?"

"I believe I will. As long as my clothing is sufficiently dry."

"I hope your letter doesn't arrive quite yet, then. It has been too long since the two of us danced."

He laughed. "The last time we danced was in the barley field."

"All the more reason to dance again."

He held an arm out to her, and she took it. "Where will you be walking today?" he inquired.

"I have no goal in mind," she told him.

"Do you walk here every afternoon?"

She placed her hand to the back of her neck. "Of late, yes."

"Where do you usually walk?"

"Up the path until it hits the road and back."

"That is quite a walk."

"Yes, well, there isn't much else for me to do."

"You don't paint anymore?"

She nearly snorted. She had never been much of a painter. For a few years, she had tried her hand at it, but the pictures in her head never turned out the way she wanted them to on paper. Funny that he should remember that.

"I'm not sure that what I did could be considered painting. My work was amateurish at best."

"But you always smiled when you painted. Well, except for the times you didn't."

That was true. While she was painting, actually putting the brush to the canvas, there was something that would settle in her. She hadn't realized that would lead to smiling, but she wasn't surprised. It was only when she stopped painting to actually look closely at what she had done that she felt frustrated by her work.

"I guess, at some point, it felt selfish for me to paint. It benefited no one. I was never truly happy with my work. One day, I ran out of parchment and simply didn't ask for more."

"One more way you grew up while I was away?"

"I suppose."

"It isn't bad to do something just because you love it."

"And Mr. *I practically ate nails for six years,* how would you know that?"

He scuffed his foot along the ground without slowing their pace. Twice in one day—it was as if he was gradually returning to the person she used to know.

"Perhaps, I know that because I spent too many years living without it."

Christine stopped him and placed both her hands on his elbows. "And now? Have you found something you love now? Is that why you sold your company?"

His lips parted; he carefully slipped both of her hands off of his elbows. "No, I didn't sell my company because of something I loved. I sold it because of something I hate."

He dropped his hands to his sides and continued walking, without holding an arm out for Christine.

"What do you hate? Nails?"

He laughed a dry, hard laugh. "How could I hate the thing that brought me to where I am today?"

"Then what?"

His shoulders drooped, and his pace slowed. Christine caught up with him in a few short steps and then matched his stride. "Hunger," he said. "I truly hate hunger. More than I have ever loved anything in my life, I hate hunger."

What had he gone through in London? He didn't look as though he had missed many meals. "Did you go hungry? You should have come back. We have plenty of food here."

"Oh, I know. I have seen of your abundance. You have more food than you need; that is for certain."

"If you knew that, why didn't you return?"

"It wasn't me that was hungry, Christine." They had reached the bend in the path where the old oak grew. He marched toward it, picked up a stone, and threw it hard and fast toward the stream. "There were a few times I was hungry, but I worked through it." He picked up another stone and threw this one even harder. It collided with a tree trunk somewhere near the stream. "There are babies that are hungry every day in London. Mothers who go without so that they can give even the smallest amount more to their children. Men and women who work long, grueling days making nails, and yet, it isn't enough. Each day, they can afford less food than the previous one, until one day, there just isn't any."

Christine's stomach soured. She had seen hunger. There were tenants on their land who hadn't been able to work, and their families had lived off of the baskets she could bring them. She had visited one family every day until she discovered the husband and father of the home was taking each basket to trade for liquor. The wife had begged her to stop coming. She would have rather gone hungry in the hopes of her husband

47

returning to work, rather than living with him too steeped in drink to keep his fists to himself.

She didn't stop bringing food, but she did get better at hiding it. Still, for the most part, people had enough to eat here.

"I'm sorry, Harry."

Harry threw the rock that was in his hand and then spun around. "No one calls me Harry anymore, you know. My name is Harrison. Harrison Chase. In fact, it should be Mr. Chase now. I sold my soul to the devil for six years. It seems I should garner that much respect, at least."

He saw her as disrespectful? It was simply habit to call him Harry. To her, that was who he was. "Mr. Chase." The words felt strange on her tongue. "I'm sorry."

"I watched a baby die in my arms, Christine." Harry's face was broken, his shoulders drooped. "He was alive one moment, too tired to cry, and then the next, he was just gone. His mother was too hungry herself to even register grief. She hadn't eaten for days, and she had a look in her eye . . ."

Christine pushed through the underbrush that led to Harry. She didn't reach for him this time. Instead, she stood in front of him and simply looked up into his face. "You love people, Mr. Chase. *That* is what you love."

"But I can't love all of them. Not really. I have to choose which people to love, and that, Miss Stone, is my own personal hell."

"You don't have to choose."

"Yes, I do."

"No, you don't."

"If I continue on the path I have started, everything I fight for will be a detriment to you."

"What do you mean?"

"I'm only telling you this because I want you to understand. When I go back to London, you may hate everything I stand for. And I want you to know I haven't made this decision lightly. I'm fighting the Corn Laws. I've vowed to myself, and I will not back down from that. Every breath that comes from this body will be spent in an effort to revoke the tariffs that make food more expensive to those who can't afford it in the first place."

"Oh." Christine didn't know what else to say. The Corn Laws were one part of many variables that kept their farm profitable. Most of their income came from tenants with dairy farms, but a portion of their land was used for grain. She hadn't spent much time thinking about the tariffs on imported grain. If Gerald hadn't mentioned them in passing, she wouldn't have even known what little she did.

"I can't love the Stone family anymore. I know everything I'm fighting for will destroy you."

"You won't destroy the Stone family."

"I don't know how much Gerald has told you—"

"I'm not completely without wits, Mr. Chase. I know the estate is in danger."

"Then how can you even look at me?"

"We aren't in danger because of you."

"Didn't you hear what I said? I know to you I am just a poor steward's son, but I have made a name for myself in London. If I join in the fight to repeal the Corn Laws, I believe we will win."

"I do, too." Harry had always done everything he set his mind to, whether it was beating Gerald in foot races or perfecting skipping stones. She had never seen him give up on anything. When he sunk his teeth into something, he never let go.

"Then you must see the danger."

"No, I see my friend who returned home for a few days. I see a man who knows what is right and is willing to fight for it. And I have known for the past two years that our estate isn't large enough to continue on for many more years. If the Corn Laws are repealed, it might speed up the demise of the estate, but it won't change its course. You are a rising star, Mr. Chase. The Stone star is a setting one. We have known that for a long time."

She bent over, picked up another rock, and placed it in his hand. "So love who you want to love, fight what you want to fight, and be the man you have always dreamed you would be. The Stones will be proud to know you. And I trust you won't waste another breath believing that Gerald and I would rather keep this land than see starving children have food to eat. You should know us better than that."

"But what should I do?"

"Gerald and I need you to laugh with us more."

"When I am about to be your demise?"

"I just told you the demise is happening regardless of what you do."

"So you want me to laugh with you?"

"Yes."

"I haven't laughed in years."

"That is not true. You laughed at me just the other day. And today, as well, if I remember."

"It feels true."

"Well, it sounds like when you return to London, you will have a fight on your hands. Let's live the days you have left here happily. Let's live them for the things we love, not the things we hate."

"Live for the things we love?"

"Yes."

He rubbed his forehead. "You are breaking down everything I have tried to build up this past year."

"If laughing and loving things breaks something in you,

then it is something that needs to be broken." Christine closed her hand over the hand she had placed the rock in. "Don't just throw rocks out of anger. Show me how well you can skip them."

Harry's mouth twisted to one side. "You want me to skip rocks?"

"I haven't seen a seven-jump skip in six years. Don't you think I deserve to see one today?"

"Neither you nor Gerald have beaten my record?"

"Not even close."

Harry's hand tightened around the rock, and his shoulders straightened. "I'm not going to be able to make this rock skip seven times."

"Out of practice?" she asked.

"No." He opened his hand and cocked his head to one side. "You gave me a very inferior skipping stone. Were you purposely trying to make it harder for me?"

A gurgle of laughter rose up from Christine's throat. The rock he held out was anything but sleek. It was nearly as tall as it was wide, and even she should have known better than to tell him to try his hand at skipping it. He smiled at her laughter and took her hand. Together, they walked to the edge of the stream.

"This may not be the best of stones, but I can make it work. I won't get seven, but I can get a few."

He dropped her hand and wound up his right arm behind him. His arm shot forward, and with a flick of his wrist—a move she had never quite been able to imitate—he sent her awkward rock flying out onto the water.

One jump, another, and a short third one before it disappeared into the water. Harry could always make anything skip. He was already bent over, scanning the ground for another stone. A better one this time, she was sure. His intense gaze eyed each rock at their feet. He picked up a few and held them in his left hand. They must have been good ones, but not quite what he was looking for. After several more adequate rocks made it into his hand, he finally found one that must have met his approval. He stood and brandished it toward her. "*This* is a rock capable of skipping six or seven times. This one will fly."

The corners of her mouth lifted. "I don't doubt it."

He handed the stone to her. "It is time someone broke my record."

"Me?"

"With a rock like that, it will be simple."

"But I haven't skipped a rock in—" Well, it hadn't been that long, actually. Probably just last month. She had gotten four skips on her best throw.

He handed her the pile of rocks he had collected in his left hand. "Practice with these first, and when you are ready, throw this one."

Christine rolled the rocks about in her hand. All of them were flat on at least one side. The one he had told her would fly was flat on both and nearly smooth. She could practically see how well it would skim across the top of the water, if only she could get her toss just right. She set the perfect one on the ground and picked one of the most flat of the serviceable rocks. If she could make this one skip five times, Harry would certainly be impressed. She tightened her grip on the stone she had picked, wrapped her index finger around the top of it, and pulled her arm back behind her.

Harry was suddenly there, one hand on her left shoulder and the other cupping her right wrist. "Relax your hand. Don't force it." His breath was on her cheek. She inhaled sharply. All the unfamiliar sensations of yesterday returned in full force. Why couldn't she react to him like she should? "I said *relax.*

You've gone even more tense. Loosen your wrist and drop your shoulder just a bit."

He shook her wrist softly, but she hardly noticed. All of her attention was focused on her back pressed against Harry's broad chest. He breathed in, and the motion of his chest brought them even closer together. How did someone come closer when they were already touching? He exhaled, his breath tickling her neck, and even though her back still rested against him, he was slightly farther away. She waited impatiently for him to take another breath, hoping for a deep one.

"Now try it like I just explained."

Christine sucked in her lips. Like he just explained? She hadn't heard a word beyond relaxing her wrist. He dropped away from her and awaited her toss.

She relaxed her wrist.

Pivoting back to put all her weight on her back foot and then transferring it all to her front, her hand flew forward.

The rock sank with a plop.

Harry looked back and forth between her and the stream. "Did you hear anything I just said?"

"Relax the wrist?"

"I didn't mean for it to flop around as you tossed."

She couldn't look at him. If she did, she was going to laugh. How had Harry Chase's close proximity caused her ears to stop working? "Sorry," she said, but there was an edge of laughter in her voice.

"Did you throw it badly on purpose?"

If only she had. "No, I can quite honestly say I did not." She dared to look at him. Both of his hands were on his hips, like a schoolmarm ready to discipline a classroom of children. The image didn't help stifle her desire to laugh. "Why would I have thrown it badly on purpose?"

"So I would teach you again."

She missed the warmth and the torture of his frame enveloping hers. "If that is all it would take, I fear my skipping will never improve."

Harry stilled. She shouldn't have said that—not when he was just starting to relax around her. He pivoted on his foot as if he would head back to the path, but then must have changed his mind, for he turned back toward her.

"I won't teach you if I know you aren't trying to improve."

"I am trying." She jutted out her chin. "I was just a bit distracted the first time. Please show me again."

"How do I know you won't be distracted again?"

"Oh, I'll be distracted," she said. He sucked in his cheeks. What was this dangerous game they were playing? She didn't know, but seeing Harry flustered by her remarks, and with her back still warm from his last lesson, she felt lighter than she had in a long time. This was much more entertaining than anything they had played as children. "But at least this time, I will listen."

She chose another rock from her left hand and, pulling her hand behind her, she turned her back to him. "Show me again," she called over her shoulder.

The crunch of his boots was slow and deliberate. This time when he took her hand, he started at her elbow and slid his hand down her forearm until his fingers wrapped around hers. "Are you listening?"

Christine nodded, not daring to trust her voice.

"Place the stone higher up in the palm of your hand." She maneuvered the stone to sit a bit higher. "Good."

"I should get a reward for managing to listen."

The few curls that had managed to escape her chignon pulled to one side as his chin came closer to her neck. "Name it."

54

A kiss at my throat.

Where had that thought come from? She jerked away from him, pulling her hand out of his. She knew herself better than to stay so close to him. First, she would think something outrageous like that, and then she would say it.

"I think I have it now."

Harry grinned. "Oh, do you?" The curl of his lips was so like his younger self, and yet all she could think of was what they would feel like against the nape of her neck or pressed against her own.

"Yes, and I will take a reward for listening."

Harry's chest expanded in the way she had hoped it would when she was standing in front of him. "What will be your reward?"

"Please don't make me call you Mr. Chase. I give you no disrespect when I call you Harry. To me, you are Harry. You always have been."

"There will be times when it would be quite inappropriate to call me Harry. At the social, for instance."

"Then I would have you trust me to know when those times are."

"You are asking me to trust you to be appropriate?"

"Is that so hard?"

"Believe it or not, no. Not when propriety truly matters."

She smiled up at him. "Then I will show you how well I listened." Christine picked out one of the better stones. "I think this rock is a three-skip rock." She pulled her arm back, relaxing her wrist but not too much, and let it fly. One. Two. Three. Then the smallest of bumps before sinking into the water.

"Was that four?" she asked.

"You underestimate yourself."

"How was my form?"

"Beautiful." Harry stepped closer to her. "Choose another rock. I want to show you one last thing."

"The best rock? I placed that one on the ground."

"No, one more for practice. Then you will be ready to break my record."

Without examining the stones, she chose one of them. "I'm ready."

For the third time, Harry stood behind her and took her hand. "This is the most important part."

She wouldn't mention a reward this time. She would just listen and ignore the way his frame made her feel small and yet protected.

"At the very last moment, flick your wrist just a bit more, outward, toward the stream. You are already doing it, but you could do it a little bit more, like this." He pushed her hand out in the familiar flick she always did when skipping stones. But he was right—he extended his hand just slightly more than she did. "I want you to know I'm not actually hurt when you call me Harry." His words made the hair at her neck quiver.

"Then why are you always asking me to stop?"

"I don't think I should savor it as much as I do. But, until that letter comes, I'm going to take up your challenge. I won't run away from the things I'm drawn to."

That wasn't what she had said. She had said *love*. The things he *loved*. "Show me that flick one more time."

He showed her four more times before she reluctantly told him she thought she could do it. She threw the first stone and managed five skips. Leaning down, she picked up his perfect stone.

She took a deep breath and concentrated on her form before letting the stone fly.

One, two, three . . . each bounce made the most satisfying *plop*. The spaces between the ripples each grew slightly smaller than the last until . . . seven skips. "Did you see that?" She jumped and kicked her legs out, first to the right and then the left.

Harry's lips turned up in a smile. "I did. Congratulations."

She ran to him and threw her arms around his bare neck. "Now, we are tied," she said into the hollow of his neck, where his cravat should have been. She pulled away quickly before doing anything more foolish. "Thank you."

Harry reached for her left hand and, for a moment, she felt that he was going to pull her to him. Instead, he uncurled her fingers and pulled out one of his less than perfect stones. He leaned back and tossed it into the stream. *Plop, plop, plop.* Four more jumps. "Blast," he said.

"You got seven as well. Why are you upset?"

"I was hoping for eight."

"You don't want to be tied with me?" A small pit of disappointment knotted her stomach.

He raised one of his thick eyebrows. "I was hoping you might need another lesson."

"Oh." She didn't know what to say to that.

"We should head back to the path. I really do need to keep an eye out for that letter."

"Yes, of course."

He held his arm out, and she took it. After all of their physical contact this afternoon, taking his arm was like returning home.

He could be gone in a day. It was impossible for her to wrap her mind around that fact when, in her heart, she knew he belonged here.

Christine's fingers curled about his elbow as Harrison led them back to the path and away from the stream. He was a fool. But he was a happy one. Christine hadn't seemed to mind his lessons. Indeed, she had seemed as drawn to him as he was to her. He didn't know what to do with this newfound hope. It didn't fit rationally into his plans. He was needed in London, he still had no disposable income despite selling his factory. If he gave up on helping the League, he would be able to live in comfort in London, comfortable enough to marry even. But, it would break something inside him that he didn't think he could ever repair to turn his back on the hungry.

Christine tightened her grip, and he pulled her closer to him. Until the letter came, he would allow himself to live for the things he loved. And as hard as he had tried to let this part of him die, he would always love Christine. If he were melted down to ore and reshaped, his core would always remain the same. He was Harrison Chase, and he loved Christine.

By all rights, the letter should have made it here by now. It must have been waylaid somehow. He hoped that wherever it had found itself, it would stay there a few more days. In the meantime, he would allow himself the opportunity to dance with Christine as a man, not a friend. And if she waited for him in front of her home each afternoon, as she had this afternoon, he would take it as a sign that she might feel for him a small amount of the pull he felt for her.

They stepped back on the path and, without discussing it, both turned toward Dorset. He wasn't ready for their walk together to end. He wished he knew if she felt the same way.

Seven

HARRISON TIED HIS cravat a second time. Mother knew how to starch a cravat, and yet it didn't seem to lie correctly after being doused in the rain. He pulled the knot just a bit to the right. Gerald's cravat was always perfect. Of course, Gerald had a valet to help him. Harrison had employed a valet for nearly two years, but until he knew how many of his funds would be needed for the Anti-Corn Law League, or a campaign if they decided to back him, he wouldn't be able to hire one again. Perhaps, he never would.

He pulled at the bottom of his jacket. His clothing would have to do. He didn't have anything better. And Christine had promised to dance with him regardless of his cravat. The few balls he had been to in London had gone tolerably. He hadn't embarrassed himself or stepped on anyone's feet. He would most likely do tolerably tonight as well.

Or he would somehow make a fool of himself.

Anyone who knew him in Dorset knew him as a land steward's son. He had become his own man in London, but no one here knew that. A land steward's son had no right to look at Christine as he knew he would do. Something had changed between them this afternoon. Or perhaps, something had gone back to how it was before. Whatever the reason for it, he was going to follow his heart—at least for the next few days.

When his letter arrived, he would have to decide whether or not to give it to her.

As much as he hated to see the Stones in financial trouble, it did open the door for him. If Christine's future was uncertain, perhaps, he could be good enough for her after all.

He kissed his mother on the forehead—she and his father had never been prone to going to socials; they hadn't even remembered that this one was planned—and marched toward Stonehouse. Gerald had sent a note that they should go together in the carriage, and the cottage path didn't have room for the horses to turn around. Not without hitting a few protruding rocks and bushes.

He arrived at Stonehouse to find the carriage outside, but no occupants inside. Not wanting to stand about waiting, he walked to the front door and knocked as if he had every right to avoid the servant's entrance.

Which he did.

The butler answered the door and showed him into the drawing room. Gerald sat on a chair near the unlit fireplace. "Ah, Harry. I'm so glad you made it."

"Thank you for inviting me to join you in the carriage. It has been a long time since I have been to a country social. It will be good to arrive with friends." And it would be good to spend time with Gerald; between time spent with his parents and keeping an eye out for the mail to be delivered, they hadn't seen each other enough.

"Compared to the soirées of London, I'm afraid our little party will seem quite small. But there is to be dancing, so I believe it will be a very satisfying evening for you."

Harrison nodded. He hoped for the same, but Gerald's shining-eyed excitement had him stepping back and forth on his legs. He was up to something.

"Gerald, what did you do?"

"Do you remember any young ladies from Dorset?"

"A few, but I would assume most of them are married by now. I never had cause to speak with many of them."

"I suppose most of the ones you would have known would be married by now. But don't worry—a fresh new crop has come up. And you have been gone long enough that you are bound to be the talk of the evening."

That blackguard. "What did you tell them about me?"

"Only that you recently sold a nail company, and selling a nail company generally makes one quite wealthy."

"Gerald, I'm living on less now than when I owned the company."

"Yes, but that is because of your morals—not because you don't actually have the money. I told no lies. You need to face the fact that you are a catch now."

"You wouldn't say that if you saw my rooms in London."

"A young wife would remedy that situation. You would see the need to upgrade at once."

"I don't want a young wife. I don't have the time for that now. I didn't tell you this before, but I've joined the Anti-Corn Law League. If they asked for half of the money I made with that sale tomorrow, I would give it to them."

Gerald's excited pacing stopped. "You are fighting against the Corn Laws?"

"Yes."

Gerald knew exactly what that meant. The sole purpose of the laws was to protect gentlemen like him.

"So that is what has made you so serious."

"I suppose it is. And I'm sorry, Gerald. I've spoken with Father about—"

"Don't be sorry. And your father doesn't know everything. There are still things that could be done."

"But the Corn Laws . . ."

"Most of our income is still generated from dairy. True, we have some alfalfa and hay, but most of that is sold to the tenant farmers to feed their cows. If the price went down on our crops, in theory, we could raise the rent, for the laborers would have fewer expenses."

It was the same economics Harrison had dealt with every day when he owned his factory. How to pay the least amount possible and still increase production at every turn. It was a dangerous kind of math that never allowed for any workers to improve their lot.

But still, he should be relieved. He didn't want to hurt the Stones. They were like family to him. "I'm glad to hear it." A foul taste in his mouth begged to differ. "I hated the idea of doing anything that would hurt your family."

He turned from Gerald and placed his hand on the mantle. He didn't want to hurt the Stone family, but there had been a spark of hope ignited by their troubles. How much of his newfound confidence with Christine stemmed from the fact that she could someday soon be in a position to ask for his help?

What had happened to the young man who had wanted to better himself in order to deserve a woman like Christine? He was a prideful fool.

The door opened, and Christine walked in. Her dark hair was swept up behind her head, and the cut of her yellow dress showed more of her shoulders than her day dresses. Her short sleeves ended in lace that draped over the top half of her upper arm. Her pale skin peeked through the delicate tatting. No wonder his hands had trembled every time he had gotten news from home those first few years. How had she remained unmarried, when she was not only enchanting, but beautiful in a way that made him want to rush to her side and spend the rest of the evening with her?

"You look quite handsome, Harry. Who would have thought when we practiced dancing in the fields that one day we would be attending a social together?"

Gerald laughed. "I always knew Harry would make a way for himself. I'm surprised you didn't think the same."

"I didn't think on it at all, I suppose. Harry has always been Harry, whether in a suit or labourer's clothing. Now come, I've a mind to dance all night, and we had better get started."

"Says the woman for whom we have been waiting," Gerald mused.

"Well," she spun in a circle, her broad skirt belling out around her, "was it worth the wait?"

"No," Gerald said, at the precise moment Harry said, "Yes."

"I will take Harry's answer to heart. Gerald, it is no wonder you are not yet married."

"I've yet to be introduced to the heiress we need to keep the estate running."

"*That* is your plan?" Harrison asked. "To marry someone who could save the estate?"

"It is one option, anyway," Gerald said. "Not the only option, but many men before me have done the same."

"What of love?" Harrison asked. Both of their heads turned to him as if he had asked if the wine tasted of arsenic. "Most women I know are deserving of love."

"That is because most of the women you know are your mother and Christine," Gerald laughed. "My father didn't marry my mother for love, and it turned out fine for them. And there are more and more merchants making enormous amounts of money who would love to attach themselves to a family of good standing."

"You would marry a merchant's daughter?"

"If it would save Stonehouse, I might be persuaded to marry the merchant." Gerald hit Harry on the shoulder. "These new standards are all good for you. There are some daughters of very strong families who will be at the ball tonight. You've been in the thick of trade. You must see how appealing money is, to anyone."

"I would far rather be sought after for my person. I hardly consider my money my own."

"It doesn't really matter what you consider it. Let's see what the ladies think tonight. Christine, have you arranged your dance card yet? You better secure a dance with Harry before we arrive, for I'm certain after we get to Jumpstead Inn, you won't have another chance with him."

"Did I misunderstand how these social functions work?" Harrison asked. "Last I heard, the men did the asking. Is it different in Dorset?"

"Oh, you will do the asking, but women have their ways of making certain their cards are filled with the men they want. And tonight, you are going to be the man every woman wants."

Miss Hubert brought her gloved hand to Harry's elbow for the third time. Or at least the third time since Christine had been watching them. She might have missed a touch or two, but it was unlikely. Christine's eye twitched. For once, couldn't Gerald have been wrong? How had he known Harry would be so popular?

Harry was tall and had a handsome, foreboding glare that she supposed some of the women would find attractive. But that was only because they hadn't seen him smile. Miss Hubert had gotten a few smiles out of him, but they weren't like the smiles he gave Christine. Not really. And Miss Hubert hadn't had to work as hard for them. Harry had been smiling at most of the women who had flocked around him the past few minutes.

The caretakers of the inn had removed all the tables and chairs from the main hall to provide room for dancing. The space was practically filled with people in their finest dresses, but whichever half of the room Harry was on always seemed to be more crowded. He was the most interesting man in the room, and both the ladies and the gentlemen knew it.

She took a deep breath—a motion made more difficult because Phoebe had laced her corset slightly tighter than what she wore for a typical day. Or perhaps because she knew she was going to have to plow her way through the circle of women surrounding Harry. Just watching him this evening wouldn't be enough. He would be on his way to London soon. She couldn't waste her time looking at him.

At least not while he spoke to other women.

She marched toward the more crowded part of the room.

A black jacket and waistcoat stopped her.

"Don't go interrupting him," Gerald said.

"Interrupting whom?" she asked, eyes wide.

"Harry. He has had so much stress in the past few years. Let him enjoy the fruits of his labours."

"But he is on my card for the next dance. And how is speaking with Miss Hubert a fruit of his labour?"

"Have you seen how she is speaking to him? For a man who grew up always undervalued, tonight is a triumph for him. The next dance won't start for a few more minutes, so let him be."

"It isn't as though anything could come from spending time with Miss Hubert. He will be leaving any day now."

"All the more reason to give him the time he has. And you never know—matches have been formed in less time than two or three days. As long as all parties are willing, there should be no impediments to a short courtship period."

"He isn't courting Miss Hubert."

"But he could be, if he wanted to. She seems quite willing, and for a man, there is nothing more gratifying than capturing a woman's interest."

"Maybe for you. Harry isn't like that. He has other pursuits. It would take a lot more than a Miss Hubert to turn his head away from those things."

Gerald turned his head to one side and looked at Christine out of the corner of his eye. "Why must you insist that he isn't interested in Miss Hubert? There is nothing wrong with her. She is amiable, well-bred, and quite good-looking."

"I'm not insistent. I simply wanted to talk to him as well. Don't you? We have hardly seen Harry in years, and we are to step aside so Miss Hubert can spend time with him?" There went Miss Hubert's fingers once again, softly touching Harry's arm. This time, she was laughing her high-pitched laugh. Surely, Harry didn't enjoy that.

"Christine," Gerald said. She whipped her eyes back to her brother. One deep line pinched between his eyebrows.

"What?"

Gerald shook his head, spun on his heel, and took three steps away from her. He threw his hands down to his sides and returned to her.

"You cannot set your hopes on Harry."

"I don't know what you mean," she lied.

"Men don't fall in love with their sisters."

"I'm not his sister."

"You might as well be. We all grew up together. There is

nothing interesting about a woman you have known your whole life."

Something tightened within her. Could that be true? Harry had always been like a brother to her as well, but the past few days had been different. Very different.

"We haven't seen each other in years," she said.

"Doesn't matter."

"Did he say something about it to you?"

"He didn't need to say anything to me about it. The man has seen you climb trees, run around with dirt on your face, and wipe mucus off the face of a tenant's child. On top of all that, the two of you embraced when he arrived. Do you think a man who was interested in a woman would so casually hold her? No. He would treat her with respect."

"What if the woman wants to be embraced? Wouldn't that be respectful?"

"He just wouldn't. Harry is one of the most careful men I know. He would take his time and put everything in place properly before so much as kissing the knuckles of a woman he was interested in."

Christine closed her eyes and once again felt Harry's warm breath on her neck, his hand over hers as he coached her on skipping stones. If Gerald was right, everything she had inferred from that interaction was false.

"Maybe you are wrong about Harry," she said. "Maybe he is different than you think."

"Well, what do you think? You've known Harry as long as I have. Would he treat a woman he loves so carelessly?"

Of course, Harry wouldn't be careless. It went against his nature. But none of their interactions had seemed careless to her.

Gerald leaned forward. "You have your planned dances. That will be plenty of time for you to spend with him tonight. Don't monopolize him. I guarantee, he won't appreciate it."

"Should I dance with him at all?" She kept her voice low, despite wanting to raise it. What made Gerald think he understood Harry so perfectly? "Considering that it can bring him no pleasure."

"It does you no harm to dance. In fact, it will increase his desirability to be seen dancing with you. Just don't take up his time. The man hasn't relaxed in years."

Christine tapped her toe inside her slipper, focusing all of her energy on that movement. This evening was not going as planned. She eyed the quartet, still settling in for their next song. She wished they would start playing. Until they at least showed signs of beginning, she would listen to Gerald and stay on this side of the room.

Several more minutes passed before the next set started. By the time Harry extricated himself from Miss Hubert, there was only enough time for him to reach for her hand and hurry her to the outer circle of dancers. Christine stood next to him, waiting for the Polka to start. For all that she had spent the whole of the evening watching him, she couldn't look at him now. The first tentative strains of the Romany Polka floated around them. Harry's fingers touched the tips of hers, and he gently pulled her hand into his. He sighed heavily and leaned toward her. "It is good to finally have my dance with you."

She turned and bowed. "You wouldn't rather still be dancing with Miss Hubert?"

He returned her bow with one eyebrow raised. "No, it is hard to relax around Miss Hubert."

The music picked up, and Harry pulled her into the first formation, his arm across her back. Nothing about touching Harry made her relax. Did he truly think of her as a sister? Someone he could touch, hold, and dance with, without inciting any emotions in him?

"Miss Hubert is quite beautiful."

"She is also quite difficult to extricate myself from." The way he turned his head into her neck as he spoke reminded her of their time skipping rocks. He hadn't seemed to mind when she hung on him. If anything, he had been the one to cling to her.

"Gerald seemed to think you wouldn't mind the women demanding your attention tonight."

They separated, her left hand still in his, their other arms extending out, then in, then back out again. Dancing in the fields with her childhood friend Harry, she never would have thought he would someday lead her so confidently about a ballroom.

The pace of the music quickened as he spun her, making conversation more difficult. "I hardly know her. She isn't clingy because of who I am. It would be different if she knew me. Or if she was a woman I was interested in."

Christine's eyes shot to his, but he wasn't looking at her. He was looking across the ballroom. She followed his eyes to find a group of women, but most of them were older. The only young woman was Miss Gertrude Gentry, and she was not much older than fifteen. Could he be interested in Miss Gertrude? Had she even spoken with him tonight? She was young and quite serious. Christine hadn't seen her smile all evening.

They spun one more time and came together. "Do you see yourself caring for a woman who is serious, or more high-spirited?"

The corner of his mouth raised, but he still wouldn't meet her eyes. "Definitely high-spirited."

He shouldn't be interested in Gertrude, then. She bit her lip. Harry didn't know any of these women, not really. Despite Gerald's warning about how quickly marriage could be decided upon, Harry wouldn't make a rash decision about something as important as choosing a wife. That wasn't his character. She had never known him to make a choice that would change his world without thinking over it seriously.

Except that one time.

When he left without telling anyone.

"Well, I don't think you should make any decisions about the women here without putting a lot of thought into it."

"Trust me. This is something I have thought long and hard about."

"How long?"

"An inordinate amount of time."

They broke apart again. Somehow, her feet managed to complete their steps without stumbling.

"I have a concern, though," he said when they came back together.

She swallowed. The places their hands met were on fire. Harry had only been home for three days. Why did his words have this much power over her?

"What is your concern?"

His eyes finally met hers. So many colors swam in them: grays and greens, dark and light browns, all sharp and alive. "My life . . . is so uncertain. I don't know what will be asked of me in the next few years. I would need to know that I am enough. Just me, because that is all I have to offer."

"You don't think Miss Hubert would think you alone would be enough?"

He scoffed and jumped to the left, and then returned to her. His dancing had only improved since their time in the fields. How many opportunities had he had to dance with women in London? "How could she? We have only met this evening."

"A woman who wanted you for who you are would want to spend time with you. She would always want you near."

Christine leaned into him. If Harry was thinking of some other girl—some woman in London—this was a risk. But it was a risk she was willing to take. Because Harry was enough for her. She had given up on marriage, certain she would spend the rest of her life as a governess in the hopes that her dowry would then be able save the estate. But if she had to choose between saving the estate and having Harry as a husband for the rest of her life, the choice was easy. His return had brought to life a part of her she had thought was dead. Becoming a governess had never been a passion. It had been a way to help her family. If she married Harry, together they would be able to find an even better solution. And one that wouldn't break her parents' hearts like her plan might have.

"Like Miss Hubert wants to be near me?"

"No, not like that."

"How can I tell the difference between a Miss Hubert and a woman who actually wants me?"

"Because a woman who loves you will search you out at any opportunity, not just those that would show her to her best advantage. She won't always agree with you, but she will always listen. And in those moments when she has sought you out and your eyes meet, you will know."

"And if I am not completely sure?"

"Then you must trust her. And if you don't, then perhaps she isn't the woman for you after all."

The music slowed and then stopped. Harry clasped her fingertips with his own and didn't let them go as he bowed. His eyes never left hers.

Trust me . . . And never leave again. If Harry understood her thoughts, he didn't say anything. But she thought he may have, and for the rest of the evening, whether he was speaking to Miss Hubert or any other young lady, she often found his gaze wandering to hers.

Eight

HARRY HAD NO right to ask to court Christine. But if she showed up this afternoon, he would. He shut the door quietly behind him as he started down the path.

He knew Christine enjoyed walking in the afternoon, but it was too much of a coincidence to believe she always walked exactly when the post was scheduled to arrive. Perhaps, she walked when she knew he would be walking as well.

His step quickened as he drew closer to the bend in the road that would show him if she waited. There was a spring in his step that none of his employers or employees had ever seen in London. What would Mrs. Ryan think of him, practically skipping down a path?

She would smile.

There wasn't a person in the world who cared about him that wouldn't want to see him this happy.

His letter should have arrived days ago. He shouldn't have been able to beat it. If it arrived today, he would give it to Christine. If it didn't, he would tell her of it anyway. As long as she had come outside to meet him again.

The road curved, and Stonehouse came into sight. Standing where the road to Dorset met the pathway to his home was Christine. The fabric of her light blue dress swayed lightly in the wind. Her hands rubbed together like they did when she was nervous.

She stood there wearing a dress as blue as the sky. His favorite colour. If it hadn't been before, it was now.

His strides grew longer and faster. He threw his shoulders back. It had been two years since the idea of marrying Christine had seemed an attainable goal. He had foolishly imagined it a possibility when he was young. And here he was, foolish once again.

Christine wasn't looking out toward the road; her body was turned toward his home. She had been waiting for him.

She had been waiting for *him.*

Ever since she had found out he would be waiting for a letter, she had been there. Waiting. He couldn't wrap his head around it.

But he would go to the devil before going back to London without knowing her mind.

"Christine," he called out when he was close enough to see the dropped pearl earrings that hung on her ears.

"Harry," she replied with a wave and a small jump. She stepped forward, almost as if to reach for his hands, then stopped herself. He found it hard to breathe. Did she sense it too? That joining hands should lead to an embrace, which should lead to a touch of the lips, which would lead to declarations of a love that would last their entire lives?

He wasn't certain, so his hands stayed to his sides—he hoped for the very last time.

"Did you sleep well after the ball?"

Christine laughed. "No."

He took a step closer, commanding his hands to stay where they were, but unable to keep his feet from moving to Christine. He smiled at her laughter. She would be out of place in London, but he would make a place for her. If she would have him.

"Neither did I." His head had been full of images of a girl

climbing trees, wading in rivers with frogs in her hair, while one image constantly remained in the background: dark hair falling over a wee babe, eyes meeting his in wonder. "Not at all, really."

"I've had much to think on," she said.

"As have I. I must confess, I am very pleased to see you here this afternoon."

Christine's shoulders rose, and her hands clasped together. "As am I."

"Should we walk?" He held out his arm, and when she took it, some of his nervous energy left. They were touching at last. He could stop digging his nails into the palms of his hands.

Her slender neck turned, and her chin rose toward him. "Do you think your letter will come today?"

"Oddly enough, I hope it does."

"You are looking forward to leaving here, then?"

"The truth is, I need to. But I am very glad I came."

"We won't have to wait another six years to see you again, will we? You will return more often?"

"I hope so."

They walked down the lane in comfortable silence. Harrison had been so busy the last few years, he had forgotten what it felt like to belong somewhere. To belong to someone. He didn't belong to Christine, but for the first time in years, he felt that he had a chance. A solid chance, and a much better chance than he had when he so hopefully penned that letter to her.

"I have something to tell you." Christine tightened her grip on his arm, this time looking down. "I have debated saying anything, but as you are perhaps leaving soon, and to London . . . I would like to tell you what I have told no one else."

Harrison's feet would move no farther. They were out of sight from Stonehouse. His heart pounded in his chest; the country air swirled about them. He placed his fingers—only slightly trembling—under her chin and raised her face so that he could look into her ever-changing eyes.

"I would like to hear it."

She furrowed her eyebrows and shrugged her shoulders, a hesitant smile on her lips. "I've been waiting for a letter as well. One I don't want Gerald to see."

He dropped his hand from her chin as if it had been burned. "What?"

"I'm telling you because I believe there is a chance we might meet again in London, if all goes according to my plan."

"Each afternoon, you have come to walk because you were expecting a letter?"

She nodded in excitement, not knowing the way her smile was hardening and cooling his heart. It had been iron only a few days ago—it was turning to iron again. "I was so worried my letter would come before yours, but now I don't care. Just don't tell Gerald about it."

There was only one reason she would hide a letter from Gerald.

"It is a letter from a man."

"Yes. And if he knew what I had planned . . ." She stopped without finishing.

"Is he not a good man?"

"He is—but a merchant in London. It is a position Gerald never planned for me."

"A merchant." The words barely made it through his ground-together teeth.

She reached her hand out to his arm, but he pulled away. For the first time since bringing up her exciting *plan*, her eyebrows furrowed. "I don't think there is anything wrong with him being a merchant."

"Obviously." He took a deep breath. If she was to live in London married to a merchant with whom he could most certainly come in contact, he needed to start hiding his feelings immediately.

"It seems to me you already don't like this plan of mine, and you have not yet heard it."

Harrison took a deep breath. He needed to hear her out, even if it meant they could never actually belong together. He would always remain hers for the taking, but she . . . she had never truly been within his reach. It was time to remember who he was: Christine's friend. "I have full faith in you, Christine. I'm certain whatever you have planned has been well thought out."

Christine beamed, her face practically glowing in the afternoon sun. He had never caused her to smile like that. How had he come to the conclusion that she could care for him as much as he did her?

"I've been in correspondence with a Mr. Wilstead. He seems very amiable."

"Mr. Wilstead, the railroad man?" Harrison nearly choked on the words. "The man is a widower with three children. His wife hasn't been dead for more than six months."

"You know him?"

"A little." The man was in trade. He had built at least three railroad lines and had done very well for himself. Harrison had sold him large shipments of nails a number of times. "He has come into his wealth through the railroad."

"You speak as if that makes him less of a man."

"I've never heard anything but good about him, but Christine—Miss Stone—" Her eyebrows furrowed at the use of her family name, but what was he to do? He couldn't keep calling her Christine, not if she was serious about this Mr. Wilstead fellow. "What has a man like that to do with you?"

"He needs someone to take care of his children."

"And you would settle for that? Can't he find some other woman to care for them?"

"Of course he could, but I hope he doesn't. Do you know what it is like for me here? I know what is going on with the lands, and I know it cannot last. It is better for me to take things into my own hands before it is too late."

"Too late?"

"If I stay any longer, we will lose everything."

And then even a wealthy merchant might not have her.

"How set are you on this plan?"

"I . . . I don't know anymore. At one point, I was very certain this was what I needed to do."

"But now?"

"Now, I'm confused. Until I receive his letter, I'm not even sure he will have me."

"If it has gotten to the point of correspondence, I would assume he will have you." Any man would have to be a fool not to want Christine. "But you hardly know him. And London? Did you have to choose a man who lived in London?"

"*You* are in London. I thought you would be happy to see me there from time to time." Christine's bottom lip quivered. "Was I wrong?"

How could he answer that? If she thought he would be happy to see her married to another man in London, Harrison had been wrong about so many things. She hadn't been waiting each afternoon to spend time with him; she was trying to intercept her own letter. A letter from a man she was arranging to marry. And they were so far off in their thoughts that she assumed he would be happy about it. Was she in the wrong? No. But he was. He was incredibly, foolishly wrong, and he had no one to blame for it except himself.

Hooves sounded up the lane, and a small cloud of dust announced an incoming rider. There was no carriage—just a man on a horse. If they hadn't been standing on this bend in the road, they would have seen him much sooner. Harrison was saved from answering any more of Christine's questions. She reached for his arm, and he closed his eyes at her easy touch. She hadn't realized what their time together had meant to him, or she wouldn't be touching him so casually now. With a tug, Christine pulled him to the side of the road.

The horseman was no one he recognized, but he pulled his black horse to a standstill beside them. "I'm looking for a Mr. Harrison Chase. I have an urgent letter from London."

"I'm Mr. Chase."

The man nodded and swung down from his horse. He pulled a satchel slung about his shoulders from behind him and opened it. Rifling through multiple papers, he found the one he was looking for and lifted it from the leather bag.

"You've a letter from Richard Cobdan. It is marked urgent."

Harrison reached for the letter and hastily broke the seal. He had only spoken with Mr. Cobdan three times: twice in living rooms of mutual acquaintances, and once in a dark office. Their conversations had been more like interviews than anything else. Harrison had done well. It hadn't taken more than ten minutes of their first meeting for the two of them to realize they had similar goals and passions. Mr. Cobdan simply had more power at his fingertips. Harrison unfolded the letter.

Mr. Chase,

The change we have been waiting for has come. Lamb has been given a vote of "no confidence" and has resigned. A new parliament will be forming in the upcoming weeks. I need you here. I am depending on your ability to work day and night on a campaign in your borough, and the League will support you in any way you deem necessary. We need to win that seat to repeal the Corn Laws, and I know you are the man for that position.

I was surprised to hear you were in Dorset. I expect you to return as soon as possible. If I don't hear from you by the end of this week, I will assume you are not interested and find another candidate for your borough.

Yours in the cause,

Richard Cobdan

"What is it?" Christine asked, bringing him back to the present.

"Lamb is no longer prime minister. I must return to London at once."

"He isn't? What has happened?"

"He has resigned; it seems this time he will actually leave his office. Peel will be forming a new government, and I'm to run for the House of Commons. There isn't a moment to lose. I will return to Stonehouse and bid farewell to Gerald."

"Will you be returning anytime soon?"

He wouldn't. His dream of visiting Stonehouse as a family member was gone almost as quickly as he had true hope in it. "Not in the near future."

He took two steps toward Stonehouse, then stopped. He spun on his heel. The man who had delivered the mail was still rifling in his bag. Christine stood watching him. Her dress billowed out to one side, and the small locks of hair that refused to stay put at the nape of her neck danced in the wind.

The next time he saw her, she would be the wife of another man. He would have no right to call her Christine or to teach her how to skip rocks. She would have her hand around another man's arm, and he would have no right to ask her to choose him instead. It would be too late.

He rushed back to her. He took both her hands in his and kissed them one at a time. "Christine." Her name was hushed on his lips. "These last few days have been more than pleasant. I hope you know I will always cherish the time, past and present, that we have spent together." He rubbed his thumb across each of her delicate, warm knuckles. She must think him a cad, hovering over her like this. But he wanted one last moment with her. "If you change your mind about Mr. Wilstead . . ." he said, without looking her in the eye. Then what? Perhaps she would consider marrying him? He was on his way to London, perhaps to spend every penny he had earned in a campaign that he might lose. "Please let me know." It was weak and cowardly of him, but he couldn't allow her to suspect the depth of his feelings for her. Not if he ever expected to set foot on Stone land again.

Her eyes scrunched together in confusion. "All right," she answered.

He couldn't leave having only said that. "And don't go to London yet. Stay here until Parliament is formed."

Every obstacle which had been so easily overlooked when he thought she might love him was brought before him full force. Even if he was elected, there was no pay for a Member of Parliament. He wouldn't know how much of his money would make it through the election until after it was over—most of it for certain—but after that there would be ongoing costs of supporting the League. He had nothing to offer Christine.

He turned and left.

Nine

HARRY NEVER LOOKED back at Christine, his march toward her home never slowing. Could the man be more aggravating? She hadn't even had the chance to finish telling him about her plans to become a governess and her hopes to see him while in London. He had dashed off with more work to do. She had thought he was learning the art of living at last, but one correspondence from London had set him back to the man he was when he arrived.

True, that correspondence had included the fact that the prime minister was no longer seated in parliament, but still . . .

A clearing of a throat sounded behind her. She wasn't alone. She had nearly forgotten the man who had delivered the letter. She turned to find him holding out a stack of several letters.

"Are you mistress of Stonehouse?"

"I am her daughter."

"Then I may leave the rest of these in your hands. I have come directly from London, but when I asked the mail coach driver directions to Stonehouse, he sent me with these letters as well. Apparently, there was a strike one town east of here and some of the mail was delayed."

He handed her the letters and, with a nod, mounted his horse. The man gave his horse a kick, and they were on their way back down the road, this time with less urgency than when he arrived. Christine covered her nose with her hand and walked away from the dust left in his wake.

She shook her head and dusted off her skirt with her free hand. Today was not turning out at all as she had expected. When she saw the smile on Harry's face as he had greeted her, she thought perhaps he had grown to care for her.

What a ridiculous thought. The only thing that man cared about was work.

Couldn't running for Parliament have waited a few more minutes while she told him her plans?

She sighed. Of course it couldn't. Harry wouldn't be Harry if he didn't focus all of his energy on objectives. Once he chose a course, he wouldn't deviate from it. If only she could have been a part of his ambitions . . . for a moment she had thought she might. But one note from London was all it had taken to put her in her place.

She glanced down at the letters in her hands. The one on top was for Papa. It would have to wait until he returned from Surrey. She slid that one to the back of the pile. The next was a letter for Gerald. She slid it to the back as well.

The next letter was addressed to her and stamped *London.* Mr. Wilstead had finally written her back.

Harry was much too far down the lane to call for him. So be it. She had started this process alone; she could certainly open the letter on her own. If Mr. Wilstead wanted her, she would become a governess and give up her chance to marry. Her father would stop holding her dowry for her, and that money could go toward saving Stonehouse. All of those things had seemed like a good idea before Harry had returned. But now?

It was simply a decision that would affect the entirety of the rest of her life.

She might as well be done with it.

She walked down the lane a few paces, then left the road to stand by an oak tree. With hands shaking, she broke the seal.

Her eyes scanned the contents of the letter. Words jumped out at her: love, leaving, missing, and the signature at the end—Harry.

A letter from Harry. She leaned against the oak and ran her fingers over the careful script.

Christine,

I'm sorry.

I have fallen in love with you. I somehow forgot my position, forgot that we grew up together, forgot that anything between us is impossible, and I fell in love with you. I can no longer stand by, knowing if I don't change something in my life, I will be forced to watch you wed another. You would leave Stonehouse, but when you returned, there would be a man with you. I could not bear it. What is more—and my hand betrays me as I write this—I want to be that man.

I'm leaving. If you are reading this, please know I have sent this letter because, at last, I have raised myself to a point that could be close to deserving you. Or if not deserving, I have made myself into a man that society would consider nearer your equal. A daunting task when I know you have no equal.

I am young, and you are even younger. I imagine this endeavor will take years, for I have so very far to go. But know this: any toil or hardship I go through from this point on will be sweet to me if it eventually brings me back to you.

I cannot ask you to wait for me.

The chances of this letter ever reaching you are small. But it is a risk I am willing to take.

I will miss you every day,

Harry

Christine's legs no longer held her. She slid down the trunk of the oak and landed in a heap. Her hand flew to her mouth, and she breathed deeply through her nose. Harry had fallen in love with her? How was that possible? When? Shaking her head, she checked the signature again. The bold strokes on his "H" were thick and definite. Every sentence had been written in clear, straight lines as if he had pounded them directly out of his heart. Only her name at the top had thin, hesitant strokes.

He wrote her name the same way he said it. Softly and with care.

Through blurred eyes and with her hands shaking, she scanned the contents again, forcing her mind to focus on the information she found there, though her eyes kept returning to his lines of love. He must have written this just as he was leaving, years ago.

She jumped up from her inelegant position on the ground. Harry loved her. She folded the letter and pressed it to her heart. All these years. He had loved her all of these years. She brushed off her skirts. Harry was preparing to leave, and the last thing she was going to do was to let him leave without telling him how she felt.

Like the sun had risen after a long, lonely night.

Like she had been starving and warm ripe strawberries had dropped into her lap.

Like the man who made her world bright, relied on her to make him whole.

She wasn't about to let Harry leave her again. Not now that she knew why he had left in the first place. She picked up her skirts and ran.

She pushed open the front door with all her might, causing it to nearly crash into the wall, but she jumped into the house and saved it from doing so. Harry was in her home somewhere, bidding farewell to Gerald. She ran first to the drawing room, but it was empty. She passed a surprised Mrs. Walter, who stepped back in astonishment at Christine's hurry.

Christine stopped and put both hands on Mrs. Walter's shoulders. "My brother . . . where is my brother?"

"He is in his study with Mr. Chase."

With a nod, Christine darted down the corridor and threw open Gerald's closed door.

Harry was speaking. "—you must tell her I was young and didn't know my mind when I wrote—"

She dropped the door handle, all the strength in her arm gone. She must have misheard. Harry couldn't mean the letter. He couldn't. To be given such tenderness, to be handed love from Harry only to have him snatch it away would be too cruel.

"Well, here she is now," Gerald said. He and Harry were standing in front of his desk. "Why don't you just tell her yourself?"

Harry's eyes went to the letter. One of his long, slender hands dashed forward and braced himself on the desk. "It came?"

Nothing about him conveyed happiness. "Yes," she said.

His eyes were panicked. "I didn't send it."

The past three days flashed before her eyes. Every afternoon Harry waiting for the post, making her promise not to look at the letters when they came. Something inside her broke. He hadn't wanted her to see this letter. "But you did write it."

"A long time ago."

Six years, could a man change so much in six years? His thick arms and well-tailored clothing answered her question. Harry had changed. He had seen so much more of the world than she had; he had danced with the wealthy daughters of merchants and sat in meetings with powerful men. One of whom was asking him to run for the House of Commons. "Did you mean it? When you wrote those words, did you mean them?"

Harry placed his hand over his eyes and rubbed them, then dragged his fingers roughly down to his chin. "Are you planning to go to London, to that man?"

Gerald pulled his head back and straightened. "Say, what is this?"

"Hush, Gerald," Christine said at the same time Harry turned to him and told him to "cork it."

"I thought I would." She had no idea why he would bring Mr. Wilstead up at a moment like this. "I would like to be in London near you."

"Near me?" Harry turned his back to her and leaned over the desk, his hands gripping the edge of it as if it were his last lifeline on earth. He hung his head. "True, you would be near me, but completely out of my reach."

"I'm certain Mr. Wilstead wouldn't command all of my time." Christine stepped forward, closer to him. "I, for one, would like to visit with you when I am there."

Harry started to laugh. A deep, anguished sound. "You think Mr. Wilstead would allow you a visit? Would you show him that letter and say, 'Look, my poor old friend from long ago is miserable if he doesn't at least get to look upon me now and again?' What kind of husband would allow such behavior?"

"Husband?" Gerald placed his hand on Harry's shoulder and spun him about. Harry wouldn't look at him, wouldn't look at Christine. "What husband exactly are you talking about?"

"Mr. Wilstead." Harry said the name low and soft, like the growl of an injured dog.

The room stilled, and a slash of light filtered in from Gerald's window. Christine bit the inside of her cheek and closed her eyes. She had been misunderstood.

Very, very misunderstood. She looked down at the letter still in her hands. Only Harry's signature was visible. She traced it with her thumb.

"Gerald, are you opposed to me marrying?"

"No, of course not. But I would like to be informed of it. I don't even know who this Mr. Wilstead is. Harry doesn't seem to like him—that much is apparent."

"My dowry will empty what is left of the estate's stores."

"Your dowry remains untouched precisely for that purpose."

"And would you mind very much if the person I married was a merchant? A man who had worked to make a living?"

"You really should be asking these things of Father. I can't believe you have gotten so far as an engagement without any of us knowing."

"Oh, I'm not engaged."

"Not yet," Harry mumbled.

Christine couldn't help it—she smiled. "Not yet is correct." She took two steps forward and leaned into her brother, her mouth near his ear. "Would you allow me to speak to Harry alone for a moment?" she whispered.

Gerald scrunched his face. "Why?"

"Oh, just leave already," she hissed. "I don't think you will want to be present for what is about to transpire."

"You aren't going to hurt him, are you?"

"No," Christine said. "At least, I'm quite certain I'm not."

Gerald nodded and, taking one last look at his friend still leaning against the desk, left the room.

Ten

THE SOUND OF the door opening and closing caused Harrison to uncover his eyes and stand straight at last. He still couldn't bring himself to look at Gerald. "Is she gone?" he asked, his eyes intent on looking out the window.

"No," Christine's soft voice answered.

He spun. Christine marched toward him, her face unreadable. He leaned against the desk, suddenly uncertain. "Where did Gerald go?"

"I asked him to leave."

"You did?" He shook his head. He couldn't be alone in a room with Christine. There was no telling what he would do. "I must go as well." He pushed himself off the desk and strode toward the door, purposely casting a wide berth from where Christine stood.

She dropped his letter onto the desk and then skipped to the side and caught him by the arm.

"Don't go."

He took a deep breath and allowed himself to look at her. Her dress was slightly wrinkled from their walk, and several strands of her hair had come loose. At some point, she must have taken her gloves off, for her bare fingers lightly pinched the fabric of his jacket. She had never been so beautiful, for which he was grateful. He would keep this image of her forever emblazoned in his mind. "I have to. I've been called back to London. I've a campaign to run."

"And I'm certain you will win."

"It will be a lot of work."

"That has never scared you off before."

"No, and I will be throwing myself into this completely."

Christine's fingers slowly walked down his forearm in the most devilish manner. One finger after another slowly stepping in front of the other until she reached his cuff. Once there, she slid her index finger along the inside of his bare wrist. He pulled his hand back as if it were on fire.

"Miss Stone. I have never before found you to be cruel."

"I am being a bit cruel, aren't I?"

If she knew what her touch meant to him, which she must, since she had read his letter, then she was.

"More than a bit," he managed to say.

"Well, perhaps, I am finally repaying you for putting frogs in my hair." She stepped forward, allowing only mere inches between them. He closed his eyes and took a deep breath, but all that did was allow her honeysuckle scent to flood his senses. No one in London smelled like that. He needed to—

Christine took hold of both of his hands. "Harry." Her voice was as soft as the dew that formed on early morning leaves.

He didn't dare open his eyes and look at her. "You should start calling me Mr. Chase."

She pulled him to her in the lightest of movements—a gentle tug on his hands, and suddenly, she was pressed against him. Her form fit perfectly next to his, as if together, they were one whole. He opened his eyes to find her smiling up at him. "I'm not going to marry Mr. Wilstead." Her hands tightened in his, and almost involuntarily, his grip contracted as well.

"But you asked Gerald about it. You told me you were going to care for his children."

She smiled and leaned farther into him, dropping his hands and wrapping hers about his waist.

"I was to be his governess. I was awaiting a letter of employment."

A quick breath escaped his lips. He brought a hand to his mouth, bit into his index finger, and released it. He was overwhelmed with a sudden rush of heat and light. Every part of his body seemed to scream for a chance to sing. He needed a focal point, even if it was a focal point of pain. "His governess?"

"Yes, and when I asked Gerald about marrying a merchant, I wasn't referring to him. I meant—"

"Me." The word escaped from his lips like a puff of air. Harrison's shoulders relaxed, and his hands dropped to his sides. The pieces of his heart, which, moments ago, had been scattered about like leaves in the wind, rushed into his chest and snapped back together. Christine tightened her hold at his waist.

"Yes," she said. "Of course I meant you."

A small laugh escaped Harrison's mouth. He slid his hands down Christine's arms to where they connected behind his back, just to be certain they were there. He needed one more witness of this moment to be certain it was real. "Of course you did? There has been no 'of course' for me. How was I supposed to know that?"

"I searched you out every day."

"You were waiting for a letter."

"Yes, and I could have done that without you."

Harry shook his head, placed a hand below her chin, and traced her bottom lip with his thumb. "Ask me again if I meant what I said in that letter."

She released his waist and cupped his hand in hers, then turned her head and kissed his palm. "Harry, did you—"

Harrison didn't wait for her to finish. Six years had been long enough. He slid his hand behind her neck and pulled her to him. Her gentle gasp as he pulled her forward was cut short as he covered her mouth with his own. She sighed into him and returned her hands to his waist. He had dreamed of this moment for years. Christine in his arms, his fingers in her hair, and his lips on her smiling ones. He had promised himself he would return a triumphant hero with more money than even the Stones had, and Christine would fall into his embrace.

This was not that. The smile of her lips pressed against his own returning smile had nothing to do with his bank account or his position in society. Christine loved *him.*

Why the devil hadn't he thought of working on that before?

He angled her head to the right and kissed her hard enough for her smile to be lost in the fierceness of his touch. He needed Christine like he needed sunlight, like he needed happiness and understanding. She was everything he had ever wanted, and he had been deprived of her for much too long. He released her only when he had run out of air, her eyes wide and dancing. "That is for pulling me into the stream," he murmured into the side of her cheek.

A small noise somewhere between a snort and a laugh escaped her throat. Harrison nipped her ear before moving down her neck to her collarbone. He slid his lips along the ridge until he reached her shoulder, where the edge of her gown hit. He kissed the last of the bare skin there. "And that is for making me think you were going to marry some widower with three children."

Christine pulled away from him. "What is this game we are playing?"

"You must admit, it is better than any we played as children." He smiled and raised an eyebrow.

"Oh, it is, but I have a few bones to pick with you as well."

Harrison smiled. "If only I had spent more time tormenting you . . ."

"Oh, I can find plenty of grievances. Don't you worry." She reached for his cravat and pulled his face down to her level. "This is for putting frogs in my hair."

Harrison closed his eyes, waiting for his blessed punishment. Christine laughed and put both of her hands in his hair and jostled them about, completely upsetting his carefully-styled hair.

His eyes opened just as she was running behind Gerald's desk. She held his chair protectively in front of her and squealed.

"Oh," Harrison said. "Two can play at this." He strode forward, and Christine jumped out from behind the chair, rushing to the window and pressing herself against it. He reached her before she had a chance to escape. In a flash, his hand was in her hair, and he pulled out two of the pins. "That is for holding Mrs. Johnson's baby when you were only fifteen, and looking so fetching, I couldn't help but fall in love with you." One side of her hair tumbled down nearly to her waist. The light from the window flashed gold into her otherwise dark hair. His eyes pivoted to hers. They were on fire.

She took advantage of his reverence, grabbed both his shoulders, and spun, pushing him into the curtains, which enveloped both of them.

"This is for leaving me here alone with only Gerald." She pressed her lips against his. Their breaths came in synchronized rushes as her fingers found the back of his neck, digging into his flesh as she pulled him harder toward him. Harry spun them again, bringing them most of the way out of the curtain.

He placed both of his hands on the wall behind her and then slid his fingertips down the length of her fallen hair.

"I'll answer your question now." He kissed the tip of her nose and then stepped back. "I feel so much more than I did when I wrote that letter. After six years, I started to forget. I talked myself out of loving you. If I had left before discovering you weren't to be married, I never would have recovered. I would have spent the rest of my days fighting to feed the hungry, all while hungering for you. I knew I loved you at seventeen, but now I know life without you would only be a hollow emptiness that no one else would ever be able to fill. You have always been the only woman I will ever love."

Christine raised an eyebrow. "I have that much power over you?"

"More."

She laughed, and her head fell forward into Harry's chest. He pushed off of the wall and curled his arms around her.

At that moment, Gerald decided to walk back into the room.

"What the devil?" he said. "Harry, what the deuce are you doing to my sister?"

They both turned to face him. Christine's hair was half undone, her lips swollen in the most provoking manner. He couldn't look much better. They stepped fully out from the edges of the curtain, and Gerald hissed.

"I thought you were going to marry some merchant from London," he said.

"I am."

"Well, he isn't going to take kindly to you acting this way with Harry."

Christine reached for Harrison's hand and curled her fingers around his. "The merchant from London *is* Harry."

"Oh," Gerald said, his face flat.

"Oh," he said again, his eyes narrowing. "This is a trick, isn't it?" He put both hands on his waist and stepped back to examine the two of them. "Are you fooling me in order to repay some old debt?"

Christine's free hand went to her mouth. "How could you think we would ever consider doing such a thing?"

Harrison laughed, and his fingers tightened around hers. Christine had suggested doing exactly that.

"See!" Gerald pointed to Harrison. "He is laughing. This is a hoax. You are having a bit of fun at my expense."

Harrison dropped Christine's hand and laid his palms on Gerald's shoulders. "We were having a bit of fun."

"Not as much fun as we were having a moment ago," Christine sniggered behind him.

He was going to enjoy having a lifetime of games with her. "But I am in earnest. I have never been more earnest about anything in my life."

Something in his eyes must have convinced Gerald. After looking back and forth between the two of them, he sighed. "Are you certain? I mean, it's Christine."

"Gerald." Christine's voice was deep with warning.

"I wouldn't expect you to understand." Harrison said. "She is your sister. But she has never been mine."

Gerald rubbed his temples and then pinched the bridge of his nose. "I suppose I can understand that." He reached for Harrison's hand and pumped it up and down. "Welcome to the family, Harry. You are a much better fit than some stuffy London merchant."

"Thank you, Gerald. It means the world to me to hear it. I hope your parents will feel the same way."

"They won't take much convincing. You have done well for yourself, and Christine is no spring chicken."

"Gerald!" Christine rushed forward with a dangerous gleam in her eye.

Gerald laughed and dodged her attack, jumping to one side and then running behind his desk just as she had earlier.

They circled around the desk. "There was no otter in the stream, was there? You made that up to get rid of me."

Gerald sniggered. "It looks as though I won't need to be rid of you now. Lucky for me, Harry will take you away to London."

Christine leaped forward, and Harrison wrapped his arm about her waist and pulled her back to him with her arms flailing about like a windmill.

"Avenge me, Harry. Look what I have had to put up with."

Harrison laughed. "I, for one, am quite happy he sent you off on that otter chase and will not be avenging you. In fact, we need to discuss what our plans are." Christine calmed down, but she didn't take her eyes off of Gerald. "I need to return to London."

Harrison slowly dropped his hand, and Christine stayed by his side. "You saw the letter I received. I cannot give up on a seat in the House of Commons if it means I could make a difference for so many families who can't afford food."

"I know," Christine said. "Of course you need to go."

He couldn't imagine leaving her now. "I will send for you as soon as the new government is formed."

"Would it be so bad if you had a wife during the process?"

"No, it wouldn't be bad." Especially for his own sanity. "Some would even see it as an asset. Once they saw you, everyone would see it as an asset."

"Then, perhaps, I might come sooner."

"Father and Mother will be returning in the next two weeks," Gerald said. "We will, of course, need to wait for them."

"And for banns to be read," Harrison reminded them. "I

will happily start that process as soon as I have received word from your parents."

"But your parents," Christine said. "We can tell them now." She reached for Harrison's hand and pulled him forward.

"I'm not certain we are ready for that," Harrison said.

"Why not?" Christine turned to him, brows furrowed.

"You may want to visit your maid first." He tugged on the loose curls trailing down her back.

"What did you do with my hair pins?" Christine asked.

Gerald shuffled uncomfortably and shook his head. "This is going to take some getting used to."

Harrison ignored Gerald and tried to remember what he had done with the pins. He had been quite pleasantly occupied at the time. He scanned the floor before finding them in his pocket. He pulled them out and held them in his open palm.

Christine snatched the pins out of his hand, rolled up her hair, and fastened the loose strands.

Both Gerald and Harrison cocked their heads to one side. Her hair was up, but it didn't look much better.

Christine reached for Harrison's hand once again. "Come," she smiled. "Let's tell your parents we are to be married."

He followed her willingly, giving his old friend a shrug as he passed his soon-to-be brother-in-law. No matter what Christine's hair looked like, her invitation was one he would have to be a fool to decline.

Eleven

CHRISTINE EYED THE six paintings in front of her. One was a tree, or perhaps a bush. A tree, she decided. Definitely a tree. She had no idea what the other five could be. She took the paint brushes her students had washed to the basin to remove the last bits of stubborn paint. After four years of marriage, she knew Harry would gladly buy her more brushes, but she didn't like to take advantage of her husband's generosity.

Not unless completely necessary.

Converting the small carriage house in their nearly nonexistent garden into an art studio had apparently been a necessity—at least, according to Harry. They had no plans to own a carriage, and he knew plenty of children who would love to learn from her.

Christine didn't turn around at the sound of the door opening and closing softly behind her. She knew the sound of her husband's step. One of the paintings was covered in gashes of reds and oranges. At first, she had thought Jim was painting nonsense, but the more she looked at it, a pattern seemed to emerge. Like a word she had momentarily forgotten, she could feel the image at the back of her mind, but she couldn't quite place it. The paint was thick, to the point of being wasteful, but ten-year-old Jim was so engrossed while painting it, she didn't have the heart to ask him to use less.

"I've brought you something." Harry's voice was low and soft, like the sound of the stream she had left behind in Dorset.

She smiled. "Of course you have."

Harry came up behind her and wrapped his arms around her middle. One of his hands held a thick envelope. Harry's head slid onto her shoulder and nuzzled her neck, his chest expanding as if he were breathing her in. She sighed into him. As much as she missed Dorset, Harry would always be home. He motioned to the thick, garish painting with his chin. "Who painted that one?"

"Jim."

"Well, he got the colors right."

She spun in his arms until her head was under his, then leaned back just enough to see his face. "What is it?"

"That is the heart of a forge, where the fire and coals are so hot they turn dark metal into bright flames."

She tried to spin back around to look again, but Harry held her tight.

"I brought you something."

His smile was subtle. He was trying to contain his excitement. This was no common gift.

"You don't need to buy me things."

"I know. But I found out this was for sale and knew we had to have it."

"It is for both of us?" She had almost said 'all of us,' but it was still early yet, and she hadn't told Harry about her suspicions. After four years of waiting, she didn't want to get his hopes up in case she was wrong.

He unwrapped his arms from around her waist and handed her the envelope. It wasn't sealed, so she made quick work of opening it.

It was a bill of sale. Land. Her heart froze for a moment.

"Harry, where is this?"

"Dorset. Father told me Mr. Cummings was selling off a good portion of his land."

Richard Cummings was a neighbor. His land bordered her parents' on the north side. Their stream crossed over into the Cummings land. Chase land, now. Their land. "This is two hundred acres." How could they afford this? She hadn't followed their finances very closely, but other than her studio, they had lived frugally in London.

"It is only land. There are no dwellings, other than the tenants' homes on it. Mr. Cummings is keeping his home and five acres to live on, but he will no longer farm or collect rent."

"But, how?" Christine could practically smell the summer flowers in bloom. The roar of the ocean only a few scant miles from home. She traced Harry's signature at the bottom of the document.

"You may remember I sold a factory before we married."

"But . . ." she stopped. They had been living off the interest that money provided each year. She hadn't forgotten it—just considered it spoken for. When they first arrived in London they had thought they would need it for his campaign, but the League had funded it. Some of the money was donated to the League, but they had saved the main portion in case there was ever another push to repeal the Corn Laws. But after months of talks with Peel, he had managed to convince Parliament to abolish the Corn Laws, practically on his own. The majority of their money was never needed.

Harry traced her cheek, a gesture that never lost its tenderness, despite years of marriage. "We have a decision to make," he said.

She nodded, still clutching the bill of sale in her hand, her mind racing with possibilities.

"We need to be in London when Parliament is in session," Harry said. She nodded again, not trusting herself to speak. "But when it is not, we could live in Dorset. We still have the funds to do one of two things. We can build a home on this land . . ." He pointed to the paper in her hands. ". . . or we can stop renting and buy a home here in London. One with room enough for all our books and space for entertaining."

"Dorset," Christine said. She clutched the lapels of her husband's jacket, the bill of sale wrinkling where she still held it. She loved their life in London, and didn't want to leave her little studio for a grander home. They could move most of the books to the country. Living in Dorset for a large portion of the year would be a dream come true.

"You don't mind staying in this small home? I never meant for this to be permanent."

Christine slid one hand up his lapel until it reached his cravat, and flicked it with her finger. "Poor me. I will continue to be stuck in confined quarters with you."

He smiled, a devilish gleam lighting up his eyes. "I knew you didn't mind the close quarters, but I did think perhaps you missed having a stream to push me into."

Christine laughed, but in her heart she agreed with him. "For the last time, I never pushed you into a stream."

"Well, push or pull, you will have plenty of time to soak me completely when we are back in Dorset. I've got some ideas that should help keep our land and your family's land profitable over the next few years. I think more and more land will be sold, now that the price of grain has gone down. If, between our two families, we can buy enough of it, we can take advantage of some of the new innovations I've been hearing about."

"You don't trust Gerald to marry an heiress?" Her brother's current passion was an heiress with a very large dowry and a small amount of respect for him.

"I'd rather he didn't feel the need to marry one. I would

offer him advice, but I'm sadly lacking in the wooing depart-
ment. I only ever loved one woman, and, fortunately for me,
she was stuck in Dorset with a positive drought of men."

"I still can't believe you left me there."

"It was only for six years." He stroked her cheek again.
"Six miserable, lonely years."

"Don't ever do it again." She narrowed her eyes and
stepped closer to Harry.

"As if I could."

He lifted her chin between his thumb and forefinger and
kissed her. She wrapped her arms around his broad chest, her
fingers barely reaching each other behind his back. The bill of
sale still dangled from her hands. Harry was solid, safe, and an
ever present force in her life. In a few weeks—once she was
certain—she would let him in on her secret. Hopefully, they
would be on their land in Dorset. After she was done telling
him, and after he was done showering her with affection, she
could push him into the stream and he would have no
recourse.

Not in her condition.

She grinned as her lips grazed his cheek. Teasing Harry
never grew tiresome. At some point, the bill of sale dropped
from her hand to the floor. They would pick it back up again
later. Life with Harry hadn't always been easy. But every aspect
of life was better when they were together, including their
struggles. Life, at times, had forced them to take some steps
backwards, but with their hands linked together, every step
was a step in the right direction.

Thank the heavens Mrs. Ryan had managed to send that
letter.

Esther Hatch grew up on a cherry orchard in rural Utah. After high school, she alternated living in Russia to teach children English and attending Brigham Young University in order to get a degree in archaeology. She began writing when one of her favorite authors invited her to join a critique group. The only catch was she had to be a writer. Not one to be left out of an opportunity to socialize and try something new; she started on her first novel that week.

Visit her at: EstherHatch.com

A Ring of Gold

-NICHOLE VAN-

God answers sharp and sudden on some prayers,
And thrusts the thing we have prayed for in our face,
A gauntlet with a gift in it.
—*Elizabeth Barrett Browning*

Ah, but a man's reach should exceed his grasp,
Or what's a heaven for?
—*Robert Browning*

Gentle Reader, we here at *The Tattler* have one burning question: Will Mr. Ethan Penn-Leith and Miss Viola Brodure make a match of it?

All of London is well-acquainted with the popularity of Miss Brodure's novels. Speculation continues regarding her latest book, *Little Lottie*, and its now infamous Chapter Eleven, in which Miss Brodure proclaims the brilliance of Mr. Penn-Leith, the celebrated Highland Poet. With the rest of London, we continue to wait and see if Mr. Penn-Leith will reply to Miss Brodure's overtures in a similarly literary fashion.

On this Valentine's Day, when we celebrate love, we hold out hope that the two literary giants of our age will write a romantic story of their own.

One

VIOLA BRODURE HAD made a monumental mistake.

There *had* to have been a better way to capture the man's attention.

An introduction through a mutual friend.

A happenstance meeting upon a country lane.

A convenient carriage "accident."

Anything other than this.

She had simply wished to make his acquaintance. That was all.

Instead, Viola had released a hydra—a monster with heads named Expectation, Public Spectacle, and Melodrama.

Worse, Viola—who blushed to meet a stranger and stammered her way through most conversations—was no Hercules. The more she attempted to dismember the hydra, the more it multiplied.

What was she ever to do—

"READ THE LETTER, GIRL!" Mrs. Prior boomed, interrupting her thoughts.

Viola flinched, nearly dropping the envelope clutched in her hand.

Mrs. Prior had reached that elderly age where one ceased to care about propriety and manners. Moreover, she was notoriously hard of hearing and incapable of modulating the volume of her voice.

"IT MUST BE FROM HIM!"

"Yes, dearest, it is surely from Mr. Penn-Leith himself." Viola's father, Dr. Brodure, smiled. He sat beside Mrs. Prior on the parlor sofa, his white hair sticking out in soft tufts above his ears, giving him an owlish look that tugged at Viola's heart. "It is postmarked from Edzell, after all."

Viola looked down at the letter. Yes, indeed, "EDZELL" was scrawled beside the penny black in a postmaster's impatient hand.

Only one person of note lived near the tiny hamlet of Edzell, Scotland:

Ethan Penn-Leith.

Viola ordered her heart to *stopbeatingsofast.* But her lungs threatened rebellion. Nerves and stress always aggravated her asthma, so to be reading a letter of this magnitude with an audience . . .

Viola darted a glance at Mrs. Prior, seated across from her. The woman sipped her tea innocently enough, but she was surely cataloging details to be reported to neighbors, friends, and (heaven forfend) the occasional journalist. The incessant curiosity about Viola's personal life only increased her anxiety.

Why could others not content themselves with her writing alone? Why must they pry into every corner of her life? She swallowed, trying to regulate her breathing, focusing on the fire popping in the grate.

Viola's father—the youngest son of a baronet—was a gentleman of letters and clergyman to a small parish in Mayfair. Their church was not a large, fashionable affair like St. George's in Hanover Square. Rather, the Church of St. Laurence sat on a side street, largely ignored by the surrounding aristocratic residents, much to her father's frustration.

Mrs. Prior was a notable exception. A wealthy widow, her

generous donations greatly assisted the parish, explaining why Viola's father overlooked the woman's ofttimes gauche behavior.

"READ THE LETTER!" Mrs. Prior repeated, and then frowned. "WHY ARE YOUR HANDS SHAKING?" She turned to Dr. Brodure. "WHY ARE HER HANDS SHAKING?"

Viola darted a glance downward. Hmm, her hands were indeed trembling. Her lungs tightened further. Mrs. Prior tended to exacerbate Viola's natural shyness. Add a letter from *him* into the mix, and it was any wonder Viola could still breathe.

She often pondered this cause and effect—did her own shyness exacerbate her asthma? Or was it a more ironic opposite . . . her worry and fear over having an asthma attack in front of strangers caused her shy tongue?

She lifted her head and met her father's imploring gaze. *Please read the letter*, it said. *It is a little thing to acquiesce to Mrs. Prior's demands.*

Swallowing, Viola nodded. The parish depended upon Mrs. Prior's largess.

Viola broke the seal, eyes scanning the lines of text.

"ALOUD!" Mrs. Prior shouted, making Viola flinch. "YOU MUST READ THE LETTER ALOUD, GIRL!"

Viola shot a panicked look to her father, who smiled and nodded his encouragement. "If you could, my dearest."

How could she refuse?

She took a steadying breath and read:

Invercairn Mains, Edzell, Angus, Scotland
February 12, 1842

Dear Miss Brodure,
I scarce know how to begin this letter. It has, in all truth,

been months in the making. Permit me to express how thoroughly I adore your work. Little Lottie *is a rousing tale of the human spirit. I find the creative turn of your mind most fascinating. I do not wish to be impertinent, but I beg you to indulge me—from whence do you draw your inspiration?*

Furthermore, thank you for your expansive praise of my humble poems. If I may be so bold as to say, though the words were placed in wee Lottie's mouth, I felt as if they came directly from your heart. I am honored to have my name included in your own work in any way.

Your most humble servant,

Ethan Penn-Leith

P.S. I neglected to mention that my sister is an ardent admirer of your novels, as well. She wishes you Godspeed in all your writing endeavors.

Viola rested the letter on her lap, hands still trembling.

He had *written.*

She paused to savor the sensation—the electric hum in her veins, the whoosh of blood in her ears—committing it all to memory. As a writer, she hoarded such moments, tucking them away to be recalled weeks or months later.

"Well, well, well." Her father sat back in his chair, his eyes widening, a giant grin splitting his face. "What an honor Mr. Penn-Leith does you, Viola. Why, Wordsworth himself praised the man's ingenuity just last month."

"TOOK HIM LONG ENOUGH TO WRITE!" Mrs. Prior harrumphed. "I HAD NEARLY GIVEN UP HOPE!"

Despite the tactless words, Viola had to agree—she had nearly given up hope herself.

Her intentions had seemed innocuous at the outset. Harmless. Simple.

Ethan Penn-Leith's first and only book of poetry had

blazed through London literary circles the year before, a conflagration of ideas and sound. Why the man's very name—Ethan Penn-Leith—rang with poetic assonance and consonance. He wrote about the moors and braes of the Scottish Highlands with such unabashed passion that one reviewer claimed to literally feel the chill wind whistling through his words. Even Queen Victoria was enamored and credited Mr. Penn-Leith for inspiring her visit to Scotland the previous year.

For Viola, however, it was the ideas contained within Ethan Penn-Leith's poems that captured her.

A popular authoress herself, Viola wrote moralizing stories of pious orphans and virtuous maidens who held to their principles even under trying circumstances. But she had recently passed her thirty-third birthday, and the occasion found her seized by an odd sort of discontent—an ache for . . . *more.*

Something in the words of Ethan Penn-Leith had altered her—his authenticity, his realism—knocking down mental walls and freeing a fierce creature that stretched restlessly inside her.

Viola was heartily sick of pious orphans and virtuous maidens. She wished to write stories that *mattered.*

Mr. Penn-Leith's most popular work, "Adjacent but Only Just," was a deeply personal poem that described his life as a farmer, a man working in the shadow of the Highlands, adjacent to wildness but never part of it. The entire poem had been heralded as a metaphor for modern life—the separation of humans from their native roots, a desire to seek one's true nature instead of simply living in sight of it . . . adjacent, but only just . . .

Mr. Penn-Leith's words profoundly summed up Viola's life.

Adjacent, but only just.

Adjacent to adventure and living.

Adjacent to significant ideas and words.

Adjacent to marriage and children.

And so, in an effort to no longer live *adjacent* to life, she had put her admiration of Mr. Penn-Leith into the mouth of one of her characters, hoping that the poet might reply with a polite thank you. She regularly received letters from admirers; such a correspondence was acceptable for an authoress.

It had seemed sensible at the time. Her shy tongue had always been a barrier between herself and gentlemen. But writing? *That* she could do without inciting an asthma attack. And if Mr. Penn-Leith replied, then Viola could respond and, in that manner, a dialogue might begin.

That had been her *sole* intention.

But then *Little Lottie* had become a runaway success; it was already on its third printing.

And in light of the novel's popularity and Mr. Penn-Leith's fame, a London gossip rag had seized on Viola's homage to him and constructed a narrative out of it: Viola Brodure and Ethan Penn-Leith were destined to fall in love and marry.

Heaven help her.

Her cheeks pinked, and her breathing tightened.

Hopefully, London broadsheets do not have circulation in rural Scotland. She could only pray Mr. Penn-Leith remained oblivious to the gossip.

Truly, Viola should have foreseen this. The broadsheets *loved* Ethan Penn-Leith—the sweeping romanticism of his poetry, the handsome virility of his person. The papers regularly printed a lithograph drawing of him—a large man with a great kilt wrapped around his chest and waist, square-jawed with tousled curls, a glint of humor in his eyes. It was rumored more than one woman had swooned at the mere sight of him.

Was it any wonder the man was so celebrated?

"SHE MUST WRITE HIM BACK!" Mrs. Prior thumped her cane—*thwap.* "NOW!"

A wave of searing heat scorched Viola's cheeks. Her chest constricted in earnest, causing her breathing to hitch painfully. She shot her father a desperate look.

"Reply immediately?" Her father smiled, ignoring Viola's alarm. "That is excellent advice, Mrs. Prior."

Oh, no. Please, no.

Viola drew in air, trying vainly to keep her nervous panic at bay. But the room was overly warm, her corset constricting.

What would Mr. Penn-Leith think of her?! To reply so quickly would imply that she had only included the chapter to get his attention.

Oh, very well, she *had* wished his attention. But she did not want Mr. Penn-Leith to know it, as well.

Where had all the air in the room gone?!

She caught her father's eye, trying to communicate her distress.

"Father—" A wheezing breath. "I have only just received the letter." *Wheeze.* "It would d-distress me to appear overly eager."

"We cannot allow this opportunity to pass." Dr. Brodure waved his hand. "You should take Mrs. Prior's advice and pen a reply immediately."

"YES! THE BLOOM IS OFF THE ROSE! YOU AREN'T GETTING ANY YOUNGER! YOU MUST ACT QUICKLY!"

Viola pressed a hand against her stomach, her lungs closing further, her asthma looming. She gasped a breath. And then another.

She loved her father dearly. She did.

But it was as if he were determined to live his life *through* her, encouraging Viola to achieve everything he had not—the popularity of a famous writer, the preaching of moral stories to a large audience.

In her father's eyes, Viola Brodure and Ethan Penn-Leith were destined to become another Percy and Mary Shelley, a celebrated couple of the *literati.*

Viola did not necessarily disagree with her father's goals, per se; she simply wished to pursue them in her own manner.

She took another distressed breath, wrapping an arm around her midsection. Why had she allowed her maid to lace her corset so tight?

Finally, her father noticed her labored breathing and her high color—signs of an imminent asthma attack.

He adjusted the fire screen, shielding her from the fire with its irritating smoke. Sliding onto the seat beside her, he reached for her hand, tugging it from her waist.

"All will be well, dearest," he said, voice low. "You will write him back, a polite reply. That is all I am asking—"

"YOU MUST VISIT!"

No!

Just . . . no!

Viola's lungs froze. She gasped, a horrific, wheezing sound.

"Breathe slowly, child. In. Out." Dr. Brodure rubbed her back. "I am sure Mrs. Prior simply means a visit for *myself.* I will begin a correspondence with a few ministers I know in that area. Perhaps, they would welcome a guest preacher in the parish, that's all." Her father's tone was angelically inno-cent. "I hear Edzell is lovely in the summer. A perfect writing retreat, I should think. So if the local cleric happens to invite me to give a sermon or two in his parish, what else can I do but bring my devoted daughter along?"

Viola closed her eyes, lungs still heaving. Her father's words were not particularly soothing. She *knew* her father, after all. Dr. Brodure would see them invited to Edzell before the summer was out. She would meet Mr. Penn-Leith face-to-face. Her father would ensure it.

You began all this with the intention of meeting Ethan Penn-Leith, remember? Does it matter how it all comes about?

And yet, the rising panic in her chest told her that, yes, it *did* matter.

She wanted to meet Mr. Penn-Leith on her own terms, not through her father's heavy-handed machinations.

"YOU MUST INVITE ME TO THE WEDDING!" Mrs. Prior announced. "I SHALL GIVE A LARGE DONATION!"

Dr. Brodure perked up at those words. "That is most kind, Mrs. Prior. Let us discuss that further."

Oh, merciful heavens!

Two

"YE MUST GIVE a reply immediately, Ethan," Aileen Penn-Leith said. Malcolm watched as his sister waved a piece of foolscap under their brother's nose. "This is Miss Viola Brodure we speak of. *Miss Brodure!* She is one of the most celebrated writers of our age."

"Aye, and so am I, in case ye forgot." Ethan replied, reaching for a potato scone. "Miss Brodure surely understands these things. I'll reply eventually—"

"Eventually?!" Aileen threw up her hands. "Everything is *eventually* with you!"

Malcolm raised his eyebrows. Aileen was not wrong.

The three Penn-Leith siblings—Malcolm, Aileen, and Ethan—were seated around the dining room table, eating breakfast. A cheery fire popped in the grate, lending warmth to the weak winter sun streaming through the large bay window.

"Ye know I love you, Ethan," Aileen continued, leaning onto the table, the dark curls framing her face bobbing in frustration, "but ye are a chronic procrastinator."

"Of course, I am." Ethan winked. "It's part of my poetic charm."

Aileen took in a steadying breath, the kind that were all too frequent when speaking with Ethan.

Malcolm pressed his lips together and reached for

another sausage. Their cook and housekeeper, Mrs. Allen, always prepared extra, bless her kind heart. She knew Malcolm loved a full Scottish breakfast—fried eggs, a juicy sausage, a slice of black pudding, and a hot tattie scone—all washed down with strong tea in peaceful, contemplative quiet.

The *sausage* and the *quiet* being the most important components of said breakfast—two things his siblings blithely ignored.

"Ethan," Aileen began again, steely patience in her tone. "Miss Brodure is not your typical admirer. Her attention to ye is *flattering*. She wrote ye most promptly—"

"*Too* promptly," Ethan countered. "The ink was scarcely dry on my own letter and, *poof*, hers arrives in reply. Such eagerness smells of desperation." He punctuated his words with an enormous bite of eggs, a lock of his famously tousled hair flopping onto his forehead. "And it's not surprising. She is older than me, ye know. Fair upon the shelf."

"So she is a year or two past thirty?" Aileen rolled her eyes. "Ye are nearly thirty. Why, Malcolm is thirty-five, and I am a year past thirty myself. Do we not deserve to marry?"

"Bother, Aileen!" Ethan stretched his shoulders, the smoothness of his accent slipping. "This isnae about our ages, per se, and ye know it. Just because I'm a poet, and Miss Brodure is an authoress, it doesnae follow that we're a matched set. I will reply when the muse strikes me."

"This is a letter, Ethan, not an epic poem, for heaven's sake."

"A man has his pride, that's alls I'm saying."

Malcolm set down his fork and shot a glance at his dog lounging at his feet. Beowoof raised his shaggy head, giving Malcolm a mournful look.

You and me both, lad.

Aileen and Ethan could be at this all day. As the oldest

and, quite frankly, most level-headed of the siblings, Malcolm was the designated peacemaker. He leaned forward, his forearms braced on the table top.

"A prompt reply to your initial letter is a mark of courtesy, Ethan," Malcolm said. "Miss Brodure, by all accounts, is a lady in every sense. She isnae courting ye. She's simply being polite."

"Ah, the silent Malcolm Penn-Leith speaks!" Ethan rocked back in his chair.

Malcolm batted away his brother's mocking tone with practiced ease. "We may no' belong to the highest levels of society, but we can be well-mannered and courteous. Ye should reply to Miss Brodure."

Naturally, Malcolm loved Ethan with all his heart and would happily sacrifice his life for his brother. That did not mean he was blind to his brother's faults. Ethan could be an utter eejit from time to time.

Aileen was of the opinion that Ethan couldn't help it.

"The world has never said, 'No,' to him," she often confided to Malcolm. "'Tis only natural that Ethan would wish for things beyond you and myself. It is what gives his poetry its grand scope. Ye remember what he was like as a child . . . so charismatic and charming."

That was truth. Ethan had always shone brightly.

Their mother, Margaret, had been a wealthy Leith from Aberdeenshire with family connections to the Earl of Aberdeen himself. Margaret's betrothal to Mr. John Penn, a gentleman-farmer well below her station, had upset her more genteel family. As a condition of her marriage contract, Grandfather Leith had required the new couple to combine their surnames into Penn-Leith. But the lowliness of their mother's marriage had always rankled Grandfather Leith.

Their mother's brother, Uncle Leith, had seen Ethan's

potential early and insisted on raising him, determined that at least one of his nephews would escape the taint of his birth.

So while Malcolm was left to work the farm alongside their father, Ethan went to live with Uncle Leith in his fine house in Aberdeen. Ethan attended school there (the same grammar school where Lord Byron had penned his first verses) and had then gone on to study at the University of St Andrews, all the while mingling with others far above his station. Uncle Leith even sent Ethan on a Grand Tour.

For all that Malcolm and Ethan were brothers, a vast ocean of experience and education separated them. Ethan had an urbane smoothness to his manners and speech that Malcolm could never match.

"I'll help ye pen a reply, as I did last time." Aileen shot Ethan a bright smile. "No muse required."

Ethan sighed, pushing back his plate. "I suspect neither of ye will give me a moment's rest until I do this."

"Likely not." Aileen shrugged.

As usual, Malcolm wondered how his sulky, often self-centered brother had managed to become such a celebrated poet.

Though, he supposed that sulky, self-centered moodiness was something of a prerequisite for any lauded poet. It took a significant amount of zeal to take one's self so seriously.

"Who knows," Malcolm added. "Ye may even find that ye like Miss Brodure upon further acquaintance. I imagine ye have a lot in common."

"Aye," Aileen agreed. "And I hear she is a reputed beauty. Mrs. Ruxton has a lovely engraving of her."

"A beauty, you say?" Ethan perked up. "Well, being beautiful *and* talented is something, I suppose . . ."

Malcolm handed a piece of sausage to Beowoof. "Write the letter, Ethan. Being a gentleman often means doing a necessary thing even when it's not convenient. It's the final step that takes a lad into manhood."

Ethan gazed at him for a moment. "*The final step that takes a lad into manhood* . . ." he repeated. "I quite like that. May I use the idea in a poem?"

"Of course."

Ethan pushed back from the table. "Very well. Aileen, let's write this letter."

And to Malcolm's relief, Ethan and Aileen quit the small dining room for the parlor, leaving him to enjoy a quiet breakfast at last.

Three

VIOLA STOOD IN the middle of a muddy road, staring at the rutted tracks disappearing into the roiling fog of the Scottish countryside.

She had been waiting for nearly two hours now, pacing up and down the lane. Their gig rested behind her, its single axle listing at an unnatural angle. Her maid, Mary, was curled up and sound asleep on the carriage seat, having grown weary of waiting.

No sound reached her; the fog had silenced the birds round about. The deathly quiet should have been unnerving. After all, Viola's entire life had played against the background of London's endless bustle—carriages rumbling, hawkers calling, people chattering.

She had worried that the fresh air, endless greenery, and animal dander of Scotland would act as irritants, exacerbating her asthma.

But instead Viola found it soothing . . . nearly freeing in a way. As if all that silence somehow allowed her lungs to finally . . . breathe.

The countryside burst with life, glimpses of vitality moving in and out of the fog—prickly gorse covered in vivid yellow flowers and lambs clambering in the field. Branches arched over the lane, the leaves bright green and newly grown despite it being the third week of May.

The series of events that had landed her here, waiting on the foggy lane, was something out of one of her own novels.

Mr. Penn-Leith had replied to Viola's second letter. A correspondence had ensued.

True to his word, her father had contrived an invitation to preach in the parish of Edzell. Dr. Brodure would spend the summer discussing arcane doctrinal points with the local vicar, leaving Viola free to write and "make acquaintances with the local population."

And by *local population*, Dr. Brodure meant Ethan Penn-Leith.

Viola blushed whenever she pondered her father's machinations. Worse, she had not informed Mr. Penn-Leith of their plans to summer in Edzell. Ironically, she hadn't known how to phrase it; the words felt too brazen.

But their arrival in Edzell had been delayed. Her father had hired a gig and horse from a local inn, but the older carriage had been unequal to the badly rutted road, the axle cracking before they reached their rented country cottage.

Dr. Brodure had unhitched the poor horse and pulled himself onto its back, riding to fetch help, leaving Viola and Mary alone with the carriage.

Which is how Viola found herself standing in the middle of a rural country lane, mist swirling around her.

She wrapped an arm around her waist, sucking in a deep lungful of soothing air and releasing it slowly.

Scotland hummed with promise, a giddy sort of anticipation that was paradoxically calming and yet exhilarating all at once. As if change itself were hidden in the whisking fog.

This! This is what she had wanted. A sense of hope. That her life *could* change.

That she no longer needed to live a life adjacent.

She would meet Ethan Penn-Leith. She did not expect

him to take a shining to her—truly she did not, despite her father's machinations.

But she *did* wish a friendship. The wisdom and philosophical depth of Mr. Penn-Leith's poetry inspired her. How delightful would it be to receive critique and discuss ideas with him? Most importantly, perhaps, he could advise her how to proceed with her own writing.

Her father insisted Viola explore topics that were appropriate to a woman's tender sensibilities, delivering novels with a sermonizing bent. Viola's middle-class readers wanted to feel pious and sympathetic toward her characters, not shame for their own culpability in enabling social ills.

For her part, Viola believed a little more guilt and public pressure on Parliament to enact reforms were needed.

She longed to advocate for societal change, rather than validating the status quo.

With each breath, that same fierce creature stretched inside her, testing the crisp Scottish air, tasting anticipation, reaching for something entirely . . . *new.*

The fog continued to flow around her, eddying across the road, trees rustling in the wind. Though how wind and fog could coexist remained a puzzle. Why didn't the wind simply blow the fog away?

In her experience, London fog was a creeping thing, settling in with a muffling heaviness that tightened her lungs and triggered her asthma.

This Scottish fog was made of more mystical forces. It swirled and blew, filling her lungs with cool, wet air that soothed and calmed.

A paradox.

Or, at the very least, another metaphor portending change.

Regardless, she committed the moment to memory. A writer could never hoard enough descriptive details.

Viola pulled her cloak tighter around her shoulders.

A shape loomed out of the fog.

She nearly sighed in relief. Surely, this was her father returning . . .

But, no . . . a large dog loped up the road, tongue lolling, tail wagging. He seemed exceptionally friendly, with an adorable face and curling, honey-colored hair. He wandered right up to her, nuzzling her skirts with an amiable sniff.

Viola froze.

She adored dogs. Unlike cats or horses, dogs were living sunshine, endlessly happy with themselves and the world. But dogs, like most animals, triggered her asthma. And so she stood still, terrified to get too close.

A loud whistle drew the dog's attention.

Viola raised her head.

A burly Scot emerged from the fog.

The man strode out from the mist like a medieval laird surveying his lands, a mythical hero of a lost age. A russet-and-brown kilt wrapped around his waist and crisscrossed his broad chest, an enormous pin holding the heavy wool in place. A more modern jacket and waistcoat rested underneath; a jaunty cap sat atop his head.

But it was the man himself—with his dark hair and dark brows over even darker eyes—that ensnared her.

He was not classically handsome, she supposed. The lines of his face were too harsh for mere prettiness. He was beyond beauty, in a sense . . . more elemental . . . unbreakable iron forged of metal from Scottish mountains.

He met her gaze, sending a tingling jolt down Viola's spine.

Gracious.

Here was a *man.*

He seemed the sort who could easily carry the world itself on those broad shoulders.

He came to a stop several yards in front of her, his kilt swinging. His eyes darted past her, surveying the broken carriage.

"Madam." He nodded a head in her direction.

"Sir," she replied with a hesitant smile.

He said nothing more for a moment, instead taking time to examine the gig listing at an angle, the maid sleeping. Viola sensed that little escaped this man's notice.

She should have been surprised or nervous or concerned or *some* apprehensive emotion—

But no . . . her odd brain chose to feel bone-deep safety and comfort.

Was this what others meant when they called Scotland a land of contrasts? Freedom fog and soothing Highland warriors?

Finally, the man brought his eyes back to her, hitching his thumbs into the leather pouch—a *sporran,* she had heard it called—that hung from his belt.

"Please tell me yer husband has taken the horse and gone for help?" His brogue rolled over her, a rumbling wave of shivering delight.

Viola's smile grew.

Heaven help her, but she loved a competent man, one who moved past self-evident matters and asked the most pertinent question.

No restating the obvious. *Stuck, are ye?*

No manly posturing. *Stand aside, lass. My muscles and superior knowledge will fix this in no time.*

No. Just simple, straight-forward competence.

Perhaps, it was his sense of strength that emboldened her tongue.

Or perhaps, it was his happy, friendly dog that put her at such ease.

Or maybe, it was simply the surreal hush of the rushing fog and fresh Scottish air.

Regardless, her terrible shyness had yet to make an appearance.

"Yes, in a way," she replied. "I haven't a husband, but my father returned to the inn from whence we hired this wretched vehicle." She motioned at the resting gig behind her.

He nodded, gaze meeting hers and then sliding away. As if he, too, were . . . shy. Or, perhaps, simply reserved.

Regardless, Viola felt even more at ease, even more curious about him.

Was he a local gentleman farmer? A lord's steward?

And the crucial question every spinster asked:

Was he married?

His dog moved forward again, whining and sniffing at her hand. She pulled back.

"He willnae bite ye," the Scot said. "He's right friendly."

Viola looked into the dog's eyes, the poor thing's longing to be petted reflecting her own wish to pet him.

"Oh, I would love nothing more than to pet him," she said, raising her head. She couldn't let this man believe she disliked his pet. "But I fear I have a sensitivity to dogs." She waved a hand in front of her face.

"Ah." The man rocked back on his heels, gaze still pensive. "Ye didnae need to worry about him. He doesnae shed. It's some oddity in his breeding. He willnae irritate your senses. Go on. Give him a wee pat."

Viola hesitated. She desperately wanted to pet the dog, but an asthma attack . . .

She met the man's gaze, her hesitation surely evident.

"Trust me." The quiet assurance of his words rumbled over her.

And . . . she believed him.

She looked back at the overeager dog. As if sensing that a good scratching might be in the offing, the animal wagged his tail more vigorously.

Heavens. He was a handsome pup.

She took a fortifying breath.

Life was to be lived, was it not? Surely, this was part of her commitment to no longer exist adjacent.

Tugging off a glove, she bent forward, holding out her hand.

"There now," she crooned. The dog ecstatically communicated his delight, sniffing her hand. Smiling, she cautiously rubbed him behind his ears as she had seen others do.

Gracious! His fur was warm and soft, curling around her fingers. The dog angled his head, giving her better access.

Most importantly, nothing in the motion appeared to irritate her lungs. Crouching on the grass that ran down the middle of the lane, she rubbed him with both hands.

She took a deep breath. And . . . nothing. No ill effects.

How many times had she longed to have a pet? To bury her face in a dog's side and simply relish in sharing space with another living thing?

Laughing in wonder, she raised her gaze to meet that of the Scot.

"How utterly marvelous!" she said, voice full of wonder.

Malcolm stared at the unknown woman scratching Beowoof's ears, an enormous smile on her face.

Utterly marvelous, indeed.

The woman was, to put it bluntly, absolutely stunning. That initial glimpse of her, standing alone on the lane, slowly coming into focus out of the fog like an ethereal dream . . . He had nearly thought her a selkie—a mythical creature said to haunt rivers and lochs, luring men to their dooms.

And then that first meeting of their eyes . . .

She had knocked the breath clear out of his lungs.

Her chestnut curls framed a dainty oval face and achingly-blue eyes, her woolen cloak not concealing the gracious curves of her body.

Her accent proclaimed her to be English, and highly-born at that. A genteel traveler, most likely visiting for the summer. She nearly vibrated with a bewitching energy, her open face full of childlike wonder.

In short, she was astonishingly compelling.

And now, she had won the affections of his dog. Beowoof basked in the attention, the shameless wretch.

The lady, still grinning, buried her face in Beowoof's fur, only to raise her head again, laughing in astonishment.

"I can scarcely believe it," she said, voice amazed. "His fur doesn't irritate my lungs. How remarkable! What is his name?" She turned to scratch the lucky dog's neck.

The shameless beast shot Malcolm a smug look, as if to say, *O'course the lovely lass prefers me, ye wretch.*

Malcolm grimaced. *Traitor.*

"Beowoof," he said.

Her face lifted, eyes glowing. "Beowulf? How charming."

Erhmm. "Actually, it's Beo*woof.*" Malcolm stressed the final syllable.

Her eyes drew down. "Beowulf?" she repeated.

Drat his thick Scottish accent.

"Beo*woof,*" he clarified.

Those impossibly beautiful eyes of hers continued to look confused.

Blast it all.

"It's Beowoof." He paused and rolled his hand . . . and then rolled his eyes. "As in what a dog says . . . *woof, woof.*"

Thank goodness Ethan wasn't here to witness this.

Malcolm would never live it down, reduced to literal barking in front of a beautiful, sophisticated English lady.

"Oh!" Her face turned incandescent with understanding. "*Woof!* Beo*woof!* How adorable." She rubbed Beowoof's cheeks, clasping his face between her palms, her voice a sing-song. "Who's the hero of the Geats? Who defeats Grendel? You do. Yes, you do, you excellent beast."

Beowoof was ecstatic, his entire body wagging in an attempt to get closer to her.

Malcolm could hardly blame the lad.

He watched her cuddle Beowoof for a few more minutes, crooning and scratching him, before finally pushing back to her feet. She brushed her hands down her skirt and turned to Malcolm.

"I should commend you on your excellent taste," she said, her smile soft. "Calling one's dog after a great hero of Anglo-Saxon literature shows a certain amount of verve. Are other animals in your care similarly named?"

No ignorant miss, this lady.

"Aye. We have a cat named William Shakespurr, not to mention Coolius Caesar, my prize Highland steer."

The lady laughed, a joyful burst of sound.

Malcolm appreciated the laugh lines at the corners of her eyes. They spoke of years lived and wisdom gained.

Here was a true woman, not some giggling lass fresh from the schoolroom.

Even more, he liked that he had made her laugh.

Malcolm permitted himself a small smile.

"Shall we introduce ourselves?" she asked. "This is no London drawing room, so I suppose we needn't stand on ceremony."

Indeed not, thank goodness.

"Malcolm Penn-Leith, at your service, madam." He

sketched a loose sort of bow. Proper formalities were not his forte.

Her dazzling smile froze.

"Malcolm Penn-Leith?" she repeated.

Ah.

He heard the recognition in her voice. He could nearly have said the next sentence with her.

"Are you a relation of Mr. Ethan Penn-Leith, by any chance?" she asked.

"Aye. Ethan's my wee brother."

Again, she laughed, as if he had said something absolutely delightful. Heaven help him, he loved making this woman laugh

"*Wee* brother?" she repeated. "Does Mr. Penn-Leith prefer to be called that, then?"

Malcolm couldn't help his own answering grin, the motion pulling at his cheeks.

"Aye," he replied, "particularly when there are lovely lasses about."

She did not miss his meaning. A charming blush flooded her cheeks, and her eyes darted away, but then came shyly back to his.

Malcolm scarcely recognized himself. Flirting was Ethan's forte, not his. And yet, this bonnie lass made it feel effortless.

"And your name, madam?"

A small hesitation and then, "Viola Brodure."

Malcolm could not stem his startled inhalation. "The authoress?"

Again, she ducked her head in apparent shyness. "The very same."

Malcolm's brain hummed in stunned silence for a moment.

This was Viola Brodure? The woman Ethan had been writing to all these months? This open, delightful creature?

Miss Brodure looked away, as if embarrassed or, more likely, finally realizing the distance between their stations in life.

Malcolm was nothing more than a gentrified farmer.

She was a gentleman's daughter and a celebrated novelist.

He hated the way his heart plummeted at the thought.

Obviously, she was a lady of quality. That had been apparent from the outset, but he hadn't understood exactly how large the chasm was between them.

Had she come to meet Ethan, then? His brother hadn't mentioned anything about her visiting. But that meant nothing. Ethan was feather-brained more often than not.

"Why does it behave like this?" she asked after a moment of silence.

The abrupt change in topic had Malcolm scrambling. "Pardon?"

"The fog," she clarified. "How can it be windy and foggy at the same time? I find it most puzzling."

Oh. *That* he could answer. "The fog is called *haar*, and it blows in off the North Sea in early summer—"

The sound of an approaching carriage stopped him short.

"That must be my father." Miss Brodure turned toward the sound, giving him a moment to stare at her unashamedly.

She was lovely. Captivating in every way.

But two facts Malcolm understood quite clearly.

One, Miss Brodure obviously had some affection for his brother. She wrote Ethan; she had journeyed to Edzell to meet him.

Two, knowing his *wee* brother as Malcolm did, Ethan was going to adore her. And life never said "no" to Ethan.

131

What Ethan wanted, he got.

Viola Brodure and Ethan Penn-Leith were a match made in heaven, destined for one another.

Malcolm had never begrudged his brother anything. He wished Ethan every happiness.

But just this once, Malcolm wished he didn't have to witness the entire thing, from start to finish.

Four

MALCOLM WAS RIGHT crabbit for the remainder of the week.

His all-too-brief meeting with Miss Brodure had affected him far too deeply. Her blue eyes and clever mind and witty tongue popped into his mind with alarming frequency, forcing him to regularly evict them, attempting to chant sense into his muddled brain.

Miss Brodure is a refined, cultured lady.

You are not a refined, cultured gentleman.

She has journeyed to Scotland in pursuit of your refined, cultured brother.

They will likely marry and have refined, cultured children.

In short, she is not for you.

You must cease thinking upon her.

But, of course, *knowing* a thing was quite different from feeling it.

And as everyone in the village wished to discuss her arrival, putting her from his mind was nearly impossible. If one more person started up a conversation with the words, "Have ye heard about Miss Brodure?" Malcolm was liable to explode.

All in all, it made a man downright peevish.

Naturally, Aileen was ecstatic when word reached

Invercairn Mains that Miss Brodure and her father had let a cottage in the parish.

"This is so marvelous, Malcolm," she crowed as they waited for Ethan to join them for dinner. "They say Dr. Brodure is to preach a sermon on Sunday, so we shall all meet Miss Brodure. Ethan will find her compelling, just you wait and see."

Ethan was less sanguine.

"I cannae decide what to do," he grumbled to Malcolm the next day as they reviewed their summer plantings. Or rather, as Malcolm reviewed the summer planting schedule, and Ethan haivered on about Miss Brodure. "Just because I'm a poet and Miss Brodure is an authoress, it doesnae follow that we will be suited. I will not be thrust into a relationship simply because Aileen thinks it a romantic idea."

Malcolm did not respond, as he could not bring himself to encourage Ethan.

Malcolm loved his brother, but he was no martyr.

Ethan continued on, accustomed to Malcolm's taciturn silence. "All that said, Tam McLean met Miss Brodure yesterday and asked me, if I didnae wish to pursue her, could he have her instead?"

That, Malcolm could not let pass. "Miss Brodure is a person, Ethan, not a parcel to be passed about."

"Aye." His brother rolled his eyes. "But Tam has refined tastes in women, and he said she's as fine a bird as he's ever seen. She doesnae look a day over twenty-five."

Malcolm nearly sighed. "Again, Miss Brodure is more than the sum of her outward appearance. She is a soul and heart and mind that should be meticulously explored. You are behaving like a hunter—viewing her as a prize to be won—when you should be donning the hat of an intrepid trail-blazer."

Ethan stilled, his eyes getting that faraway, pondering look. "*You are behaving like a hunter, when you should be donning the hat of an intrepid trailblazer . . .* I quite like that. May I use it?"

"Of course. But get to the point, Ethan?"

"Oh, 'tis simply this: If Miss Brodure is as lovely as they all say, I would be a fool to dismiss her out of hand. Only a child refuses something simply because others wish him to have it."

It was a rather startling bit of self-awareness from Ethan.

"Besides," Ethan continued, giving Malcolm a sly side-eye. "Someone, as of late, has been encouraging me to take that final step into manhood. Figure I might as well give it a try."

Malcolm barely stopped a grimace. Just his luck that, after years of turning a deaf ear, *now* Ethan decided to heed his brotherly advice.

Worse, even God appeared to smile upon Ethan's plans, as Sunday dawned to encouragingly blue skies.

Malcolm, Aileen, and Ethan arrived early at the church, only to find that most of the parish had the same idea. The churchyard overflowed, villagers blethering with one another in their colorful Sunday finery—top hats and feathered bonnets and lacy parasols.

It took Malcolm a moment to locate Miss Brodure in the gathered crowd. But a group of matrons turned to greet Ethan, affording Malcolm a brief glimpse of the church door.

Ah. There she was.

Miss Brodure stood between the vicar—Mr. Ruxton—and her father, all three welcoming parishioners as they entered. It was an unusual circumstance, to be sure, but gracious of her to greet members of the parish personally. She ducked her head and blushed as she was introduced to Lord and Lady Hadley.

Miss Brodure was decidedly bonnie in a dusky blue gown that cinched her trim waist. Malcolm was sure Aileen would gnatter on about the intricacies of it: *Did you see the vandyked edging along her sloped collar? Most charming. And not an ounce of puff to her sleeves! Thank heavens that ridiculous fashion has finally ended.*

Malcolm waited patiently with Aileen for their turn to greet the authoress.

Ethan, however . . .

Well, *patience* had never been Ethan's strong suit. His brother bounced on his toes or leaned to the side, determined to get a better look at Miss Brodure.

Finally, the crowd parted, offering Ethan a clear view.

His slack-jawed reaction was everything Malcolm had predicted.

"I say, Malcolm," his brother murmured, angling his head for a second and then a third glance. "She *is* a fine lass. A real stunner."

Malcolm heartily agreed, for all the good it did him. He had learned long ago that Ethan always received what he wanted.

"Do ye ken Uncle Leith might choose me to live with him?" Malcolm asked his father while standing on tiptoe to reach the horse's saddle. "I've been ever-so-respectful around him."

"I cannae rightly say, lad." His father brushed the mare. "'Tis your uncle's choice, no' mine."

"I'd like to go to a proper school and learn Latin and Greek." Malcolm desperately wanted an education, to learn more of the world. "Uncle says he may even travel to Italy."

"Och, yer uncle be filling ye with ideas far beyond yer station. Let it be, lad."

Of course, in the end, all of Malcolm's wishes and earnest

words amounted to nothing. Ethan with his handsome looks, winning smile, and easy charm was chosen, not him.

The very reasons Miss Brodure would surely choose Ethan, too.

Others in the parish clearly thought the same. Several matrons spoke in low voices, eyes moving back and forth between Ethan and Miss Brodure.

Finally, Malcolm and Aileen reached the church door.

Miss Brodure darted a glance in their direction, her eyes going to Aileen before skimming up to meet Malcolm's gaze. She flushed and demurely lowered her head.

Mr. Ruxton made the introductions, Malcolm and Aileen bobbing their heads in murmured greetings.

But Miss Brodure kept her gaze averted.

Such maidenly modesty was somewhat at odds with the engaging woman Malcolm had met along that foggy road. Where was the charming lady who had laughed in delight over Coolius Caesar and William Shakespurr?

Frowning, Malcolm stepped aside, pulling Aileen with him, as his sister tended to linger.

Ethan took their place, facing Miss Brodure.

The entire churchyard leaned forward, intent on watching the celebrated Scottish poet greet the famous English novelist.

"Miss Brodure," Ethan said, expression nearly awestruck.

"Mr. Penn-Leith," Miss Brodure replied. She raised her head and met Ethan's gaze briefly, before flushing and looking down at her hands clasped at her waist.

They made a striking pair—Ethan with his wind-swept, Highland gallantry and Miss Brodure in her refined, ladylike modesty.

Malcolm was sure this moment would be talked about for years to come. In fact, he would likely see it in some magazine—"The Highland Poet Meets Miss Brodure"—

printed alongside a lithograph of Ethan in kilt and cap, bowing romantically over Miss Brodure's hand, just as he was at present.

"Miss Brodure, permit me to say," Ethan said as his head rose, "how ardently I admire your writing. You grace us with your presence."

A sigh ran through the gathered crowd.

"How romantic," a female voice murmured somewhere near the churchyard gate.

Miss Brodure clearly heard the woman, as her blush deepened, eyes downcast. "Mr. Penn-Leith, you are too kind. Your own works are to be esteemed and lauded."

She curtsied, still not raising her head fully to look at Ethan, as if she were . . . *shy.*

Malcolm nearly grunted in surprise.

Was Miss Brodure shy?

She certainly hadn't seemed shy during their conversation on the lane. But given the number of people waiting to speak with her, he supposed it would be natural to feel overwhelmed.

But why did the thought of Miss Brodure being shy seem ill-fitting to him?

He pondered the question as Ethan and Miss Brodure finished their conversation, as he and his siblings entered the church to sit on the family pew, and as Dr. Brodure delivered his sermon.

Miss Brodure sat close to the lectern, her body perpendicular to Malcolm, enabling him to study her profile during the long, often tedious discourse. She repeatedly ducked her head, surely feeling the weight of so many eyes on her.

Like many in the congregation, Malcolm had read Miss Brodure's novels and found her writing engaging, even if her topics tended toward the overly didactic and sermonizing.

For example, her most recent novel, *Little Lottie,*

followed the adventures of Lottie Lawrence, a pious, orphaned girl forced to live by her wits while investigating her guardian's murder. The book had received glowing praise—one reviewer in *The Atheneaum* had called it, "A needed physic in our era of ever-loosening morals."

Dr. Brodure certainly seemed to agree. He praised his daughter's writings over and over. " . . . As little Lottie entreats us, 'Do unto others, as you yourself would have done unto you . . .'"

With each mention, Miss Brodure would blush anew and take in deep, fortifying breaths.

Was she truly shy, then? After that first meeting, *shy* was the last word he would have used to characterize her.

Joyful. Effervescent. Fierce. Enchanting. Intelligent.

Those were the words he would choose. Not shy. Not bashful. Not retiring.

And why did the discrepancy bother him?

An hour later, Viola stood in the churchyard, listening to parishioners chatter around her, all the while fighting to keep her breathing slow and steady.

Her dratted shyness had reared its head with a vengeance today. Though she was grateful so many loved her novels, her tongue knotted when meeting new people, aggravating her asthma. Her hands had trembled throughout her father's sermon, her breathing tight in her chest, as literally every eye in the church had studied her.

Outside in the fresh Scottish air, she could breathe more easily. Now if only her hands would cease their trembling.

"We must have you for dinner," Lady Hadley was saying at her side. "Muirford House is lovely in the summer."

The countess was beautiful, the gray threading through her auburn hair only adding to her regal bearing. Lord Hadley looked at his wife with intense fondness, though a sense of mischief glinted in his gaze.

"Och, ye know we are for London tomorrow, *mo chridhe*," he reminded her gently.

Lady Hadley laughed. "Yes, well then, Miss Brodure must promise she will remain here until we return." Lady Hadley shot her an expectant look. "Will you promise, Miss Brodure?"

"Of course." Viola bobbed her head, heat rising in her cheeks. "I would be most honored, my lady."

"It is settled then," Lady Hadley smiled. "We shall dine in midsummer, when we return."

Lord Hadley nodded his agreement, reaching for his wife's hand and threading it possessively through his elbow. Would that Viola could find someone who, after possibly twenty years of marriage, would look at her as Lord Hadley looked upon his wife.

Would Ethan Penn-Leith be that man?

Viola was no fool. She had passed into spinsterhood many years ago, and her shyness had always hampered her tongue. As a young woman, just the thought of a man speaking with her would have sent Viola into a full-blown asthma attack.

But now ... now she was determined to change. No more living in shadows.

As if sensing her thoughts, Ethan materialized at her elbow, a broad smile on his face. He was charm personified, a roguish lock of hair escaping his hat to tumble across his brow, framing his earnest, dark eyes.

"Miss Brodure, what a delight it has been to make your acquaintance." Ethan bowed low—an extravagant, courtly gesture.

"Likewise, Mr. Penn-Leith." She curtsied.

Lady Hadley leaned into her husband's arm—to better observe Ethan and Viola?—an expectant look on her face.

Did the entire county assume that Viola and Ethan would make a match of it?

And did she find that thought exciting? Or suffocating?

"Ah, Malcolm, excellent to see you!" Lord Hadley fixed his gaze on a point beyond Viola's shoulder.

She turned to see Malcolm Penn-Leith strolling up behind her, shoulders back, kilt swishing with each step, his expression unreadable.

He paused at Ethan's side, shaking hands with Lord Hadley and bowing over Lady Hadley's hand before turning to Viola with a smile and a rumbled, "Miss Brodure," that rolled over her like warm, summer sun.

But as had happened earlier, before she could exchange another word with him, Malcolm was quickly relegated to the background as Ethan stepped forward, taking center stage.

Ethan was clearly at ease with himself and the world, his charismatic energy wrapping around the gathered crowd. Before long, he began telling the story of his recent pilgrimage into the Cairngorms to commune with nature.

As Ethan talked, Malcolm stood unmoving beside his brother, hands clasped atop his walking stick, jaw firm, a slight breeze stirring his kilt.

In the days since their first meeting, Viola wondered if she had exaggerated her sense of initial attraction to him.

She had not.

Heavens, but Malcolm was every whit as compelling as he had been several days past.

Seeing the two brothers side-by-side was illuminating. Her writer's brain could not stop comparing the two.

Malcolm gave the impression of steadfast immovability,

feet spread apart, face impassive. The man radiated competence. As if he would face a raging inferno, a formal ballroom, or the very hounds of hell with unflappable *sangfroid.*

Ethan was . . . what she had expected him to be . . . charming, silver-tongued, a bit of a rogue. The energy of his poetry was clearly reflected in his person, in his current dramatic recounting of watching a sunrise from the top of Glenshee.

Both men had a similar look; anyone could see they were clearly brothers. But it was the small details that told their larger story.

Malcolm rested his palms atop a well-worn walking stick. He wore no gloves. Scraped knuckles and thin, white scars crisscrossed the back of his hands, a silent testament to years of hard labor, of determination and focused duty. Of a life not bound by custom and endless etiquette.

Ethan's hands, however, were encased in supple kid-leather, the gloves protecting his skin from the harsh conditions of life. Such gloves were the mark of a gentleman, of refined manners and etiquette.

Before this moment, Viola would have said gloves were a necessity, a trait of true gentility. After all, a similar set of soft gloves covered her own hands. A lady always protected her skin from exposure to the sun and elements.

Why, then, did her gloves abruptly feel like a token of her confinement? A symbol of her life adjacent? That instead of allowing her hands to get dirty—worn and used and scarred from the heavy business of truly *living*—she chose to remain unscathed. Sheltered. Pampered.

Similarly, next to Malcolm's solid strength, Ethan appeared . . . unfinished. His excitement was like that of an eager puppy—full of energy and vigor, but lacking in deeper substance and direction.

Surely, there was more to Ethan than this bubbling surface?

He was the Highland Poet, after all. The same man who penned the lines:

I am adjacent,
But only just
A falcon's flight away
From feral moor and heather'd scent,
A prisoner of the malcontent
Of life lived in delay.
I am adjacent,
but only just.

Surely, the man's florid personality hid intense depths of feeling?

As Ethan's story wound down, Viola squirmed in her silence, the lines of his poetry humming in her ears.

A prisoner of the malcontent/Of life lived in delay.

Her shyness seemed a cage, a glove smothering her, causing her to retreat instead of engaging with life.

Enough.

No more.

Despite the press of the people around her, the staring eyes that rendered her so nervous, threatening to trigger her asthma . . . she placed a mental hand on her fears and forced her tongue to speak.

"Your story is most captivating, Mr. Penn-Leith." *Heavens!* Why was her voice so breathless? "Was it during your hike that you realized the Cairngorms could be a metaphor for life in general? That living adjacent to wildness symbolized the human quest to find deeper meaning in life?"

She *had* to know, she realized. She had to see that flash of insight and genius that surfaced in his poetry.

Her question caught him seemingly off-guard. Ethan paused, head rearing back slightly.

But he quickly recovered, donning a magnetic smile. "That is a most perceptive question, Miss Brodure. I should love to call upon you and recount the whole of my artistic process. I adore nothing so much as communing with a fellow writer."

Two female voices sighed behind Viola, and someone else murmured, "What a perfect couple they make!"

Ugh. For the love of—

"I should be most honored, Mr. Penn-Leith." Viola curtsied. "Please call at your leisure."

Out of the corner of her eye, she caught Malcolm's grimace, a fleeting look.

Why that reaction?

And why was she focusing on Malcolm Penn-Leith's random facial expressions instead of basking in the thought of Ethan Penn-Leith calling upon her?

Five

ETHAN PENN-LEITH made good on his promise to call upon Viola.

The man appeared in her front parlor the very next afternoon, his sister, Miss Aileen Penn-Leith, on his arm. They burst into the room in a bustle of hats and overcoats and walking sticks, stripping off those ever-present gloves and handing all to a hovering maid.

"Oh, Malcolm never makes social calls," Miss Penn-Leith said when Viola asked about the older Penn-Leith sibling. "He's far too busy with the summer planting at the moment."

"Aye," Ethan waved a dismissive hand. "I cannae imagine Malcolm in a parlor, sipping tea and settling in for a long blether."

Huh. Neither could Viola, she supposed. Instead, her mind supplied an image of climbing the rugged moor above Edzell, Malcolm reaching back a hand to help her up the steep path.

She shook the idea away. How ludicrous.

Ethan Penn-Leith was here, in her front parlor.

Focus on the handsome man in front of you, Viola. This is why you allowed yourself to be dragged to Scotland in the first place.

Surely, her preoccupation with Malcolm was an anomaly. *Ethan* was the brother that mattered. He was the

Highland Poet, after all. Viola simply needed to know the man better.

They spoke of inanities for a moment. Or rather, Ethan and Aileen discussed the unseasonably warm weather, the departure of Lord Hadley for London, and the prospect of taking a drive to St. Cyrus Bay for a picnic on the beach there.

Viola poured tea and nodded at the appropriate times.

Ethan's gregariousness was a bit like stepping from a dark room into bright sunlight. Viola expected it to be warm and welcoming, but it mostly left her blinded and blinking, unable to see the way forward.

In short, Ethan heightened her native shyness.

But she *needed* to overcome this. She could not spend her life cowering in the shadows. Surely, she would adapt to the bright vivacity of his personality given time.

And so, as she had the day before, Viola placed a firm hand on her nerves and opened her mouth.

"I have long appreciated the ingenious turn of your mind, Mr. Penn-Leith. As an author myself, I find it fascinating to discuss writing endeavors with a fellow writer. How do you go about writing a new poem?"

"What an excellent question, Miss Brodure," Ethan replied, stretching his feet out before him, clearly relaxing into his subject matter. "Before beginning any new poem, I must find a suitable subject." A smile stretched wide across his face, the appreciative gleam in his eyes stating that *she* was his subject of the moment.

Ah. He was flirting with her in earnest now, it seemed.

Why did that fact not cause her heart to skip and dance? The man was exuberance and enthusiasm personified.

Who didn't adore an exuberant enthusiast?

What was wrong with her?!

This was Ethan. Penn! Leith!!

Aileen sipped her tea and smiled, obviously enjoying their tableau.

Focus, Viola. Get to know him.

Viola swallowed and gave Ethan what she hoped was an encouraging smile. "And then what do you do?"

His returning grin turned more self-deprecating. "And then I think and walk and think some more."

"Ye also make endless lists of rhyming words," Aileen interjected.

"That, too. Though my poetry does not rely heavily upon rhyme as much as rhythm and meter."

That was true. "And depth of thought," Viola added.

"Aye." Was Ethan's grin now more forced? "That, as well. In fact, allow me to recount an anecdote that happened while sailing from Montrose to Arbroath last September that I think exemplifies my process . . ."

He spoke on and on, hands waving, his handsome face flashing from expression to expression.

And still, Viola felt only polite amusement and interest. How could that be?

Ethan Penn-Leith was exactly as Viola had supposed him to be: charismatic and clever. He was everything she thought she had ever wanted in a suitor.

But instead of elation, she felt a certain . . . hollowness.

Mmmm. She searched for the right metaphor to describe it.

Once, many years ago, when she had been wrestling with a particularly thorny plot problem, she had taken a hackney cab to Westminster Abbey. There, she had spent the afternoon sitting on a bench in the Poet's Corner. Surrounding oneself with the graves of dead literary greats—Chaucer, Spenser, Dryden—seemed a rather morbid way to find inspiration, and yet, the experience had been transcendent. The cool, moist air of the abbey soothed her lungs. The quiet hush allowed the energy of the place to penetrate her soul. It had been a silent conversation of sorts, a rejuvenation, filling her mind with ideas and renewed zeal for her project.

Viola had supposed that spending an afternoon with Ethan Penn-Leith would be a similar experience. That they would feed off one another's creative energy, practically finishing each other's sentences in the race to connect ideas. That with Ethan, she would feel alive and finally *living*.

But the reality of being with Ethan was rather the opposite. He spoke of *his* interests and *his* writing and *his* work. After a while, Viola felt as if she were sitting on a park bench and watching the world go by. It was interesting, to be sure, but lacked any true connection.

How could this be? How could Ethan Penn-Leith *himself* make her feel adjacent to living?

Was that not the pinnacle of all ironies?

And after Ethan and Aileen finally took their leave, Viola was left with one lingering thought: Would she have felt the same hollowness had Malcolm Penn-Leith accompanied his brother and sister?

Malcolm received a moment-by-moment recounting of his siblings' visit with Miss Brodure over supper later that evening.

"She was utterly charming, Malcolm," Ethan said around a mouthful of roast beef. "Gracious, ladylike, with the most delightful blushes."

Malcolm grunted his agreement, slathering butter on a warm bap. Viola Brodure was certainly all those things and more. He could hardly fault Ethan for having eyes in his head, now could he?

"Aye, she and Ethan got along famously," Aileen agreed, reaching for the bowl of tatties. "Ye should have seen them, Malcolm. Like peas in a pod, talking about metaphor and such."

"Miss Brodure is quite perfect, I think." Ethan beamed.

Malcolm couldn't let that comment pass. "No one is perfect, Ethan. 'Tis unfair to place perfection upon the lady—"

"Bah! I willnae hear anything ill of Miss Brodure. I have spoken my truth."

Malcolm let it drop. From what he had seen and heard so far, he supposed Viola Brodure *was* close to perfection.

"I'm fair on my way to being madly in love with her, I ken," Ethan continued.

He spoke the words with his typical casual bonhomie, much as one would declare, *This meal has been delightful,* or *You should pop in on a Tuesday.*

Malcolm gritted his teeth. Miss Brodure deserved songs of praise or bouquets of flowers or—

"Ye should write Miss Brodure a sonnet, telling her all this," he said.

A brief silence ensued as Ethan seemingly pondered this, chewing his beef slowly.

"Aye," his brother said after swallowing, expression somewhat glum. "I supposed I *should* write a sonnet about it."

"Why the dour face, then?" Malcolm grunted in reply. "You're a famous poet, are ye not?"

"Aye, I am." Ethan tossed his fork down, shrugging his shoulders. "It's just . . . 'tis more enjoyable to bask in the fame of being a celebrated poet than to actually do the work required to *be* one, is all."

Malcolm's eyebrows flew to his hairline.

That was likely the most self-aware statement Ethan had ever uttered.

Malcolm wasn't sure whether to rejoice that his wee brother was finally (*finally!*) growing up . . .

. . . or lament Ethan's terrible timing.

Six

ETHAN PENN-LEITH'S social call left Viola feeling off-kilter.

How could that be? Should she not be thrilled, cast into rapturous alt?

Her father certainly was ecstatic.

"Mark my words, my dear," he said. "This is just the beginning. Mr. Penn-Leith means to court you in earnest. I cannot wait to see it in the broadsheets. Ah, what a glorious couple you two will make."

"Papa!" Viola could not keep the panic from her voice. As usual, a blush scorched her skin.

"No, I will not stop to save your maidenly modesty, Viola. You *must* realize the import of this connection. We preach the Lord's word through your books. A marriage to Mr. Penn-Leith would cement your position among the greatest novelists of our age."

"I thought my *writing* would do that, Father, not my choice of husband," she countered, tone as dry as the Sahara.

"Bah! You know as well as I that Mary Shelley would not have amounted to much had she not married Percy—"

"That is debatable."

"—moreover, I thought you *liked* Mr. Penn-Leith?"

Viola covered her face with her hands, giving her head a shake.

She *did* like Ethan. She did.

He was handsome and charming—the very definition of a romantic suitor—and any other woman in her place would have given Ethan her heart by now.

But it seemed that some part of Viola's heart longed to know his brother.

Malcolm had an intensity, a *gravitas*, that she had yet to see in Ethan. She sensed Malcolm hid heights of thought and feeling within his craggy surface—a mountain of ideas waiting to be explored.

Yet . . . surely, she could not simply walk away from Ethan? How could she have traveled to rural Scotland—and at such risk professionally and personally—only to give up when she and Ethan did not immediately form a bond?

She raised her head. "I *do* like Mr. Penn-Leith." *Both of them.* "I simply wish to allow our acquaintance to progress at its own pace."

But, of course, in that wish, Viola was utterly thwarted.

Just like Dr. Brodure, Miss Aileen Penn-Leith and the other ladies of Edzell were determined to foster a match between Viola and Ethan, pushing them together at every opportunity. At least no one in Edzell subscribed to the *London Tattler*, so Viola was spared *that* added embarrassment.

Ethan, of course, readily accepted and encouraged his neighbors' matchmaking. Viola often felt like unexplored territory. A *terra incognita* that Ethan, the intrepid explorer, had flung a flag over, declaring her his for the taking. As if she were a possession and not a fellow explorer in her own right.

Worse, Viola did not discover a miraculous sense of connection with the man.

The opposite occurred, in fact. The more time she spent with Ethan, the more she thought of Malcolm.

Had that instantaneous connection she felt been a one-time coincidence? If she spoke with him again—alone, one-on-one—would things be the same? She couldn't deny the magnetic attraction of him, the power of his raw masculinity. Was her fixation with Malcolm strictly a physical thing, then? (And if so, how humiliating to be thus swayed by a pair of broad shoulders.) Was it merely a passing infatuation? Or was it based on an actual similarity of thought and heart?

Unfortunately, the rules of society being what they were, Viola could hardly walk over to Invercairn Mains and call upon Malcolm specifically. And when Viola and her father *did* call upon the Penn-Leiths, Malcolm was nowhere to be seen.

"Oh, Malcolm is never at home during the day," Miss Penn-Leith said over tea. "The farm requires his full attention, particularly during the summer months."

Finally, desperate to at least *speak* with the man, Viola resorted to the best tool in a woman's arsenal: the subterfuge of planned coincidence.

Miss Penn-Leith had mentioned that Malcolm kept several prized Highland cattle—Coolius Caesar among them—in a small glen on the edge of his property. Most evenings, Malcolm strolled down to check on his cattle before returning home along the lane.

Viola determined to wait for him there.

Sadly, she did not know the precise time at which he would pass, so she had to stoop to a stratagem straight from a Gothic tale.

Finding a part of the path where she could see a convenient distance in each direction, Viola sat herself upon a log and partially unlaced one of her half-boots. The entire scenario made perfect sense, she supposed. Malcolm would come up the path, and she would be in the process of retying her shoe, making it seem as if their meeting were entirely happenstance.

Heavens, the contortions she went through to speak with

the Penn-Leith men. First traveling to Scotland for Ethan, and now this.

Fortunately, it was a lovely evening in early June, the sun lingering long in the sky.

Unfortunately, Malcolm was not quick to appear.

A half-hour passed.

Squirrels darted up and down a tree opposite where she sat, chittering at one another.

Another half-hour passed. Viola's leg had gone quite numb.

Was Malcolm not coming, then? Had he returned home along another path? Or was her information faulty?

Perhaps, she should abandon this idea? It had been silly in the first place, she supposed.

That initial encounter with Malcolm had likely been an anomaly. And even if it had *not* been, Malcolm struck her as the kind of man who would not encroach on his brother's "territory."

Finally, after another quarter hour and no sign of Malcolm, Viola bent to retie her shoe in truth.

He would not be coming. The entire idea was a mistake anyway—

Beowoof abruptly appeared, loping toward her at a good clip.

Viola sat up higher, seeing Malcolm's form trudging up the lane at a distance.

Oh, heavens.

Her heart panged in her chest.

Somehow, he was even taller than her memory, broader in the chest, his ever-present kilt swinging as he walked.

And in that moment, she had an answer to her question—

Why did *this* particular man dominate her thoughts so?

Because he was simply that—a *man*.

A *mature* man, with shoulders strong enough to bear burdens and admit mistakes and be relied upon.

In comparison, Ethan appeared a glass-house orchid. Lovely and exotic, to be sure, but temperamental and finicky.

Malcolm was hardy heather, able to bloom and thrive in the harshest of conditions. Why did women underestimate the power of competence? Why did men underestimate its appeal?

He appeared lost in thought, but then, as if sensing her gaze, he raised his head.

Oh!

That first moment. The locking of their eyes. The jolt of electricity down Viola's spine.

His dark hair ruffled in the slight breeze. Faint lines radiated out from his eyes, evidence of years spent in fields, squinting against the wind. Evening whiskers shadowed his jaw; he was the sort of man who would have to shave twice a day in order to remain clean-shaven. And somehow, that small fact endeared him to her.

Seeing him . . . it was like surfacing from underwater. Suddenly, for the first time in days, she could breathe again.

But with that breath came an almost overwhelming sense of physical awareness. During their previous encounter, speaking with him had felt effortless.

However, today—likely due to her enormous machinations and the questions buzzing in her mind—her hands abruptly shook, her native shyness threatening to tie up her tongue.

She had achieved her goal.

Now how was she to manage it?

Malcolm nearly stumbled when he realized it was Miss Brodure sitting beside the lane, retying her boot.

Beowoof had barked and ran ahead, alerting Malcolm to someone's presence—someone Beowoof knew. But Viola Brodure had been the last person he expected to see.

Granted, Ethan talked of little else. Malcolm had rarely seen his brother so taken with a lady.

But even knowing that, Malcolm couldn't help the way his own heart lifted to see her.

He was an utter *eejit*.

The lady had traveled from London with the intention of making Ethan's acquaintance. No one was fooled by Dr. Brodure's insistence that their arrival here was simply happenstance. The entire *village* was working behind the scenes to ensure that Ethan and Viola Brodure plighted their troth before summer's end.

The longings of Malcolm's own heart were completely irrelevant. Honestly, did he think a fine lady like Miss Brodure would ever be taken with *him*? Particularly when Ethan was about?

Keep a steady head, he chided himself, swallowing the bitter taste in his mouth.

She finished tying her shoe and stood to greet him, a tentative smile on her lips.

"Miss Brodure." He bowed.

"Mr. Penn-Leith." She curtsied before looking down at Beowoof. The poor thing remembered only too well her affection from the previous week. He wagged his tail and nudged at her skirts.

Smiling more openly, Miss Brodure sank down, scratching the dog behind his ears.

"Your animal is utterly shameless, Mr. Penn-Leith." She shot him a wry look, her blue eyes sending a dagger straight into his chest.

How was he to manage this? He liked Miss Brodure far too well. She took up an inordinate amount of his cranial space.

Malcolm might share Ethan's same background in theory, but his brother's life had been vastly different— education, travel, and fame placed Ethan and Miss Brodure on more equal footing.

The most Malcolm could hope was to call Miss Brodure his sister-in-law.

And what a depressing prospect *that* was. To spend years as a quiet witness to her marriage to Ethan.

What a disaster.

"Beowoof is a bit of a flirt, I am afraid," he said. "Like most Scottish men, he likes the lasses."

Malcolm said the words without thinking, but given how quickly Miss Brodure's eyebrows flew to her hairline, she read more into the words than he had intended.

Like most Scottish men, he likes the lasses.

Instead of saying flirtatiously in return, *Indeed. And do you like the lasses as well, Mr. Penn-Leith?*, Miss Brodure ducked her head and buried it in Beowoof's fur, as if embarrassed or . . .

Shy.

That word surfaced again.

Miss Brodure was truly . . . *shy.*

Why had no one else in the village noticed this? Or commented on it?

But voicing the question in his head, he knew the answer. Most were so overwhelmed to be in her presence, to actually speak with the lauded Miss Brodure, they neglected to see the woman behind her words.

How difficult had the past week been for her?

An aching sort of tenderness wound its way through his chest. Shyness, a reticence to speak up, was something he understood well. There had been a time when his younger self had struggled to even form sentences when talking to a stranger, particularly a woman. His tongue would stick to the roof of his mouth, and a buzzing energy would fill his ears.

Maturity had helped with that. The nervousness rarely surfaced now, but the reticence to speak still remained. He wasn't like Ethan—delighting in being the center of his own world. He had no desire to dazzle with charm and make small talk for hours with patrons and admirers.

Malcolm had never bemoaned the lack of those skills in himself. He had never wanted them.

Until now.

Until her.

Would that he had a glib tongue and could set Viola Brodure at ease.

She continued to bury her face in Beowoof's fur, rubbing his jowls, and murmuring to him. Two bright spots of color on her cheeks were the only outward indication of inner turmoil.

Malcolm hated her distress.

Sitting down on the log beside her, he ran a hand over Beowoof's back.

Miss Brodure—Viola, in his heart—sat back, her color climbing higher.

"Thank you for letting me pet him," she said, the words coming out in a breathy rush. "I never imagined that there would be a dog I could touch with such ease." A small tremor afflicted her hands as she stroked Beowoof's jaw.

"Aye." Malcolm flitted through ideas, anything to ease her nerves. "His story is a bit unusual, to be honest. Beowoof was actually a gift for Ethan from Her Grace, the Duchess of Buccleuch."

This admission startled a laugh out of Viola. "Ethan? A Duchess?"

"Oh, aye. The Duchess is quite enamored of our Ethan, she is. So she wrote, intent on gifting him one of the Duke's prized Labrador Retrievers."

"A Labra . . . what?"

"A Labrador Retriever. 'Tis a new breed of dog His Grace has been developing for the past decade or so. We Scots are always casting about for better dog breeds to withstand the marshy hunting grounds of the Highlands. Anyway, years ago, the Duke brought over some water retrievers from Newfoundland and bred them with his favorite hunting dogs here and created an entirely new breed."

"And Beowoof is one of those dogs?"

"Nae, actually, he's not." Malcolm smiled. "Ethan doesnae like dogs all that much."

"He doesn't like dogs?" Viola placed her hands over Beowoof's ears, as if to prevent him from hearing her words. "How can anyone not like dogs? What's not to love about a dog?" She slid her hands down to Beowoof's jowls and bent her nose to his, her voice going singsong. "How can anyone not love you, you adorable thing?"

Beowoof wagged his tail in joy, clearly thinking that Viola herself was the most adorable thing.

Malcolm could not agree with him more. The man who married this woman would be a lucky dog, indeed.

"So how did you end up with Beowoof?" she asked, raising her head.

"Like yourself, Ethan told the Duchess that he had a sensitivity to dogs—even though he does not—thinking that would end the exchange. Not even a week later, Beowoof shows up in the arms of one of His Grace's grooms. Apparently, His Grace's prized Labrador Retriever had escaped his pen and enjoyed a—shall we say romantic?—encounter with Her Grace's favorite French poodle. Beowoof and a litter of similar puppies were the result. Surprisingly, the puppies retained some of the best qualities of both dogs—the loyalty and energy of a water retriever mixed with the tighter fur of a poodle, which reduces sensitivity."

Viola laughed in delight, rubbing Beowoof's head. "How very clever of you, you darling dog."

"Naturally, Ethan could not refuse the gift at that point. I was all too happy to claim Beowoof as my own."

"I cannot fault you. He is magnificent."

Silence hung for a moment. But it wasn't an awkward thing.

Far from it, in fact.

The stillness spoke of comfort. Of ease in their shared shyness.

Viola's hands had stopped their trembling.

Malcolm considered it a victory.

"Come." He stood and extended his hand to her. "Allow me to escort you home. Ethan would never forgive me if some harm came to you."

He *had* to say the words, to remind himself—and her, he supposed—that everyone considered her to be his brother's property.

Given the way Viola's smile dimmed, she did not miss his implication. Was it due to some lingering guilt that she was speaking with Malcolm without Ethan present?

Or, dare he hope, that she was perhaps not as enamored of being Ethan's property as the rest of the village wished her to be?

Regardless, Viola placed her gloved hand in his, her slim fingers sliding over his gloveless ones. He was a farmer, after all. A gentrified one, but a farmer, nonetheless. He had never bothered with gloves.

But now, the contrast spoke of everything that stood between them.

Her hand resting overtop his, fingers sheathed in elegantly-stitched kid leather, buttery soft. Beautiful. Protected.

His palm like a rough-hewn oak, clean but nicked and worn in places. Rugged. Uncouth.

She stared, too, her breath hitching, as if the moment were significant to her somehow . . .

Or perhaps, she was simply horrified at the stark difference between them?

He was no London dandy, no rarefied rake to charm and dance attendance.

Some emotion he didn't understand flitted across her face.

And then . . . her fingers tightened around his. Not gently. Not shyly.

But rather a vise of a grip.

Nearly a possession of a sort, as if claiming all his scarred and rugged and silent pieces for herself.

The heat of her hand burned where it touched him, the light weight of her fingers scalding his blood. His heart soared, beating a rapid tattoo in his chest.

What a magnificent creature she was!

Why had he assumed that Ethan owned this woman in any way? How male-centric of him.

Viola Brodure would never be a man's property. Not Ethan's. Not his.

She would only ever belong to her fierce self.

He responded in the only way he could. He tightened his own grip and pulled her to standing.

She wobbled slightly, and he slid his other hand up her arm to grasp her elbow, steadying her.

"Thank you," she whispered, eyes rising to meet his.

Her thanks seemed more than mere words, more than his hand raising her up.

He felt as if she were thanking him for being . . . himself.

Which, as a thought, was quite absurd. Why would Viola Brodure be grateful for *him*, of all people?

But at the moment, he only cared that he stood near her. So close he could see himself reflected in her eyes. How else was he to learn that all that glorious blue was edged round in soft gold?

She had a touch of the angelic, it seemed. A ring of angel dust around her pupils.

Hah! Poetic, that.

Ethan couldn't have that thought. Malcolm wanted it for himself.

She still hadn't moved out of his grasp, her eyes continuing to search his. He felt physically incapable of releasing her, as if some unspoken communication was happening, soul to soul.

Or perhaps that was just his fanciful wish, because eventually she smiled and took a step back, severing the contact.

His hands mourned her loss.

She gave her head a little shake, as if loosing cobwebs . . . bringing herself back to . . . herself.

"Thank you," she repeated.

"'Tis my pleasure." He offered her his arm.

She slid that same elegant, gloved hand through his elbow, the touch of her fingers just as scalding even through the layers of his coat.

He whistled to Beowoof to attend them. The dog loped out of the woods.

"Would you be so kind as to tell me about the life of a gentleman farmer?" she asked as they began to walk. "I have only ever lived in London."

"Indeed? And how are ye finding Scotland then? Too wild for your tastes?"

"Quite the contrary. I am starting to believe that I never took a true breath of air until coming here."

"Is that right?"

"Oh, aye." She drawled the word just as he would.

He laughed. "We'll make a Scot out of ye yet, Miss Brodure."

He felt her smile. "So tell me about your life, Mr. Penn-Leith."

Malcolm needed no further encouragement. "I will happily, Miss Brodure. But when your eyes glaze over as I discuss corn shares, I willnae apologize. Ye have been duly warned."

She laughed, a delighted, intoxicating sound.

He spent the rest of the walk up the lane telling her about his take on crop rotation, the reasoning behind the animals he bred, and the endless worry of pests and weather.

If he bored her to tears, it did not show. She asked intelligent questions and seemed genuinely interested in his answers, words and ideas flowing easily between them.

Of course, in the end, he neglected to ask the most obvious question: Why was Miss Brodure on the lane in the first place?

Seven

THE NEXT DAY, Malcolm tried to not think about Miss Brodure *every* passing second.

Viola crooning to Beowoof, her eyes alight with joy.

Viola laughing as he told tale of Coolius Caesar getting loose and rampaging through a line of fresh laundry.

Viola tilting her head as she asked yet another perceptive question.

He did manage to go a minute or two without images of her popping into his head . . . though only a few.

How was he to endure watching Ethan woo and marry this woman?

Because Ethan was utterly taken with Viola Brodure. He had already cornered Malcolm twice today, wanting ideas he could use to describe love.

Unsurprisingly, Malcolm was less than helpful. It was one thing to watch Ethan woo Viola. It was something else entirely to expect Malcolm to actively participate in damaging his own heart.

Viola might ask polite questions about Malcolm's life as a gentleman farmer, but it did not follow that she wished to marry into it. She had traveled to Edzell for Ethan.

Malcolm kept repeating these thoughts as he headed home at the end of the day, trudging up the same lane.

She will not be waiting again.

She is not for you.

Cease this foolishness.

And yet, his stupid heart still hoped, leaping and lurching at the possibility of seeing her again.

So when Beowoof barked and set off up the road, Malcolm had to forcibly stop himself from chasing after, equally desperate to see what was ahead.

Was she there? Had she come?

He forced his feet to walk at a normal pace, ignoring the blood thumping through his veins.

He came up the low rise . . .

And there she was, sitting on the same log as the day before, rubbing Beowoof's chops. An errant ray of sunlight broke through the trees, rimming her head in golden light—a nearly angelic punctuation mark.

She *had* come. But why?

Coincidence, again?

Perhaps.

But Malcolm was all smiles as he bowed in greeting, asking about her day. And like the previous evening, conversation flowed easily between them.

He asked her about her writing.

She asked him about his Highland cattle.

He returned home with a head nearly in the clouds.

Why had she been waiting? Did she seek him out because, unlike the rest of his neighbors, he tried not to heap expectations upon her? That, with him, she could just be?

Or did her interest in him go beyond that?

Regardless of the reason, the next day, she was sitting on the same log.

His mind struggled to fully understand. For some reason, this incredible woman was waiting for *him*. Not Ethan. Not some London beau.

His heart nearly burst at the sheer wonder of it.

The fourth day after meeting Malcolm along the lane, Viola was a bundle of nerves.

Ethan, the wee brother, had become more and more forward in his attentions. He visited nearly daily, ensconcing himself in their small parlor, talking endlessly.

Viola found Ethan . . . perplexing.

On the one hand, he was a skilled conversationalist. He could monologue for hours about rhyme and meter (though, ironically, never about philosophy and meaning, which Viola found much more interesting). As a shy person, she preferred listening to talking anyway, and she appreciated the viewpoint of another creative mind.

But on the other hand, Ethan Penn-Leith was *exhausting*.

Like her father, Ethan basked in her praise and affirmation, something that Viola excelled at due to years of experience. But she sensed that Ethan needed the validation for its own sake and not because he actually wished her genuine opinion.

In short, the reality of the Highland Poet was not on par with the power of his poetry.

Though with regards to poetry, Ethan had sent over a poem the previous morning. It had been clever, comparing courtship to exploring a foreign land rather than a hunting expedition, saying:

> Carry onward, bold soul, to that heart-land
> Of ready marvel and mystery,
> Where gorse lies waiting to understand
> Why you lay no flag of victory.

The poem had softened her slightly toward him; clearly,

there were hidden depths within Ethan Penn-Leith. Pity Viola never saw them beyond words on paper.

When she asked him how he conceived such touching metaphors, Ethan had babbled some nonsense about communing with the Goddess of Inspiration and listening to her dedicated muse.

What balderdash. In her experience, writing was more hard work than meditation and lightning bolts of genius.

But one thing she did know: She did not wish to marry Ethan Penn-Leith.

There.

She had admitted it to herself.

He seemed the perfect suitor. She *knew* this, and yet her heart simply could not like him beyond polite friendship.

Ethan simply felt like so much surface. She wanted more than a pretty veneer over life—wit and charm were no substitutes for substance and true depth of feeling.

Unfortunately, this knowledge left her in a bit of muddle.

She had traveled to Scotland specifically to meet Ethan. The entire village was practically pushing them together—

Scratch that.

If the *London Tattler* was to be believed, the entire *country* wished Viola and Ethan to marry.

How could she extricate herself at this point? Rejecting Ethan Penn-Leith would not commend her to his supporters. It would not endear her to her *own* readers nor her publisher.

Heavens, what a mess.

Of course, none of this stopped her daydreaming about Malcolm. The rugged Scot was Ethan's opposite in many ways. Silent and observant. Intelligent and profoundly insightful. His presence was a soothing balm, a space where she could drop pretense and simply . . . live.

Being around Malcolm was more than mere chemistry or

animal attraction. When they were together, she felt as if she were learning her own soul anew.

Viola had been honest when she claimed she hadn't really breathed before coming to Scotland. Before meeting *him*.

She thought about Malcolm all through Ethan's meandering stories, through her father's sermonizing, through her own distracted attempts at writing.

Eager to meet him on that fourth day, she had donned her bonnet and gloves and had one foot out the back door when Mrs. Ruxton stopped by for a quick visit. Viola could not be rude to the vicar's wife. And so, she had removed her bonnet and gloves, requesting tea be sent to the parlor. Through a small miracle, Viola managed to get the lady out the door after a brief thirty-minute visit, but she knew she would be too late to catch Malcolm along the lane.

Heart heavy, she nonetheless hurried out the door—bonnet forgotten, gloves abandoned—down the narrow path and on to the lane that lead to the far fields.

She walked quickly, fearing that the exertion of running would be too much for her lungs, that it would aggravate her asthma.

But, oh, how she longed to run!

Had she already missed him?

Please be there.

Please wait for me.

She turned down the final lane, the one that had the log where she had met him the previous three days. She hoped against hope that perhaps Malcolm would still be walking up the lane, that perhaps she hadn't missed him entirely.

But he was nowhere to be seen.

No bark from Beowoof. No whistle from Malcolm.

Lungs heaving, she continued on. Just a little farther. Just to their log. Then she would know for sure that she had missed him.

She rounded the last corner, steeling her heart to find an empty road.

Beowoof's joyous bark greeted her instead.

Viola's chest heaved with joy.

There he was.

Malcolm.

Standing tall, a foot propped up on their log, a slight breeze ruffling his kilt. His eyes swung to hers.

Oh, heavens.

Gracious.

Electricity crackled between them. The very air charged with a fluffing, hopeful sort of wonder.

In that look, she saw it—

He *knew.*

He knew she had been racing to see him.

And . . .

Now *she* knew.

He had been waiting for her.

He had hoped she would come.

A painful sort of jubilation thrummed in her chest, jittery in her blood.

She slowed her pace, continuing up the lane and stopping five feet in front of him.

She smiled.

He gazed at her, eyes warm and thoughtful, before a slow grin stretched across his face. It was quite like a sunrise, glorious and full of promise.

"Miss Brodure." He nodded his head, his voice rumbling over her.

"Mr. Penn-Leith." She dipped a small curtsy, the wind ruffling her uncovered head.

His eyes darted over her person, noting her missing bonnet, her lacking gloves, surely understanding that she had raced out the door to meet him.

Viola should have been chagrined, at the very least.

But instead, all she felt was freedom. Blessed, blissful freedom. The joy of having hands and head as unencumbered as his own.

"A pleasure to see ye," he continued, that same smile tugging at his lips. Beowoof nudged at her skirts, demanding a greeting of his own.

"And you, too, sir." She bent and scratched Beowoof's ears.

"I take it my discourse on the differences between Highland and Angus cattle didnae put ye off yester evening. Come back for more, have ye?"

Viola couldn't help her wide grin. "Quite. I find cattle endlessly fascinating."

That garnered a huffed chuckle. "Now I know ye be bamming me. *No one* finds cows fascinating."

"No? It must be something else, then," she laughed, meeting his dark gaze.

That same energy bounced between them, the moment stretching, growing in portent.

He did not ask the obvious question: *Why did ye come then?*

And she did not give the clear answer: *Why, to see you, of course.*

But the exchange seemed to happen nonetheless.

"Come," he motioned. "Allow me to escort ye home."

"Thank you."

"Dinnae thank me quite yet, lass. I have stipulations."

"Stipulations?"

"Aye." He nodded, crossing his arms over his chest, gaze most serious. "I dinnae wish to speak of cows."

"No cows?"

"None. Nary a word about feed or beef or market prices.

Chickens, pigs, sheep, and other barnyard animals are also prohibited topics of conversation."

Viola affected a put-upon sigh. "I suppose goats, ducks, and swans are also forbidden?"

"Ye suppose correctly. Might as well throw in all crops, as well. Barley and oats and such."

"Even potatoes?"

"*Particularly* potatoes. A wretched business . . . potatoes."

That piqued her curiosity. "Truly? Why are potatoes wretched?"

"Have ye not heard? They say there is a blight affecting them at the moment, though it hasnae reached Scotland as of yet."

"How dreadful!"

"Aye, it is. I cannae think what we'll do if—" He stopped mid-sentence, fixing her with a look. He wagged his finger. "Hah! I see what you're doing there, lass. I willnae be distracted into discussing tubers."

"You misunderstand, sir. I truly am interested—"

"Nae. I'll have none of it. I wish to know more about your writing, about why ye choose the topics that ye do."

"Sincerely? That is quite a lengthy discussion, I fear."

He offered her his arm. "Then we shall walk slowly."

In the years to come, Malcolm would remember the weeks that followed as snippets of conversation with Viola.

Every day, if possible, one or the other would be waiting at the same fallen log. He would leisurely walk with her along the deserted lane, leaving her at the end of the long path to the house Dr. Brodure had let.

Their conversations covered a wide range of topics, but Malcolm loved most hearing Viola talk about herself.

"Why did ye decide to become a writer?" he asked her one evening as they strolled arm-in-arm up the lane.

She smiled and shrugged. "To be very honest, I cannot actually remember a time when I did *not* wish to be a writer."

"Aye?"

"Aye," she mimicked back, causing him to smile. He did that more nowadays, almost anytime the thought of her passed his mind.

A smile rarely left his face, it seemed.

"I fear storytelling is in my blood," she continued. "Our last name, Brodure, comes from the French *brodeur*, or embroiderer. As a family, we have always loved to embellish things. My mother said that I came out of the womb telling stories and never stopped."

"She sounds like a fine lady."

"That she was. She died of a fever when I was fifteen. I've missed her dreadfully ever since."

"I am sorry. I know I miss both my own mother and father."

"I grieve for your loss."

"Thank you, but it was a verra long time ago. Though, I must say, ye dinnae truly become an adult until ye bury both your parents. That's when true adulthood settles on ye."

"Are you implying that I still have some growing up to do, Mr. Penn-Leith?"

"Perhaps," he teased. "But first, I wonder if it isnae time for ye to call me Malcolm?"

She tut-tutted her tongue. "Such informality, Mr. Penn-Leith. What would all my fine, genteel London acquaintances say to such a thing?"

"That ye count me a friend, Viola?"

She smiled, wide and delighted. "That I do, Malcolm. That I do."

Eight

THOUGH HE GREATLY enjoyed his evening strolls with Viola, Malcolm did not relish dining with his family.

Ethan's endless chatter about the lady ensured that.

"I think Miss Brodure is quite attached to me now. She fair hangs on my every word," Ethan said one Tuesday morning over breakfast. "I cannae imagine how our courtship could be any more perfect."

"Oh, Ethan," Aileen beamed, eyes glassy, "I am so happy for ye."

Malcolm grunted, unequal to the task of encouraging his brother.

His heart whispered that Viola liked him specifically. That Malcolm himself was precious to her.

Did Viola light up the same way when Ethan walked into a room? Did she smile wide and welcoming?

Malcolm thought not.

But a lifetime of watching every lovely thing simply fall into Ethan's lap had him questioning his own understanding. Perhaps, Viola merely found Malcolm to be a kind listening ear.

"Did ye know the London broadsheets are saying we'll make a match of it yet?" Ethan said, delight in his voice. "A university mate of mine sent up a clipping from *The Tattler* or some such. The author says all of London hopes Miss Brodure and myself will write our own love story."

"Heavens! How dreadfully romantic," Aileen laughed.

"It is," Ethan grinned, spearing sausage on his plate. "Miss Brodure came all this way just to meet me. Think of what the papers will print when we marry! How famous we both shall be—"

Malcolm pushed upright from the table, rattling the silverware.

"I say, Malcolm, you off to check on the south field?" Ethan asked, obliviously cheerful.

"Something like that," Malcolm mumbled, all but storming out of the room.

Despite Ethan's words, Malcolm himself wasn't convinced Viola Brodure truly preferred his wee brother.

The more Malcolm observed, the more he saw that she accepted Ethan's attentions, but she did nothing to seek them out.

Furthermore, she did not confide in Ethan. Whenever Malcolm asked Ethan basic questions about Viola—*Is her mother still alive? Has Miss Brodure always wanted to be a writer?*—Ethan could not answer them.

And yet, she readily shared her innermost thoughts with Malcolm.

"I cannot say that I truly like my own writing," Viola said one sunny evening in mid-June.

Malcolm felt his eyebrows raising at the admission. "How can ye not like yer own writing?"

She walked at his side, her hand a soft weight on his

elbow, her skirts occasionally brushing that bare strip of skin between the bottom of his kilt and the top of his stockings.

He adored being with her like this—the ease of their camaraderie, the sense of belonging. Though their lives had differed vastly—he in rural Scotland, she in urban London—there was a sameness in the way they each saw the world.

A harmony of thought.

"Truly, Viola? How can ye say such a thing?" he continued. "Your writing . . . why, it's fair brilliant."

That got her attention. Viola stopped abruptly, sending her skirts to swinging. He turned to her. She angled her head, her blue eyes scrutinizing his. The barest of smiles touched her lips.

"You've read my work?" she asked.

"Aye. A'course, I have."

"Oh!"

"I particularly liked *Little Lottie*. Those descriptions of London." He shivered. "I could practically feel the creeping fog."

"That's very kind of you to say."

"There's nothing of kindness about it. 'Tis truth."

Two spots of color appeared on her cheeks. Utterly charming. She looked at him for another moment before her eyes darted away, gaze taking in the countryside around them. She wrapped her left hand around her narrow waist, a motion Malcolm was coming to understand meant she was feeling some strong emotion.

But what emotion might that be?

He continued, "Why write if ye dinnae like what you're saying?"

She sighed. "Unfortunately, the life of a lady, no matter how privileged, is always scripted by a father or a husband."

"Your father dictates your topics?"

"Often. He likes me to be his voice, after a fashion. He feels quite strongly that a lady should not sully her mind with the baser parts of humanity. So I may allude to deeply distressing behaviors, but I should never delve into them."

"Like the child labor you touch on in *Little Lottie*? I liked those passages best."

"Me, too." She bit her lip. "I think that might be part of the problem. The writing that feels most authentically me—not the silly moralizing bits that I know I must include as examples of the tenderness of my sex to appease my father"—she rolled her eyes—"but the descriptions that touch on the troubles of the world, on the dark recesses few dare to explore . . . *those* are the things I wish to discuss."

Her voice rose, vibrating with passion and conviction. "A hidden wrong—like the abuses of child labor—is allowed to continue because we, as a society, refuse to discuss it. We cover it over and hide it away. Child labor is a difficult topic, liable to incur feelings of guilt and helplessness—emotions we all would like to avoid feeling—and so we sweep it aside, telling ourselves that it doesn't exist or that it isn't as bad as we suppose, relegating it to sanitized snippets in stories like *Little Lottie.*"

Ah.

Viola refused to meet his gaze, eyes staring sightlessly over the surrounding fields, clenching her fists over and over, obviously trying to rein in her emotions.

This woman and her magnificent heart.

"I couldnae agree more, Viola," he said, voice low and earnest. "Such ills do need to be addressed. And I think ye are the person to do it."

She whipped her luminous blue eyes back to his, expression wide and surprised.

"Truly?"

"Aye. Why not tell such tales? Shine a beacon of light into the worst of human ills; force society to see and act."

She laughed, a bitter, caustic sound. "If only it were that easy. Taking on such topics will surely alienate many of my readers." A pause and then, "I am so heartily sick of gloves!"

That had Malcolm rearing back his head. "Pardon?"

"Gloves!" She raised her hand, brandishing her fingers in their kid leather as if they were a taint upon humanity.

Frowning, she tugged at the fingertips, vehemently stripping the offending garments from her hands, one at a time.

Free of their shield, her hands were pale and fragile-boned. *And likely impossibly soft to the touch*, an unhelpful part of his brain noted.

A perfect lady's hands.

Malcolm stood in perplexed silence. "Why would ye remove your gloves? Your poor hands should be protected."

"Hah!" She shook the gloves at him. "That is precisely the point! I am so tired of being coddled, of people saying I should shield myself from ugliness. That I should keep to more palatable topics for a woman. Women are still human beings and cannot—nor should be—protected from life's ills. Ugly things happen to us all. Why are we metaphorically covering our souls in gloves"—she slapped the gloves against her hand—"and pretending such horrors don't exist instead of openly showing our pain and discussing harsh realities? Just as I cannot sew or eat with gloves on, I cannot write effectively when topics are forbidden me!"

She held herself still, as if waiting for the blow of his condemnation.

Malcolm was having none of it. He liked her like this—impassioned, vehement, fiery.

This was what he missed in her writing. *This* was the woman the world needed to hear.

"Ye are a crusader, lass."

"A marauder, you mean."

"Nae, a *crusader.* Ye are Eleanor of Aquitaine or Joan of Arc, intent on freeing her people." Taking a chance, Malcolm reached out and plucked the gloves from her hands, tucking them into his sporran. She stared at him, wide-eyed, chest heaving.

Taking a further liberty, Malcolm held out his hand, palm up.

An invitation. *Take my hand.*

Viola bit her lip, and then lifted her right hand.

She paused, and then slid her palm across his.

Just as before, the contrast between their hands was astonishing—her porcelain skin resting atop his weathered, brown one.

But this time, it was the heat of her touch that seared him, that sent electricity arcing up his arm.

And like before, she wrapped her fingers around his and held on tightly—claiming him—the firmness of her grasp mimicking the fierceness of her heart.

"This," he said, lifting their joined hands. "This is what I mean by ye being a crusader. Ye wish to use your hands for good. To get dirt under your nails and scrapes across your knuckles. Or, more specifically, to have your scrapes and dirt *acknowledged* as such. Gloves only ever offer the illusion of protection, after all. I would argue that women often experience *more* of life's ills than men. They bear bairns and tend to the sick and stretch food and make a home amid squalor and neglect. And all this while trying to please their menfolk and having few legal rights of their own." He tightened his grip on her hand. "So, yes, lass, I consider ye a crusader."

She said nothing for a moment, eyes blinking rapidly, her left hand wrapping around her waist, fingers fidgeting. But her palm in his held true.

She cleared her throat before speaking again.

"I fear not much will come of it." Her low contralto voice skimmed across his skin in a soft whisper. "I am far too shy to be an effective revolutionary—"

"I disagree."

"—moreover, who would wish to read such a thing?"

"Those who seek truth." He squeezed her hand. "Those, like myself, who enjoy your writing, the clever turn of your phrase. I predict ye will be surprised who lauds such writing if ye do it."

"But many will lash out and denigrate it, too. It will tarnish my current body of work."

"Perhaps. There will always be critics. So why refuse to say what is in your heart? Particularly when it is so very vital to the greater good?" He tugged on her hand, helpless against the need to have her closer to him. "I contend that ambition is not an end result to be achieved. Ambition is a *wish*—the ultimate desire of our heart. 'Tis the sum of what we *would* do, not what we actually accomplish."

Viola continued to hesitate—eyes blinking again, chest heaving, gaze fixed on his sternum. She swallowed, throat rolling.

"Viola, listen tae me." He said the words softly, gently, willing her to look at him.

He pressed her hand to his chest, wanting her to feel the steadiness of his thumping heart, the truth of his words.

He waited. Birds sang. Trees rustled. Beowoof sniffed about in the grass.

Finally, she brought her eyes back to his, glimmering with unshed tears that nearly unmanned him.

Who had *dared* to tell this woman she could not have the world? Who had forced her to wear gloves, to remain confined to a narrow sphere? He wanted to smash down walls for her.

"Ye have so much fire, lass," he said, still holding her

hand over his heart. "I feel it every time we talk. Ye practically *burn* with it. It's a conflagration of ideas and passion inside ye." He thumped his free hand against his chest. "But I fear for ye, too."

She continued to bite her lip. A single tear dropped onto her cheek. "Y-you do?" The barest whisper.

"Aye. Such fire . . . 'tis a dangerous thing, I think. If ye ignore it, it may very well end ye. I ken that ofttimes literal death isnae the way we die most."

She absorbed this with an audible inhalation.

She mouthed the words back to him—*ofttimes literal death isnae the way we die most.*

He lifted her hand from his chest, pressing a kiss to her knuckles.

"Take on the world's ills, Viola Brodure," he urged. "Shed your gloves. Sing your heart. People *will* listen."

She nodded her head, tears falling in earnest. She swiped them from her cheeks, digging in her skirt pocket for a handkerchief but not finding one.

Malcolm retrieved his own from his sporran. She took it with a watery smile.

"How did you become so wise?" she sniffled, dabbing her face.

"Farming in rural Scotland, a'course." He grinned, cheeky and mischievous. "Have ye not heard? All the greatest poets are doing it nowadays."

Malcolm was entirely too proud of her startled, guffawing laugh that followed.

Nine

MALCOLM'S WORDS WOULD not leave Viola alone.

She stripped off her gloves and all but threw them at him, and instead of laughter or recrimination, he returned with . . .

I understand.

I see.

The man instinctively knew the language of her soul.

Poor Ethan had never stood a chance with her.

The brothers were, in a way, utter opposites.

Ethan had the persona and words of a poet, but she had yet to see any true depth of insight or feeling from him. When she was with him, she felt more appendage than self. She existed *adjacent* to his dreams and wishes, watching and supporting, but not actually participating.

But with Malcolm, she could fully . . . *be.* He wanted her to engage in life, to get her hands dirty in the business of finally *living.*

Ironically, she felt like Malcolm had the heart and soul of a poet, even if he lacked the ability to put it into so many words.

His encouragement to write weightier stories haunted her.

Literal death isnae the way we die most.

Did he understand how thoroughly those words would resonate within her breast?

She could not stop them running through her mind, over and over, an endless wheel looping round.

She had a vision of herself stuffed inside a glove labeled with expectations and etiquette and the scores of things society demanded from a woman . . . restricted to the point of suffocation, the words she wanted to say dying on her tongue, lacking air to live.

A death, in truth.

She could not—she *would* not—be that woman any longer.

Malcolm Penn-Leith had lent her the courage to take this step. To leave behind a life of watchfulness—of existing adjacent—and enter into the "feral moor."

Her mind, set free from its fetters, hummed with activity. She made list after list of ideas and storylines. Where to begin?

She settled on exploring women in poverty, and the ofttimes horrific decisions they had to make. She had seen so much, both in her research for books such as *Little Lottie*, and also through her father's work as a vicar. Life could be cruel to a woman with little education and even less ability to provide for her children. If the men in her life declined to help, a woman was left with very few choices, indeed.

Viola found herself writing in a near frenzy of creative energy.

Her days settled into a steady rhythm—frenetic writing in the morning, calls and visits in the afternoon, and her "evening stroll" to regenerate her creative muse, but which was, in actuality, a meeting with Malcolm.

Of course, throughout it all, her father was oblivious to the changes occurring within her. To the true longings of her heart.

She knew that he would feel betrayed when she informed him of the direction of her writing.

Worse, the dear man still thought she might marry Ethan Penn-Leith.

"He is simply the most marvelous of men," her father said one afternoon in July as the door closed on yet another visit from Ethan. Despite the cloudy, gloomy day, Ethan had not missed an opportunity to call upon them.

Viola was careful during Ethan's visits to not encourage him. Thankfully, her father usually joined them, eager for the poet's company, making it more difficult for Ethan to woo her in earnest.

But Ethan had become less oblique in his references to a possible union between them. Viola knew she needed to have a frank conversation with him—at the very least, she needed to make it clear that she preferred his elder brother—but with her father always about, the opportunity never arose.

And Viola, being shy and doubly-so around Ethan, found it difficult to force the issue.

She knew she had two fraught confrontations in her future: one with her father, the other with Ethan. How could she resolve them peacefully?

"Mr. Penn-Leith is to be commended," her father continued. "I hope you have not been remiss in noting what a dedicated and devoted suitor he has been to you, Viola."

"I have noticed it, Father, but—"

"The man can scarcely tear his eyes from you," her father nattered on, cheerfully oblivious. "I fear you have not been suitably encouraging. You need to be more doting."

Oh, dear. This was precisely what Viola feared.

She *had* to say something. Her father had to understand that she only felt friendship for Ethan. Nothing more.

"Father," Viola began, "though I do like Mr. Penn-Leith as a friend, I cannot say that I wish for a further measure of his regard. Friendship is sufficient for me."

"What is this?" Her father froze, his brows drawing down. "How can you not wish for his deeper regard? We journeyed to Scotland specifically for *this.*"

"Perhaps initially, Father. But—"

"Don't be foolish, child. You have been on the shelf for years and are unaccustomed to male attention. I assume that this is some fit of maidenly restraint that touches you. But you must set aside your own innate shyness and encourage Mr. Penn-Leith to declare himself."

"But that is just it, Father," Viola pleaded, desperate for her father to truly *see* her wishes and respect them. "I do not wish to have Mr. Penn-Leith as a suitor."

"Pardon? How can you say such a thing?" Her father began to pace the room, his words more agitated. "You have led Mr. Penn-Leith to have expectations. Why, everyone anticipates you two will marry. Even the *broadsheets* think that you and Mr. Penn-Leith are a perfect match. Two months ago, all you could speak of was Mr. Penn-Leith and how much you admired his writings! Is your heart so very fickle, daughter?"

"No, but all this was before I actually *knew* Mr. Penn-Leith—"

"The man *improves* upon making his acquaintance! I certainly think more highly of him now." Dr. Brodure paused, staring at Viola. "You do not see, child, so I shall be very clear. You are no longer a young woman, Viola. How many offers of this caliber do you think you will receive?"

Viola inhaled, a sharp, staccato sound.

Dr. Brodure did not relent. "I have tried to spare you the bald truth of this, Viola, but it is time you faced facts. You are a woman writing in a man's world. There are those who will always think less of you because of your gender. An alliance—a marriage, in truth—to a man of Mr. Penn-Leith's talent and renown will ensure you a place with the literary greats of this country. I am trying to *assist* you in this."

Viola wrapped her hand around her waist. Her breathing was tight in her chest. Her father's frustration and her own agitation constricted her lungs, threatening a full asthma attack.

But this confrontation had been too long in coming. She would not back down now. She swallowed, forcing herself to take slow, measured breaths.

"I *do* understand what you are saying, Father," she said, "and I know the realities of my gender and age only too well. But I cannot agree with your ambition. I do not wish to rule the literary elites in London. I do not wish for greater fame or fortune—"

"Balderdash! Everyone wishes for more fame!"

"Perhaps you do, but *I* do not. I do not need fame." She took in a fortifying breath. "But I *do* need to make a difference." She continued on, forcing the words past her numb lips. "I wish to write tales that focus on the *true* ills of our society. I wish to expose those things that most would prefer to ignore. I want to be remembered as a woman who braved difficult things, not one who hid behind moralizing and platitudes—"

"Enough!! I will hear no more on this matter!" Her father's face had turned nearly purple with rage. Spittle hit her cheeks. "We settled this *years* ago. Such topics are not for women to discuss. A *true* lady would remain ignorant of such matters."

"But we are not!"

"Your father, and someday, your husband—should you choose to show an ounce of feminine sensibility and natural maternal longings—will shelter you from the ugliness of the world—"

"But I do not wish to be sheltered!"

"—and will instruct you as to what you should think and believe!"

Viola flinched, her father's words striking her like boiling water.

Her mind tumbled down a crevasse.

This was what he thought? These were the beliefs lurking underneath all her father's support and care?

That she was to remain naive her entire life? That she needed to be *told* what to think?

Viola could scarcely speak for the trembling of her limbs.

"How c-can you s-say that?" she bit out, teeth chattering with suppressed emotion, her breathing winding tighter and tighter. "My m-mind is sharp and keen. I d-do not require *instruction*"—she leaned on the word with a scalding bitterness—"to know what to think. I am c-capable of independent th-thought on my own."

How could her own *father* believe such ridiculous things of her?

She tapped her chest with a shaking finger. "I am a p-person of worth!"

It was all too much. Her lungs seized up; spots hovered in her vision, and the room darkened at the edges.

Her father instantly noted her troubled breathing.

"Enough of this, daughter," he said, concern in his tone. He led her to the sofa, sitting her down. "You will kill yourself one day with such talk. This is why we must not discuss it."

"I will n-not be s-silenced, Father—"

"Hush, child. I love you, dearest heart. I truly do. But we are better to pretend the conversation never happened. I'll have the maid fetch some coffee for your throat."

He left the room, but Viola still struggled to breathe, her eyes stinging.

How could she help her father to understand? The topic didn't distress her! No, it was her father's intransigence which caused this reaction.

Why would he not listen?

She could not continue like this . . . to accept her father's vision for her life, to live as a reflection of his ambition. To bite her tongue and play the demure lady and pretend that she didn't long to scream her own truth.

Literal death isnae the way we die most.

But what was she to do? Without her father's support, what recourse did she have?

She could not stay in this room, in this house . . . in this place where she was not *seen*.

Malcolm.

The thought scorched her.

With Malcolm, she could breathe. With him, she did not have to pretend. She could strip off the glove of decorum and simply . . . *be*.

Viola was off the couch and down the lane before her father returned.

Ten

LATER, VIOLA WOULD marvel that she managed to walk such a long distance, her corset restricting her breathing, her asthma threatening to overwhelm her. But, as usual, the cool, damp air of Scotland eased her breathing, opening up her lungs just enough for her to carry onward.

She wiped tears as she walked, the conversation with her father going round and round in her head. How could her father so callously disregard her own feelings? How could he truly believe that she needed a *man* to determine her very thoughts?

But . . . in a sense, he was *right.*

She relied on her father for a great many things. He was her liaison with her publisher, he saw to her financial interests, he negotiated contracts on her behalf.

She was, indeed, a woman in a man's world.

Oh, how that stung!

What was she to do if her father withdrew his support?

Viola passed the log where she and Malcolm usually met, as it was too early in the day for him to be there yet. She continued down the lane, intent on waiting for him at the far pasture where he kept his Highland cattle.

She cleared the trees and crossed a wee burn, the pasture coming into view. Viola raised her head.

Oh.

Malcolm's broad shoulders appeared, his back to her, latching the gate shut. The wind ruffled the hair poking out from underneath his cap and sent the heavy weight of his kilt swaying slightly to the left.

Beowoof sat beside his master, tongue lolling out. He let out a joyous *woof* when he saw her, instantly loping to her side. The dog's unfettered happiness made her vision go blurry again.

Malcolm turned at the sound, his eyes meeting hers. His brows drew down, and he strode toward her, a towering thunder gathering.

"What is it, lass?" His concerned voice undid her. "What has happened? Ye've been *greetin'*. I see it in yer red eyes."

Oh, this dear, sweet man!

Viola closed the remaining distance between them and threw herself upon his chest, weeping uncontrollably. The motion felt impossibly natural, as if Malcolm's strong shoulders had been created simply to hold the weight of her tears.

His arms wrapped tightly around her, pulling her close. Viola rested everything upon him: arms and body, hopes and fears.

He bore her burden with comforting ease.

"There, lass," he murmured. "There, there. Has someone died?"

Viola shook her head.

"Ah. Then I only have one other question." He paused to push back her hair, his rough hand cradling her face. "Who do I need tae give a good thumping?"

That was the last straw.

The final thing that sent Viola tumbling head-over-heels, giddily, ridiculously in love with Malcolm Penn-Leith.

Unfortunately, the realization was one too many.

Her father's constraining beliefs and castigation.

Her long walk taken much too quickly.

Malcolm's kind words and patient understanding.

The longings of her own heart.

Her poor body was not up to the task of actually *breathing* through it all.

Her chest spasmed, and her lungs constricted, sending Viola gasping for air.

Malcolm's expression instantly turned alarmed.

"Viola?!" He grasped her head with both hands, looking into her eyes, trying to ascertain what was happening.

She continued to suck in labored breaths, desperate to get more air into her lungs. Her vision went dark at the edges.

Viola figured if she died here and now . . . staring into the eyes of Malcolm Penn-Leith was an acceptable way to go.

Naturally, Malcolm, being Malcolm, would have none of it.

"Will anything help this?" he asked, voice urgent. "Do you know?"

Bless Malcolm and his ability to always ask the correct question.

"Air," she gasped, chest heaving. "Cool. Wet. Air."

She had scarcely finished before Malcolm swept her up into his arms, a mass of billowing white petticoats and darker skirt, carrying her across the uneven ground in steady strides.

Viola wrapped her arms around his neck, resting her cheek on his shoulder, eyes closed, mind focused on her lungs, on the simple act of drawing air in and out.

The air turned cooler. The sound of a babbling stream reached her, the world becoming heavy with humidity. The change was most welcome. She felt herself sinking down but still supported against Malcolm's chest. Viola's lungs eased fractionally, her body relaxing into his strength.

She did not know how much time passed, but her

breathing eventually freed, the tightness in her chest clearing. The cool, damp air relieved the worst of her symptoms.

Viola opened her eyes to find herself resting on a grassy riverbank.

Well, *Malcolm* sat on the riverbank, his back against a tree trunk, legs stretched out in front of him.

Viola was curled upon his lap, a jumbled ball of petticoats, her head resting on his sternum.

Even though the worst had passed—she certainly did not need his physical assistance any longer—she could not bring herself to move.

His heart beat a steady rhythm under her ear. His arms wrapped loosely around her, holding her in place—firm but not constricting, supporting but not binding. She knew he would loose her the second she asked. And would hold her again just as quickly.

Tears pricked once more.

How could any woman—any human being, for that matter—want more from life than this? To have another person who so supported you just as you were?

She had never really understood love until now. True love. Love as it *should* be.

Her father said he loved her. And she believed that he genuinely did, in his own way.

But Dr. Brodure's love was a heavy, stifling thing. It required her to hide and cajole, to give up parts of herself, over and over. He clipped her wings—kept her ignorant of her own affairs, silenced her voice—and told her it was love.

Malcolm, however, was the opposite of that. She voiced a wish, and he handed her the tools to accomplish it.

She was not so vain or sure of her own charms to suppose that he loved her—*truly* loved her, as a man loves a woman, as she certainly loved him—but she could not deny that Malcolm was, as the very least, a constant friend.

And that friendship was everything to her.

Within it, she saw what true love should be. Healing and giving. Uplifting and encouraging. All without judgment. Malcolm did not require her to hide parts of her soul. With him, she could be her most authentic self.

She adored the person she was in Malcolm's eyes. That he made her want to be the strong, brave woman he saw.

Tears pricked again.

Could this be the rest of her life? Could she simply never return to London and instead stay with Malcolm, curled into the comfort of his support? Adored simply for being ... Viola?

Malcolm held Viola for far longer than was wise. He held her long after her breathing eased—so long that his legs went numb, the damp seeped through the thick wool of his kilt, and Beowoof had vanished to heaven-knew-where.

Malcolm could not remember when he had been happier.

The soft curves of her body melted into his chest, a heavenly torture. How many days had he ached to hold Viola like this? To offer comfort and support?

Often, he had wondered if a moment like this would ever occur. Ethan continued to fill Malcolm's head with the details of his courtship of Viola, their conversations, and her reserved encouragement. How perfect Ethan considered them to be for one another.

And yet, in an hour of crisis, she had come running to Malcolm.

Finally, she stirred, pushing back and sitting up.

She was a dreadful mess, her cheeks tear-stained and splotchy, her hair bedraggled and bonnet-less, an errant curl or two sticking to her temples. His Viola would never have a good *greet* without it being painfully obvious.

He was desperate to kiss her, to confess his affection and remove this terrible uncertainty.

But Malcolm was no green lad, led by passion and emotion.

Now was not the time to declare his heart to her. Viola did not need more drama at the moment.

And so he held his tongue.

Instead, he helped her to her feet, stretching out his own stiff legs.

"Do ye wish to discuss what so upset ye?" he asked after a few minutes. "My fists stand ready to knock sense into someone's thick skull. Or, at the very least, to teach ye how to throw a solid punch yerself."

That, at least, elicited a hiccupping laugh. She shook out her skirts, smoothing the worst of the wrinkles.

"'Tis only what we have already discussed. I am afraid that physical punishment will do no good."

She recounted the conversation with her father, the older man's refusal to listen to Viola's personal aims and wishes, his insistence that the men in her life should guide her thoughts and actions.

"I know that my father loves me, that he is simply acting as he thinks is best," she finished, "but I am so tired of being what *he* wishes me to be."

"Why must you listen to your father? Ye are of age. He cannot control where or with whom you publish."

"True, but he does administer to all my business dealings. So it is not as simple as leaving. Moreover, I dislike hurting him. He is my *father*. He has always been good and kind to me in his way."

Ah. "And so his betrayal is a double wound. Once, for your love of him. And twice, for your love of your art."

She sighed, soft and low, pinning him with those sky-blue

eyes. "You sum up my situation so beautifully. You are so wise."

"A'course I am," he grinned, tone teasing. "I'm right glad you're starting tae understand this."

She matched his smile. "I suppose I could write under a pseudonym, something manly like Bertram Noble—"

"Nae, I wouldnae have ye hide yerself, lass. The gloves come off, remember?" He lifted her bare hand in his. Her skin was just as soft as he remembered. "No hiding."

Viola bit her lip and then nodded. She leaned forward to place her free palm against his chest for a brief moment. The pressure scalded him. She shifted her weight, intent on removing her hand, but he instantly pressed his own over it, holding her palm in place.

"Believe in this, lass." He waited until she met his gaze. "Your father, like most caring parents, wishes ye to be remembered. He wishes greatness upon ye. For ye to have a legacy. The problem, of course, is that history never remembers the weak and timid, those who never wandered too far from shore or took true risks. No, history only celebrates the brave. The voices who dared to flout rules and conventions for something greater than themselves."

Viola inched closer to him, as if helplessly drawn by his words.

"Write what is calling to ye, Viola." He met her gloriously blue eyes. Her tears had only heightened that ring of gold around her pupils. "If ye do, I predict that history will remember ye not for the safety of your words, but for the courage of your ideas."

She searched his gaze. What she sought, he did not know. Finally, she swallowed. "My father will never relent—"

"Then write anyway."

"People will criticize me. They will say I betray my sex."

"Write anyway."

"I may find myself ostracized. I will certainly lose friends."

"Write anyway. Those who walk away were never true friends in the first place."

A lengthy pause.

Viola licked her lips. Had she just canted that much closer to him?

"Will I be able to call you a friend?"

"Always."

Her eyes focused on his mouth. Malcolm's heart pounded in his throat.

How he ached to kiss her!

But . . . this incredible woman had experienced a difficult day. She was grateful to him for his support. Her normal defenses were lowered.

He could not take advantage of her heightened emotional state.

And yet . . .

He found himself stepping closer to her, his kilt brushing her skirts. He pressed firmly on her hand, still trapped between them, longing to hold all of her against him.

Her eyes went hazy, surely as his own were. He stared at her mouth, the perfect rosebud arch of her top lip, the plump pout of her lower.

Heaven's above, the woman was made for kissing, for risks and passion.

He knew he should *not* kiss her. And yet . . . he found himself listing forward, nonetheless . . .

Close . . .

Closer . . .

A wet nose on the back of his bare knee jerked him back into reality. Malcolm let out a surprised yelp, staggering back a step.

Beowoof danced out of the way, yipping in happiness.

Malcolm turned to look at his blasted dog.

"Beowoof!" Viola crooned in delight, crouching to give the naughty scamp a good scratching.

Part of Malcolm was furious over the interruption.

But another part was profoundly grateful.

Viola clearly liked him as a friend. Their friendship was an enormous, unexpected gift, one that would pain him greatly to lose.

But it did not follow that she felt anything *more* for him.

Case in point, Ethan was certain Viola cared for him. Malcolm heard about it endlessly. Perhaps, Viola simply had a way of making men feel special when around her?

Malcolm had avoided being around Ethan and Viola, not wishing to witness his brother's courtship first-hand.

But maybe that needed to change . . .

Perhaps it was time to ascertain, once and for all, which Penn-Leith brother held the key to Viola Brodure's heart.

Eleven

BY THE NEXT afternoon, Malcolm mostly regretted not kissing Viola Brodure when he had the chance.

Yesterday, he had succumbed to a fit of gentlemanly propriety, like an old lady having the vapors. Why, a good dose of Scottish charm and rousing kiss might be all that was needed to convince Viola to remain with him in Scotland, right?

Right?!

Or . . . upon further reflection . . . perhaps not.

Did he truly believe that Viola—the famous, brilliant, talented, Miss Brodure—would leave her comforts and literary friends and travel hundreds of miles north to rural Scotland, to enjoy writing and living as a farmer's wife in Invercairn Mains?

Mmmm.

When put baldly like that . . . even Malcolm could not deny the absurdity of it all.

He and Viola were friends, of a surety. But friendship and even deep regard did not automatically lead to romantic love and marriage.

No matter how much Malcolm might long for exactly that.

The fact remained that Ethan was a better match for Viola than himself. Ethan would help Viola's writing career in ways that Malcolm never could. It was no wonder that everyone encouraged a match between the two. Did Viola truly regard Ethan as deeply as his wee brother assumed?

Tonight might hold answers.

Lord and Lady Hadley had returned from London and made good on their promise to have Dr. and Miss Brodure dine at Muirford House. Malcolm and Ethan were to join them, along with Mr. and Mrs. Ruxton and a few other gentrified families in the area.

In short, Malcolm would likely witness Ethan's courtship of Viola Brodure up close this evening.

Wanting to put his best foot forward, Malcolm had decided to forgo wearing his usual great kilt. Instead, he donned a well-cut suit of dark wool that Aileen had insisted he purchase on a rare trip to Edinburgh. He was shrugging into the tight-fitting evening jacket when Ethan burst into his room, several sheets of foolscap clutched in his fist.

"I say, Malcolm," his brother began without any preamble, "what would be a good metaphor for love?"

Malcolm turned toward Ethan, eyebrows rising. "Pardon?"

"Love. A metaphor."

"Why do ye need my help with a metaphor?"

"I *always* need your help with metaphors. Ye have the best suggestions." Ethan tapped the papers in his hand. "I'm trying to write yet another sonnet for Miss Brodure, but I've run plumb out of ideas."

As usual, Ethan's discussion of his courtship of Viola grated. Malcolm fought for patience.

"Why not just write what ye feel?" Malcolm suggested, turning to his mirror and attempting to adjust his evening cravat. He wore them so irregularly that getting the thing to lie properly was a monstrous task.

"Yes, yes." Ethan waved the papers again. "That's all well and good, but I need a proper metaphor to capture the depth of my affections."

Malcolm tugged on his cravat, allowing Ethan's words to roll over him. What was it he had said to Viola weeks earlier? "Why not say something about how living without her love would be a death, that actual death isnae how we die most or some such."

"Bah! That's a bit morbid for Miss Brodure, I think. I need something more refined." Ethan sat down on Malcolm's bed. "With a genteel lady like her, a man has to be daring."

A man has to be daring? Was that Malcolm's answer? Instead of waiting for Viola to choose, Malcolm needed to be bold in declaring his affections? His heart galloped and leaped, clearly agreeing with this idea.

Malcolm still wasn't quite so sure.

Taking love advice from Ethan was likely unwise.

"I need a grand gesture, Malcolm," Ethan continued, as if reading Malcolm's thoughts. "That is the root of the problem with my courtship of Viola—"

"Miss Brodure, you mean?" Malcolm interrupted. Were Ethan and Viola using their Christian names, as well?

Ethan rolled his eyes, ignoring the jab. "Regardless, I have been too hesitant with *Miss Brodure*"—he leaned sarcastically on her name—"and I fear she does not understand the depth of my regard. She is naturally timid and shy, and so I have moderated my passions to suit her temperament. But no more. I have determined to be bolder, starting this evening."

Timid and shy? *Viola?!*

Malcolm nearly snorted, still fussing about with his cravat.

Yes, Viola was shy in crowds, but that ceased once she got to know a person. Anyone who knew the true Viola would never describe her as shy.

Which begged the question: How well did Ethan truly know her?

"I ken that love isnae best shown through opposition, Ethan," Malcolm replied, frustration in his tone. "Ye must meet yer lady-love as she is, not as ye suppose her to be, or as ye yourself are."

Silence for a moment.

"*Love isnae best shown through opposition* . . ." Ethan repeated behind Malcolm. "Hah! I knew ye would be good for an idea or two, Malcolm. I quite like that. May I use it?"

Malcolm barely suppressed a growl. "Why must ye always pass off my ideas as yer own?"

Ethan chuckled, unrepentant. "Och, they say creativity is simply the art of covering over the source of your inspiration—"

"Are ye sincere with this?" Malcolm turned back to Ethan. "I tire of being your muse, Ethan. So, *no*, ye may *not* use my thoughts. They're my ideas and my musings and my soul. Ye're going to have to find your own blasted inspiration this time."

Malcolm stormed out of the room. But not fast enough to escape Ethan's voice.

"*My ideas, my musings, and my soul* . . ." he repeated, voice carrying down the stairwell. "That's bloody brilliant. Are ye sure I cannae use that?"

Had any dinner ever been so long? Viola wondered. She was quite sure she had been sitting for weeks at this table.

And yet, the clock showed that scarcely ninety minutes had passed.

The guests chatted, and cutlery clinked against china dishes. Someone chuckled. Lord Hadley laughed at something that her father said beside him.

In truth, all Viola wanted to hear was the conversation Lady Hadley was carrying on with Malcolm at the other end of the table.

But that was not to be.

Viola fanned herself. Sunlight streamed into the room, the last gasp of the dying sun. At this latitude, the sun set late in the summer, allowing them to dine in sunlight well into the evening hours. The attending footman had drawn translucent shades to block the worst of the light coming through the terrace doors, but the shimmery curtains did nothing to block the heat. The room had warmed several degrees over the past hour.

At Viola's elbow, Ethan kept up a steady stream of conversation, on everything from his love of a good walking stick to the beauty of a winter sunrise.

His attentions had been more marked than usual this evening, more intense. Viola did not know what it portended for her.

Across from her, Mrs. Ruxton looked at Viola and Ethan sitting side-by-side and abruptly exclaimed for the ninth time—yes, Viola was counting—"I say, Lord Hadley, what a bonnie couple Miss Brodure and Mr. Penn-Leith make!"

Lord Hadley smiled, both his lordship and Dr. Brodure turning in Viola's direction.

"Indeed, Mrs. Ruxton," Lord Hadley boomed. "We have all agreed on this point, have we not?"

Her father chuckled, shooting Viola his most fond look. "Yes, your lordship, but I think it bears repeating."

"Oh, aye." Lord Hadley laughed.

Viola ducked her head, mortification scalding her

cheeks. How was she to navigate this? Stand up and shout to the room that she and Ethan would never become the couple they all envisioned?

Her breathing constricted at the thought.

It didn't help that she had spent the morning tiptoeing around her father. They hadn't resolved their argument from the day before. Viola had no intention of apologizing or backing down from her point of view.

Worse, her maid had laced Viola's corset too tight, determined to show her mistress to best advantage. Perhaps, that was the root cause of Viola feeling out of breath?

She managed to raise her head for the briefest moment, catching Malcolm's gaze at the bottom of the table, not missing the concern there.

Did it upset him that everyone assumed she belonged with his brother? Why had she never asked Malcolm that question?

And now . . . she was desperate for an answer.

She had been startled to see Malcolm in the evening dress of a London gentleman, rather than his habitual kilt. He wore the black evening coat and loose trousers with the easy grace of a man comfortable in his own skin. The sight had sent heat flooding her veins.

Ethan shifted beside her, his breath tickling her ear. "Have I told you how beautiful you look this evening? I daresay the very angels in heaven are brought to shame by your presence."

Viola barely stifled a sigh. As metaphors went, that one was fairly trite—Ethan, bless him, was persistent.

"You flatter me too much, Mr. Penn-Leith." She turned toward him. "I fear such words could easily lead to blasphemy."

"Blasphemy?" he scoffed.

"I am hardly as perfect as an angel of God. I should not like to be the cause of such a blemish upon your soul."

He leaned into her. "Adoring you could never be counted a blemish upon my soul—"

"I say, Dr. Brodure, aren't they simply the bonniest of couples." Mrs. Ruxton leaned forward, calling to Viola's father.

Ah. Ten times. They were on to double-digits now.

"Most certainly, Mrs. Ruxton." Her father lifted his wine glass in their direction.

Ethan beamed. Viola bit her lip.

She would have to say something, she realized. Not here. Not now. But tonight. She would find a way to have a few words alone with Ethan and convince him that there would never be anything beyond polite friendship between them.

The cheese course was cleared, and dessert ice was brought in by footmen carrying silver trays. Just as the last glass of ice was placed before guests, Ethan unexpectedly rose, taking his wine glass with him.

All eyes turned his way.

He stood confident and tall, his glass in one hand, the other hand folded behind his back. Ethan had not foregone his kilt for the evening. He looked every inch the Highland Poet, hair the precisely perfect amount of tousled.

The Viola Brodure she had been three months ago would have swooned at the sight.

Now, Ethan Penn-Leith in all his glory—clearly intent on saying *something*—merely filled her with an anxious worry.

"My lord, my lady." He nodded toward Lord and then Lady Hadley. "Esteemed guests." He shot a triumphant smile at Viola and then Dr. Brodure. "Ladies and gentlemen." He swept his glass to indicate the rest of the room. "Please forgive this interruption." Ethan's unrepentant expression stated that no one ever found his presence an interruption. "But I cannot sit in silence any longer. We have all been the most fortunate recipients of Miss Brodure's company over these past seven weeks. I believe I speak for us all when I say that I have never met such a gracious, kind lady."

"Hear, hear!" the vicar encouraged.

Ethan smiled indulgently. "Miss Brodure is a credit to her gender, the most mild and modest of ladies. Is it any wonder we look to her tales of morality and virtuous sensibility to guide us?"

Someone snorted, soft and faint, but Viola heard it nonetheless.

She lifted her eyes slightly, catching Malcolm's burning gaze.

Oh!

His eyes said it all.

I see you.

Ye are not the woman Ethan describes.

Ye burn with fire, lass. Ye were made for more than pretty stories.

Her heart sped up.

She darted a glance at Ethan. What was he leading up to?

"I have been pondering as of late," he continued, "some of the truths of life, particularly those pertaining to love."

That got a lively laugh from the room.

Oh, no. Please say no more, Viola pleaded.

But Ethan continued on, oblivious, "I have often pondered how living without love, true love, is like a death." He paused. "That actual death isnae how we die most."

Viola gasped—a startled shock of sound. Ringing filled her ears.

What had Ethan just said?!

Surely not . . .?!

An idea blasted its way to the forefront of her brain. Her heart sped up, her breathing constricted more.

Surely, that wasn't the case.

And yet . . .

Her eyes flew again to Malcolm at the bottom of the table.

She could practically hear him saying the same thing in his gravelly voice, thick with Scotland.

Literal death isnae how we die most.

Malcolm met her gaze—eyes pained, expression drawn—and in that moment . . . she *knew.*

He was Ethan's muse.

Malcolm was the source of Ethan's profundity.

How could she have missed this?

Abruptly, everything snicked into place.

Why she was so drawn to Malcolm instead of Ethan.

Why Ethan struck her as unformed. Why she struggled to connect with him.

Clearly, Ethan had talent. Viola strongly doubted that Malcolm was the author of Ethan's poetry. But the ideas behind them, the philosophical depth . . .

How had she not seen?

Mentally reviewing all of Ethan's poems, she could practically hear Malcolm's words weaving through them, his unique view of the world.

But . . . why would Malcolm allow Ethan to appropriate his ideas?

Well, she supposed that answer was obvious. Malcolm *did* love his wee brother. He wanted Ethan to succeed.

Dimly, she realized Ethan was still speaking. ". . . celebrate having this lovely lady in our midst, I should like to propose a toast. To Miss Brodure. To her vision. To her modest morality."

"How delightful!" Mrs. Ruxton enthused to her

neighbor, loud enough for the entire room to hear. "They truly are the bonniest of couples."

"Mrs. Ruxton, you speak such truth," Dr. Brodure chuckled.

The dinner guests laughed, Lord Hadley's voice booming over them all.

It was all too much.

Ethan's words.

Malcolm's soul.

The heavy expectations of those around her.

An errant ray of sunlight slipped through the filmy curtains, blinding her.

The heat of the room closed around Viola, her lungs seizing.

No!

She could *not* have an asthma attack.

Not now.

She took a deep breath. And then another.

She caught Malcolm's eye, noting his drawn brows, his thunderous expression.

Just breathe.

Why, oh why, could she not simply breathe?!

Twelve

MALCOLM CLUTCHED THE arms of his chair—anything to stop himself from lurching to his feet.

Viola had gone so very pale, her eyes downcast, her cheeks a scorching red. She strained in her dress, clearly struggling to breathe. Who had laced her so tightly into the blasted thing?

How could his eejit of a brother be so heedless of her distress?

But Ethan nattered on, oblivious, beaming at Dr. Brodure.

"I am thankful for your approval, sir." Ethan lifted his glass in Dr. Brodure's direction. "I feel duty-bound to say that I anticipate asking you, good sir, for leave to give my addresses to your daughter."

Dr. Brodure laughed, gazing at Viola's bowed head with fondness, blind to her labored breathing, the high color on her cheeks, her white fingers pressed against the table edge. "My daughter is too modest to express the depth of her emotion at the moment, Mr. Penn-Leith, but I know she returns your regard."

Malcolm hissed as if he had been slapped.

Viola's lungs heaved.

These *eejits*! She was clearly in distress. They needed to stop.

"I thank you for your blessing, good sir," Ethan laughed, all good humor. "I should like to raise my glass to the hope of Miss Brodure seeing my humble self as more than just a sometime dinner companion." His tone dripped with emotion. "But perhaps, if her ladylike sensibilities would allow it, I propose making Miss Brodure a dinner companion of a more permanent sort."

Viola pressed a shaking hand to her chest, lungs heaving.

Did no one else see her distress? Did no one understand?!

"Enough, Ethan!" Malcolm surged to his feet, voice hard and quiet.

Every eye in the room swung his way, weighty and puzzled. Malcolm felt every inch of his uncultured upbringing—his country manners, thick accent, and rough, calloused hands—all stark foils to Ethan's urbane sophistication.

But then Viola raised her head, her eyes instantly locking with his, those two spots of color flushing her cheeks.

Her chest heaved again.

Help! her expression said.

That was all the encouragement he needed.

"Ethan," he looked at his brother, "ye are distressing Miss Brodure with your declarations."

"Nonsense, brother." Ethan glanced down at Viola, brow scowling. "Miss Brodure is simply being her decorous self—"

"She's on the verge of an asthma attack!"

Viola struggled to take in a gasping breath.

Every eye whipped toward her, only making the situation worse. She needed to be free of all these weighty stares, removed from this stuffy room.

"Asthma?" Ethan asked, voice confused. "Miss Brodure has asthma?"

For the love of—!

Malcolm was already moving around the table and to her side, pulling out her chair.

"I say, Malcolm," Ethan said. "She is none of your affair!"

Malcolm ignored him, gently assisting Viola to stand. "She needs cool air. Now!"

Viola clung to his arm with a shaking hand as he led her toward the tall, terrace doors. An obliging footman pulled the door open, blasting them all with fading sunlight. Once outside, Malcolm helped Viola cross the terrace and down the wide, flagstone steps to a large fountain bubbling in the middle of an Italianate garden. He crossed to the shaded side of the fountain and guided her to sit on its stone edge. The cooler, wet air flowed around them.

But Viola continued to struggle. Her wheezing constricted his heart.

"Breathe, lass," he encouraged. "Deep breaths. Suck in from the bottom of your lungs."

Was she hearing him? Her chest continued to heave, shallow and labored.

"Viola? Malcolm?" Lady Hadley said at his elbow. "What is wrong?"

Malcolm lifted his head, meeting Lady Hadley's concerned, blue-eyed gaze. Lord Hadley stood behind his wife.

Dimly, Malcolm noted that nearly all the guests had followed them out of the dining room . . . so many curious, staring eyes. Did Viola feel their weight, as well?

"She cannae breathe," he said, voice quiet and anguished. "I fear she panicked over Ethan's wee speech. The asthma has closed off her throat." He darted a glance at the gathered guests. "She needs privacy, more than anything right now."

Lady Hadley nodded, shooting a glance at her husband. Lord Hadley instantly clapped his hands, asking the guests to return to the drawing room for after-dinner tea.

Malcolm felt some of the tension leave Viola's body as all the watching eyes turned away from her.

But the reprieve was short-lived.

"What in heaven's name is going on?!" Ethan roared, pushing through the retreating guests and striding toward Malcolm and Viola. Hadley turned and stopped Ethan with two hands on the younger man's shoulders.

"What has happened?" Peering around Hadley's large frame, Ethan struggled to catch Malcolm's eye. "Why are you caring for Viola, Malcolm?"

Hadley murmured something that Malcolm couldn't hear.

"Och! This is ridiculous!" his brother's reply rang through the garden. "*I* should be the one helping Viola at this moment, not Malcolm."

"Steady, lad," Hadley rumbled. "Give your lass some space to breathe."

Your lass.

The moniker sent a painful shard through Malcolm's heart.

Lady Hadley sat on the opposite side of Viola, running a soothing hand up her back.

Clenching his jaw, Malcolm focused on Viola. Her health was all that mattered. He wet his handkerchief, wringing out the water before pressing it to her cheek, anything to soothe her lungs.

"There, lass," he murmured. "In and out, slow and steady."

Viola nodded, eyes closed. Lady Hadley murmured encouragements.

Finally, her breathing appeared to be flowing more easily.

Malcolm went to stand, assuming his help was no longer needed.

But Viola would have none of it.

She wrapped her hand around his, bare skin to bare skin, clutching tightly. Tethering him to her. Holding him as if she never intended to let go.

Malcolm clenched her hand in return, communicating his support—he would remain by her side as long as she needed him.

He met Lady Hadley's eyes over Viola's bowed head. Her ladyship's gaze flicked to their joined hands, clearly noting how Viola clung to him.

"How fares my daughter?" Dr. Brodure arrived at Ethan's side, trying to see around Hadley as well. "And why is Malcolm Penn-Leith with her? Shouldn't that be Ethan's task?"

"Yes!" Ethan said.

Lady Hadley gave Malcolm an understanding smile and then rose in a flutter of petticoats.

"Nonsense!" She brushed her hands down her skirt. "Miss Brodure appears most comfortable at the moment. I would not see her disturbed. Perhaps, we should join the other guests inside."

Lady Hadley beamed at Ethan and Dr. Brodure, shooting her husband a telling glance.

Malcolm was not quite sure what that glance was meant to communicate, but Hadley somehow understood.

"Quite, my lady," his lordship agreed. "We should return to the drawing room."

"Rightly so," Lady Hadley clasped her hands together before turning back to Malcolm. "Malcolm, would you be so kind as to escort Miss Brodure inside? There is a comfortable chaise in the blue drawing room that she can rest upon."

Bless Lady Hadley! "Of course, my lady. I should be honored."

Malcolm stood, helping Viola to her feet, their hands still clutched together.

Ethan, however, was having none of it. He immediately jumped to Malcolm's side and tried to take Viola's hand.

"Ethan!" Malcolm shouldered his brother back.

"This should be my task, Malcolm." Ethan glared at him. "Miss Brodure is my bird, not yours."

"Yes, indeed," Dr. Brodure agreed. "'Tis only appropriate that Mr. Ethan Penn-Leith should have the honor of escorting Viola inside."

"I am f-fine, Father," Viola managed to stammer, her grip on Malcolm's hand tightening. "I s-simply need to rest."

Ethan, however, was not about to relent. Again, he moved to take Viola's hand.

Malcolm put out a staying arm.

The brothers exchanged a tense silence.

"Stop this, Malcolm!" Ethan finally hissed. "You are frightening Miss Brodure!"

"*I* am frightening her?! Do ye even hear yerself?!"

"Yes!" Ethan turned to Dr. Brodure. "As we all know, Miss Brodure's naturally timid nature is a credit to her sex, but it makes her hesitant to express her more delicate feelings—"

"Miss Brodure is fully capable of expressing her feelings!"

Ethan scowled at Malcolm before turning a bright smile on Viola. "Allow me to escort you, Miss Brodure, as I wish to protect your tender sensibilities from this . . . *unpleasantness.*" He shot a dagger-laden glance at Malcolm.

That was it.

The end of Malcolm's tether.

For the first time in . . . *ever* . . . Malcolm Penn-Leith—stalwart, stoic, unmovable—lost his temper.

"Timid? Hesitant? *Tender sensibilities*?!" Malcolm's voice rose with each word. He took a step toward Ethan.

His brother reared back. "Malcolm—"

"If that's how ye describe Viola Brodure, then ye dinnae know her at all! She is *none* of those things!" Malcolm roared.

He glared at Ethan, jabbing with his finger. "Miss Brodure is fire and passion. She is fair-brimming with courage and spunk. She isnae a timorous wee beastie, fearful of the loud noise of life. She doesnae need to be protected and coddled, like some fussy, delicate flower."

"Malcolm . . ." Ethan gave a stuttering laugh. "Are your wits all about ye?"

"Viola is heather and gorse," Malcolm bellowed, "sturdy and stalwart, able to face the harshest winds of the wild moor. She blooms in adversity and thrives most when faced with opposition."

Malcolm looked at her, at this beautiful, shy woman wiping a tear from her cheek. How could everyone else be so blind?!

"Viola is *elemental*," he continued, voice cracking with emotion. "She has a vagabond heart and a banshee soul. She longs to wail a lament for lost souls, to scream her truths to the world, demanding change and justice. She has only *begun* to explore the greatness of her talent. She doesnae need me to proclaim her truths." He paused, expression surely as anguished as he felt. He turned back to Ethan. "She is all these incredible, magnificent things and, yet, ye see none of it. How can ye say that Viola is yours when ye cannae be bothered to truly *see* that which ye claim?"

"Enough, Malcolm." Ethan whipped his gaze between the two of them, stepping closer to hiss, "Give over. You are acting the jealous fool!"

"Of course, I'm jealous, wee brother!" Malcolm shouted, not about to be silenced. "Viola Brodure is a queen among women! What man wouldnae treasure being entrusted with her heart?!"

Malcolm's words echoed through the garden.

Viola Brodure is a queen among women!

Viola was quite sure the tableau before her would be permanently seared into her memory.

Lord and Lady Hadley rimmed in the last gasp of fading sunlight.

Her father's look of consternation.

Ethan Penn-Leith with a scowl upon his handsome face.

And Malcolm—her beloved, fiery Malcolm—laying himself bare . . . having the maturity to be vulnerable.

To defend her. Too *see* her.

To shout her truths for all to hear.

Enough.

Something simply . . . *cracked* within her.

Some sense of self-consciousness that had been fueling her shyness, exacerbating her asthma. It all simply . . . fled.

Perhaps, it was her father's willing blindness to the reality of her.

Perhaps, it was the weight of the moment, the sense that this was the fulcrum upon which the rest of her life would hinge.

Or, perhaps, it was simply seeing herself through Malcolm's eyes, feeling the steady warmth of his hand in hers.

This man.

She has a vagabond heart and a banshee soul.

But . . . this was *her* fight.

She had been too silent for too long.

She longs to wail a lament for lost souls, to scream her truths to the world, demanding change and justice.

If she wished to take on the problems of the world, she needed to start with her own life.

And so, despite her asthmatic lungs and the shaking in her limbs, Viola Brodure threw back her shoulders and said what needed to be said.

She did not, however, release Malcolm's hand.

Her father finally met her gaze, his eyes dipping to Malcolm's fingers in hers.

"My child?" he began, taking a step in her direction, expression confused. "Perhaps, *I* should escort you inside."

Steadying her nerves, Viola shook her head. "That will not be necessary, Father." She was proud of her steady voice. Malcolm squeezed her hand in encouragement. "I prefer Malcolm to escort me."

A nearly audible gasp rippled. Ethan's head reared back.

No one missed the import of her words.

Viola swallowed. Now what to say?

She looked at Ethan, taking in his stunned expression. "I would like to publicly apologize to you, Mr. Penn-Leith. I know that the manner of my arrival here in Edzell gave rise to certain expectations. Though I consider you to be a wonderful person, I cannot say that my heart holds anything other than friendly regard for you. I am sorry if you had any further wishes for our relationship. Know that I only want the best for you and your future."

Malcolm squeezed her hand again.

Ethan's gaze dropped again to their joined hands, expression still puzzled.

"I . . . I dinnae understand," he said.

Viola shrugged. "I know. I scarcely understand it myself. But I have come to realize that what we *think* we want and what we *actually* want are often not the same thing. Someone very dear to me recently said, 'Literal death often isn't the way we die most.'"

She leveled a laden look at Ethan. His eyes widened; he took a fractional step backward.

He, at least, had the courtesy to not mistake her meaning. He understood that she knew the truth of his poetic "muse."

She paused to wipe a fugitive tear from her cheek.

"I am a writer. And as such, I have a metaphor for you." She dabbed at her cheek, and then dug around in her dress pocket with her free hand. They all likely thought that she was looking for a handkerchief, but instead, she pulled out the pair of silk evening gloves she had removed before eating dinner.

"Lately, I have considered my life to be a hand in these gloves—sheltered, protected." She held up the gloves by one end. The silk shimmered in the dying light. "And like these gloves, I understand the purpose of shelter and protection. It is done out of love and kindness." She smiled softly at her father. "But gloves are not to be worn ceaselessly. I refuse to force myself into a casing any longer." She threw them over her shoulder into the cascading water at her back. "I want to feel the cool breeze on my skin. I want to stretch and grow without a shell to confine me. I know that I have surprised you here tonight, but I cannot be sorry for my words. I *will* not. I may not be the Viola Brodure you supposed me to be. But I am the Viola Brodure that *I* wish to be."

Silence greeted her.

Lady Hadley wiped a tear from her cheek. Lord Hadley nodded, eyes wide.

"And now, Mr. Penn-Leith," she gave Malcolm a wan smile. "I fear my lungs are feeling tired. I would greatly appreciate you escorting me inside, as Lady Hadley suggested."

Malcolm nodded.

Lady Hadley smiled softly. "Of course. This way."

She waved Viola and Malcolm to follow her back into the house.

"She is elemental heather and gorse," Viola heard Ethan mutter as she passed. "That's quite good. I'll be using that."

Thirteen

MALCOLM FOLLOWED LADY Hadley back into the house, Viola's hand still clutched in his.

"In here." Lady Hadley motioned for them to enter into an empty drawing room. "The sofa is most comfortable there." She pointed to a blue velvet chaise before the fire.

Viola still held firmly onto his hand.

Lady Hadley nodded her head once, a small smile tugging at her lips.

"Congratulations," she murmured. "You both have excellent taste."

"Thank ye, my lady." Malcolm permitted himself a ghost of a grin.

Her ladyship looked back at the door, expression pondering.

"I do believe that I need to tend to my coiffure," she said after a moment, patting her perfectly styled hair. "I shall return in, let's say, twenty minutes, shall we?" She darted a glance at the clock. "Yes, twenty minutes, but not a second longer. I shall see that you are not disturbed."

She swept from the room, latching the door with an audible *snick.*

Malcolm nearly laughed. Lady Hadley had just gifted him twenty minutes alone with Viola.

He turned to look down at Viola, who sported a matching, wondrous look.

She pulled on his hand, tugging him toward the rumored comfortable sofa. Malcolm was no slow-top. He instantly sat down beside her on the chaise. She clutched his hand tighter, the pressure of her fingers burning his own.

"Are ye quite recovered, lass?"

"Nearly," she murmured, taking a deep, testing breath. "Merely somewhat tired, which is to be expected. Your quick thinking spared me the worst of it."

"'Twas nothing."

"I disagree. You saw. You understood." She brought her other hand around, trapping his one hand between two of hers. "And then to hear you defend me so. It meant everything." Her breath hitched. "You knew that I do not wish a future with Ethan." She paused, as if fully registering what she had said. "I did not mean to give offense, of course. I know that Ethan is your wee brother."

"No offense taken, Viola. I know Ethan's weaknesses, as well as his strengths. I do not fault you for refusing his suit."

He *rejoiced* in it, truth be told.

She took another slow breath. Her gaze dropped to their joined hands.

"I cannot do this any longer," she said, the words a seemingly abrupt change of topic.

"Pardon?"

She pressed her hands together, squeezing his. "I cannot stomach this . . ." A pause. "Us. Together like this."

Malcolm froze, his heart leaping into his throat.

What did she mean? Did she intend to toss him out with Ethan?

"I thought we had agreed to be friends, you and I?"

Something of his anguish must have come through his

tone. She raised her eyes, coaxing him to drown in those glittering blue pools.

"Ah, Malcolm." She raised her hand to cup his cheek, some glorious emotion shining in her eyes. "I fear you misunderstand me. Yes, we are friends. And I hope we will always be friends."

"Good, because I cannae let ye go. Not yet."

She smiled, her gaze going radiant. "I like how you think, Mr. Penn-Leith. Because I cannae let ye go either."

"That was a terrible Scottish accent, lass. Ye likely shouldnae attempt that again."

She laughed, a glorious bubble of sound. Malcolm's heart felt near to bursting.

"Aye, it was. I fear I will have to find myself a brave Scottish lad to help me suss it out properly."

"Ye will, will ye?"

"Aye."

"And who do ye have in mind?"

She smiled then, wide and welcoming.

"There's a man, you see," she began, tracing a finger down his cheek.

"Aye?"

"Aye. He's devastatingly handsome and has the most adorable dog."

"Is that so?"

"He's kind and gentle—"

"The dog?"

"The dog, too. The man is also most competent."

"Competent?!"

"Never underestimate the power of manly competence, Mr. Penn-Leith," she laughed, cupping his face again. "It's a much-overlooked quality."

He grinned, happiness turning his blood to champagne.

"But most importantly," she continued, "I know, without a doubt, that this man perceives me as I am. Not as the world perceives me. Not as he would have me be, or as I feel I *should* be. But he accepts me as I am, at this very moment, with all my faults and flaws and weaknesses—"

"There is nothing weak about ye, lass."

Her eyes went suspiciously bright. "*See?!* That is precisely what I am referring to."

"Just to be clear. Ye were talking about myself, correct?"

She huffed a laugh. "Of course! You said I have a banshee soul! You called me a queen! Who else could be as wonderful as you? I love who I am when I'm with you. I love the woman you see in me. You make me a better person just for being in your presence—"

"Ye paint me a saint, lass. I assure ye, I'm not quite a saint."

"I don't want a saint, Malcolm Penn-Leith. I simply want you."

Malcolm closed his eyes, the pleasure of that moment nearly too much.

"And I want you, *mo chridhe.*"

"*Mo chridhe?*"

"My heart," he whispered. "My love."

"Oh!"

"I'm going to kiss ye now," he said.

"Really?"

"Aye. I thought it fair to warn ye."

She answered by smiling and pulling on his hand, urging him down to her.

Malcolm was no slow-top.

His head dipped down. Viola raised up. Their lips met in the middle.

He had imagined kissing her for weeks, the feel of her pillowy lips against his, the sheer newness of it all.

But kissing Viola felt less like a novelty.

No . . . it was a homecoming. As if he had spent his entire life wandering in foreign lands, and only now returned to the place where he belonged.

At her side.

In her arms.

In her heart.

Viola wanted to weep.

Why the blissful happiness racing through her could only come out as weeping, she could not understand. It simply seemed the only place so much *feeling* had left to go.

Malcolm was kissing her.

She was kissing Malcolm.

Her Malcolm.

Kissing.

When he would have pulled back after a gentle peck, she raised a hand to clutch his head, refusing to allow him to retreat.

"I love you," she whispered against his lips. "I love everything—"

He silenced her words with his mouth, his adoration a palpable thing. He devoured her, leaving her no doubt as to his own affection.

She reciprocated in kind.

Silence reigned for the next ten minutes, as Viola acquainted herself with the glorious pleasure of kissing Malcolm Penn-Leith.

Finally, knowing their time was short, she kissed him one last, lingering time before pulling back.

"Ah, lass," he breathed against her mouth, "how I adore ye. I dinnae want to scare ye with the force of my affections—"

"Impossible!" Viola laughed.

"Impossible?"

"Aye. I shall never fear your love, Malcolm Penn-Leith. 'Tis mine that might send you running—"

"Never!" he scoffed.

"Then what are we to do?"

"Marry me?" he murmured. "Could ye do that, lass?"

"Yes," she whispered, licking a tear from her lip. "I would love nothing more in this world than to marry you, Malcolm Penn-Leith."

His eyes went bright. He took a slow breath, swallowing loudly. "Are ye sure? My life is here. I cannae imagine leaving Scotland, but I also feel I cannae ask ye to leave your life in London."

Oh, the foolish, dear man!

"Ask me," she ordered, laughing.

He paused, looking at her with a face so serious that she had to peck his lips.

Which lead to more kissing.

Which lead to Viola mildly panicking that Lady Hadley would return before they had finished saying what needed to be said.

"Ask me," she repeated.

He swallowed and then said, "Viola Brodure, will ye leave your friends, your literary colleagues, your amusements, and every other aspect of your life in London to marry me and move to the backwater of Scotland to spend your life as the wife of a gentleman farmer who loves ye more than life itself?"

"Yes!" she all but shouted. "I would love nothing more than that."

"Truly?"

"Aye." She kissed him. "I love you, and because I love you, I adore the Scotland that formed you. I long to be a part of it myself, to weave Scotland into my own narrative—the crisp fresh air, the soaring vistas, the wildness creeping in at the corners—"

"Careful, *mo chridhe*. Scotland will make a poet of ye."

She laughed in earnest, her heart on wings.

"No," she replied. "I think one poet in the family will be plenty. In all honesty, I think I greatly prefer to live my life firmly in reality. The poet can remain adjacent."

"Poet adjacent it is, then." He grinned, dipping for one more lingering kiss. "But only just."

What a whirlwind this summer has been for literary enthusiasts! First, as dedicated readers certainly know, Miss Viola Brodure has begun a serial novel (after the style of Mr. Charles Dickens) entitled *A Ring of Gold.* We have heard mumblings that the topic of this new novel—the life of a young woman bound to debtor's prison for losing her mistress's gold ring—is perhaps too dark for a woman's sensibilities. But if the first three installments of *A Ring of Gold* are any indication, the authoress has delivered another *tour-de-force.* We predict the novel will be Miss Brodure's most popular to date.

Naturally, the change in Miss Brodure's style could be the result of her recent nuptials. The lady did indeed marry a Mr. Penn-Leith last month. But to our puzzlement, the groom in question was Mr. *Malcolm* Penn-Leith, elder brother to the celebrated Highland Poet. How this came about, we are at a loss to explain. Regardless, Mr. Ethan Penn-Leith supported his brother and stood as best man. Both groom and brother were reported to be dashing in their full Highland regalia. Miss Brodure was radiant in a white silk gown trimmed with Venetian lace. The bride's father, Dr. Brodure, officiated the ceremony. We at *The Tattler* wish the newlywed couple every happiness.

We cannot determine if Mr. Ethan Penn-Leith is heartbroken over Miss Brodure's choice of husband, though he has tellingly left Scotland and taken up residence in London. His latest poem, published in this month's *Atheneaum*, will surely earn Mr. Penn-Leith a place beside the literary greats of history. In the poem—entitled *Elemental Is My Love*—Mr. Penn-Leith compares his lady-love to the moors of Scotland, wild and primal, a woman who he describes as, "Her of the wandering vagabond heart and lamenting banshee soul." As one critic enthused to *The Tattler*, "Mr. Penn-Leith's comparison of his love to the battered heather and gorse of the moors positively thrums with the savage vitality of the Highlands."

If this is a taste of things to come from both our Highland Poet and Mrs. Penn-Leith *née* Brodure, we count ourselves lucky to be living in this age. Or, as Mr. Penn-Leith has said, "*Let us embrace the heather'd scent/A wanderer no more adjacent.*"

An Amazon bestselling author, **Nichole Van** is an artist who feels life is too short to only have one obsession. In former lives, she has been a contemporary dancer, pianist, art historian, choreographer, culinary artist and English professor.

Most notably, however, Nichole is an acclaimed photographer, winning over thirty international accolades for her work, including Portrait of the Year from WPPI in 2007. (Think Oscars for wedding and portrait photographers.) Her unique photography style has been featured in many magazines, including Rangefinder and Professional Photographer. She is also the creative mind behind the popular website Flourish Emporium which provides resources for photographers.

All that said, Nichole has always been a writer at heart. With an MA in English, she taught technical writing at Brigham Young University for ten years and has written more technical manuals than she can quickly count. She decided in late 2013 to start writing fiction and has since become an Amazon bestselling author.

Nichole currently lives in Utah with her husband and three crazy children. Though continuing in her career as a photographer, Nichole is also now writing romance novels on the side. She is known as NicholeVan all over the web: Facebook, Instagram, Pinterest, etc. Visit http://www.NicholeVan.com to sign up for her author newsletter and be notified of new book releases. Additionally, you can see her photographic work at http://photography.nicholeV.com and http://www.nicholeV.com

A Rose by Any Other Name

-ANNETTE LYON-

One

AS SHE HAD done a hundred times before, Rose Sayer had been hired to work as extra help in the Withey family kitchen in preparation for a dinner party. While she enjoyed the opportunities to teach the younger girls at the Foundling Hospital, she secretly preferred the occasional nights when she was hired by a local family as an extra domestic servant for a day, as she was that very evening. Working in a family home felt *almost* like belonging to a real home and family, something she'd never known. Oh, at the Foundling Hospital, where she'd been abandoned as a babe, she'd been clothed and fed and educated, but that existence was a far cry from *belonging*.

Here in the Withey home, she felt a filling of that hole in her heart, if but temporarily. Granted, much, if not all, of that sense of happiness and belonging came from interacting with the Withey sons: Mortimer, the younger, and Oliver, the elder. The younger brother would sneak downstairs and beg Mrs. Phelps, the cook, for an extra pastry or other sweet. It wasn't long before the much older Oliver joined his brother, ostensibly to supervise the boy's interactions with the servants. Over time, his visits seemed more aimed at spending time with Rose and play-acting chores that were so far beneath his station that his mother would have become apoplectic if she'd known that her son—the heir to the Withey fortune—had *swept* the *kitchen,* let alone that he'd done so many times.

Rather, those feelings come from spending time with Oliver far more than with Mortimer, she thought as she stirred the filling for her famous lemon tarts.

"How soon will the filling be done?" Mrs. Phelps, the cook, asked as she peered over Rose's shoulder.

The latter shook her head with a laugh. "In plenty of time, I assure you," Rose said. "I haven't yet finished the tart shells. Mr. Dawson and his wife aren't expected for another hour, and dessert will be at the end of the meal. We've plenty of time."

Thoughts of the dinner party guest did make Rose nervous, however, though she hoped her tone did not betray her anxiety. But how could she not be a little nervous, when the dining room just above the kitchen would soon be visited by Charlie Dawson, a celebrated new novelist?

He would soon be sampling *her* lemon tarts. So yes, she felt every inch uneasy, much more so than for any other dinner party she'd helped with here or at any other family's domain. But horses could not drag that information out of her when Mrs. Phelps was near. Disaster led in that direction.

Young Mortimer had planted himself on a bench by the kitchen table to watch Rose work. After some time, he looked at her with a pensive gaze and asked, "What's it like living at a hospital?"

Rose glanced up from her work and chuckled slightly. "*Hospital* isn't quite the right word for it. It's mostly an orphanage."

"What's that?" Mortimer had his elbows on the table and his chin resting in his hands.

"An orphanage is a home for children whose parents have died. The Foundling Hospital is the only home I've known. I've spent my whole life there."

"Your *whole* life?" Mortimer repeated, as if he couldn't comprehend such a thing.

Rose moved to butter and flour the tin tart shells. "Yes, indeed. I've lived there my whole life aside from a few weeks right after I was born, which I don't remember, of course. I was brought there by a servant after my mother passed away."

Or so Rose had been told, but who knew if any rumors about a foundling that were whispered among the children were truth, gossip, or a strange mix of both.

"But you're not a baby or a little girl. You're grown."

His words made Rose's eyes mist slightly, and her hands paused in the air as she forced back her emotion. She didn't love the Foundling Hospital, but it *was* the only home she'd known. And leaving would mean no longer having the chance to work at the Withey home and feel, but for a day, that she belonged there.

"You're right, Master Mortimer. Clever boy." She put on a grin for him. "I won't live there much longer. I've been teaching the school-aged children while one of the faculty members has been sick. But soon, I'll leave to work for a family who is looking for a housemaid or a cook or some such."

"What about the boys? Do they become cooks or maids? That doesn't seem right." Mortimer's little face screwed up in confusion.

"As I said, you're a clever boy." Once more, Rose was completely composed. She laid down one buttered tin and took up another to brush butter into it. "The boys receive similar reading, writing, and arithmetic educations, but they're also prepared for careers in the military so that they, too, can care for themselves when they are grown."

Rose used a wooden roller to spread the tart pastry and began cutting out the shapes. She was grateful that she'd made the sweets so many times that she could do it without much concentration, for her mind was very much distracted by Mortimer's line of questioning.

The sad truth was that the uniforms for the children reflected their likely futures: the girls' resembled what a domestic servant would wear, and the boys' uniforms hearkened to that of a soldier's.

No other girls her age remained at the hospital any longer; they'd all been hired out. Rose had volunteered to stay until some of the younger girls knew enough to fulfill neighboring calls for help—and until Miss Tandy was able to return to the classroom. But Rose's day to leave would come, and soon. Now that the gauzy future was about to become reality, the thought of leaving for good, heading who knew where, felt far more unnerving than exciting. Her image of the future was threaded with sadness and loss.

She cut the pastry into the correct shapes, then unscrewed the lid from a jar of marmalade and spooned it into the center of each portion, all with such a steady, deft hand that an outsider—nay, even Mrs. Phelps in her own kitchen— would never have suspected the heaviness weighing on Rose's mind.

"Mortimer!" came Mrs. Withey's voice from upstairs. "Come up from there at once! I've told you a thousand times that you are to focus on your studies and *not* on the servants!"

The boy slunk off the bench and shuffled out of the kitchen, leaving with a sad wave, which Rose returned.

The room was silent save for the sound of kitchen implements doing their jobs, which made Rose's mind wander to her life at the hospital. She'd miss precious little. Certainly not the classrooms where her knuckles had been swatted, nor calisthenics in the courtyard—girls walking in a large circle one direction and the boys in a circle going the other way, walking for hours until their feet ached and, in winter months, until their toes were numb.

Nor would she miss Sabbath services in the hospital

chapel, where she'd always longed to gaze at the beautiful arched windows and feel the peace of heaven streaming through on the morning sunlight, but instead had to sit ramrod straight and never look anywhere but at the minister for fear of punishment. She couldn't move or make a sound, even if mean Matilda Harris, who somehow always sat beside Rose, pinched the soft spot under her arm just to get such a reaction that would get Rose into trouble. Back then, Matilda had been her nemesis, but Rose thought of her now as a lonely girl desperate for any attention at all. She'd died of scarlet fever six years past, and Rose had never gotten over the guilt of declaring to Matilda that she'd hated her.

Despite the strict rules, boys across the aisle made faces to catch the girls' attentions. Oh, how all of the children were starved for the compassion and love a family could provide. The very warmth and belonging she'd found at the Withey townhouse—but must soon bid farewell to.

She put a tray of tart shells into the oven and glanced at the clock above the door to determine when to check on them.

She'd found a home at the Withey residence, but not with the parents. They'd had very little interaction with her; she was merely the help. But Oliver had begun to come downstairs more and more often when she'd been hired, and he no longer bothered with the old excuse of coming to watch over his younger brother. He came to see Rose.

Dear Oliver had won her heart, but it was only a few days prior that he'd grasped that their future might be in danger—something she'd been cognizant of from the moment she'd met him. Just last week, when she'd seen him on her way back from a meat merchant, she'd told him, and he'd promised to speak with his father about their love and plans for a future together. They'd wait to marry until he finished his university studies, but they'd promised themselves to each other.

As Rose returned to the table and began tidying up the crumbs and other messes from the tart shells, she worried, knowing that she was not the kind of match a wealthy family would desire for their son. Hopefully, they'd approve of her character and give their blessing, no matter how reluctantly. She glanced at the clock for likely the tenth time since putting the tarts into the oven only a few minutes ago, but this time, she calculated how long she'd been at the Withey townhouse without seeing Oliver: four hours. Much longer than usual.

With a deep breath, she tried to think of things that wouldn't make her miss him, but failed. All her mind conjured was memories of Oliver's warm hand around hers, his kind smile, his contagious laugh, his tender lips on hers. *Think of something else,* she ordered herself. *I'll miss working for Mrs. Phelps.* There. A different subject.

The Withey kitchen was clean and warm, with all of the modern conveniences. Her future employers might well have the same conveniences and an even larger kitchen. That would be most exciting. But the idea of leaving this modern kitchen wasn't the cause of her melancholy, and trying to avoid thinking about the real reason was proving near impossible.

Oh, Oliver. Thinking of anything else was clearly impossible. She surrendered to the sadness, if only a little, which made her vision grow blurry as worry and anxiety washed over her. She beat some cream with a whisk, so they'd have whipped cream to dollop onto the tarts later. As she did so, she pictured Mr. and Mrs. Withey refusing to accept a lowly orphan into the family no matter her good character. A few tears fell, so she turned to face the wall of dried herbs in hopes that no one had seen them.

Where is he? He still had plenty of time to come down and had likely been delayed. With such an illustrious guest in attendance as the novelist Charlie Dawson, he might have been expected to stay longer than usual. As an avid reader, Oliver might have wanted to stay longer.

She cleaned the bowl and set to washing a serving platter, but even that brought thoughts of Oliver; when he came down after dinner parties, he often removed his dinner jacket and helped with minimal tasks that wouldn't leave evidence on his clothing. One time, he'd helped with washing dishes, but a few splatters of water had gotten onto his trousers and shirt, and they'd had to find a way to sneak him upstairs without his mother or Mr. Arnold noticing. That hadn't deterred him from helping; he truly did not see himself as above the servants, though his family was quite wealthy.

Granted, theirs was *new* money, which some in society sniffed at, as if old pounds could buy things new pounds could not.

Typically, Oliver tried to behave as one of the servants. Sometimes that meant sweeping, other times putting away dishes. However, Mrs. Phelps utterly refused to let him empty the cockroach trap or clear cinders from the fireplace, though he'd managed the latter one time and one time only. That was the day she'd met him, in fact.

When the clock indicated that the proper amount of time had passed, Rose removed the tray of tarts. Soon, they'd cooled, then had been removed from their tins, filled, and finished off with whipped cream. All of those things were indicators that the guests' visit would come to an end soon—she hoped—and then Oliver would visit her in the basement.

Well past the time that all of the dinner dishes had been cleared from the dining room, there was no sign of Oliver. Rose had been hired to help until eight o'clock, and that time had long-since gone, but she stayed on, helping Mrs. Phelps with any other tasks she could justify. She stayed long after the sounds of a carriage and horses clopped off into the night, carrying the Witheys' guests away.

Still no Oliver.

Should she go back to the hospital? Even knowing they could write letters to each other, she could not bear the thought of leaving without being held tight in his embrace once more, not knowing how soon she'd leave the hospital. She needed one more stolen kiss by moonlight. They'd kissed only twice, and the memories were vivid in her mind. Oh, what she would give to kiss him one more time.

At length, the work was complete, and the Withey servants retired for the evening. Rose promised to lock the door behind her and slip the key through the mail slot on her way out.

The night's employment came with a fixed payment, with the understanding that she was officially relieved of her duties at eight o'clock. Ever since she and Oliver grew close, she'd stayed far longer than necessary. Being in close proximity to him, often touching arms as they worked, was a pleasant result.

Many a night, they'd sat in a corner of the kitchen and talked for hours. Sometimes, if enough people were out, or Cindy, the scullery maid, was available to come along as chaperone, they'd walked the paths of the park across the street. Sometimes, they returned when the other servants were asleep. Cindy, exhausted, also retired, and that left Rose and Oliver—somewhat scandalously, if anyone were to stumble upon them—sitting at the table and talking even longer. They'd spent more hours than she could count in the little courtyard that was the servants' entrance, out of sight from the street as well as those in the house. That was where he'd first professed his love, held her face in his hands, and kissed her.

Any time Mrs. Withey sent for Rose, Mistress Holdaway never batted an eye at how late she returned, no matter how far past curfew she arrived. She assumed that Rose had been working the entire time, and wanted to continue to have the hospital and its girls maintain their reputation for excellence in training their girls for domestic work.

Tonight, Rose scrambled to invent reasons to stay on when Oliver wasn't there. Normally, Mrs. Phelps would have gone to bed by now, but she dropped off to sleep right there in the kitchen, her cheek still propped up by her hand.

Such an environment wouldn't suit for a private conversation with Oliver, assuming he did come downstairs. Perhaps she should return to the hospital. Reluctantly, she put on her wrap and headed to the door, wondering if this was her last time in the Withey kitchen and dreading the possibility of soon leaving London forever. As Rose reached for the door handle, she closed her eyes and breathed a prayer that she would see Oliver before she left.

Footfalls sounded on the staircase. Rose hesitated, listening to determine whether they belonged to a servant who hadn't gone to bed after all.

"Rose." It *was* Oliver, then.

Her heart pounding with relief, Rose whirled around, ready to run into his arms, only to see his face as white as the proverbial sheet. "Rose, I spoke with my father."

"And?" Her stomach dropped to her toes.

"He refuses to allow us to marry. My mother concurs. I did everything I could to convince them—ever since the Dawsons left . . ."

"That was hours ago," Rose whispered.

"Yes, it was." He looked defeated and weary. Oliver shook his head, and only then did she notice his bloodshot eyes, which testified that he'd shed his own tears. "Rose, I am *so* sorry. But we cannot marry."

Two

OLIVER STOOD IN the basement, looking at Rose and feeling as ashen as she appeared. She'd always been pale, with very fair hair and blue eyes, but now, everything about her seemed paler still, as if not just blood but life itself had drained from her.

She stood by the door with her hand outstretched for the handle, halted mid-step, as if a painter had captured her portrait and held it frozen in time. The sight of her looking stricken, wounded, made him ache. He wanted to find a way to make her happy again, when her cheeks were pinked with pleasure at a compliment as she lowered her gaze to her lap shyly.

He wanted to sit with her as she taught him something, like the night he'd learned to sew on a button. He wanted to talk beside the kitchen fire and discuss politics with the girl who always challenged his mind. So many memories flashed through his mind, as if he knew this might be the last he'd see her. He recalled the girl who'd laughed when, at fourteen, he'd tried to impress her by coming to the basement with his father's walking stick, only to trip and fall on his face. At first she'd gasped, but when the only thing injured was his pride, she'd laughed so hard she'd had to brace herself against the wall to collect her breath. He'd laughed with her, knowing that airs wouldn't impress her. Intelligence and sincerity, however, had held the key to her heart.

He wanted, more than anything, to avoid hurting her, but alas, that last wish had been shattered by his declaration.

For a few breaths, neither of them spoke, but he couldn't bear the silence. This was his burden, his duty to accomplish, however much he was loath to carry it out.

"My parents refuse to see reason." Oliver stepped fully into the kitchen. The room, which once felt warm and liberating, now felt cramped and restrictive. Everything about it seemed to taunt him, pointing out the differences in class between him and Rose, reminders that his birth and his father's wealth meant that she could never be his.

Rose clasped her hands together. "Perhaps, with time—"

He shook his head firmly, sadly. Felt a tear slip from the outer corner of one eye. The drop trickled in front of his ear and down his jaw and neck. "Father will not hear of any kind of marriage contract for me unless the young lady has a dowry and a family of name."

Oliver didn't have to define his father's version of *young lady*; they both knew it was enough to disqualify Rose. To Oliver, she was the gentlest of ladies. But as a foundling, she had neither family nor name. "My mother—" His voice cut off. Loyalty to family warred with love for Rose. His mother was bent on increasing her social standing and reputation at any cost. *Her* grandchildren, she said, would be respected even without titles. They wouldn't be looked down upon because of how recently the family came into money.

"I suspected your parents would object," Rose said quietly.

He nodded, the weight of the past hours feeling like a lead cape draped upon his shoulders. His mother was fond of Rose and spoke highly of her, but as a *servant*—someone who one day might do well for herself by marrying a nice boy from the countryside, and barring that, had the skills to make a living wage as a cook or maid, never to marry or have children of her own.

At the very suggestion of Rose ever being part of the family, his mother's face had become such a deep shade of red that the image would have been laughable if the cause hadn't been so tragic. His father, while not so visceral or vocal, was of a similar opinion. He insisted that Oliver must marry someone equal to or above his station. Doing any less would be not living to one's potential—a crime indeed, in the minds of Mr. and Mrs. Withey.

Progress, my boy, his father had said. *The modern man moves forward, and so shall you.*

Then why, at the mere thought of not sharing a life with Rose, did Oliver feel as if he were sliding into a dark pit? He couldn't imagine ever agreeing to a "suitable" match with some young woman he did not know and cared nothing for.

He and Rose had somehow moved closer together, though he hadn't consciously stepped toward her, and she'd seemingly unconsciously moved closer to him, too. They stood by the table, where she'd had him stir ingredients and taught him to chop vegetables. Below the table, he and Rose had carved their initials—a small gesture that now seemed foolish.

As if she was remembering the time spent together at the table, and perhaps the carving beneath it, Rose's hand trailed along the edge. She didn't meet his eyes as she said, "We could run away and marry."

"Oh, Rose." He closed the remaining distance between them and took her hands in his, waiting for her to look into his eyes, for she simply *had* to listen to what he had to say next.

She stared at their hands for a moment, then slowly lifted

her face to his with an expression that seemed equal parts despair and hope.

"Rose," he said again. "An elopement would be disastrous. I could never do that to you."

"I don't care about scandal. My reputation—"

"That's not why," he said.

"But—"

He lifted her hands to his and kissed her fingers. "You deserve to be protected by a fair contract. If we ran off, nothing of mine would ever be yours, and if I passed before you, everything would go to my brother—nothing to you. You would lose everything—every penny, your home. I cannot risk putting you or our future children in such a position."

Our children. Which will never be. He held her hands tightly, hoping she understood that he could not elope *because* he loved her so much. He could not risk a future for her of homelessness or debtors' prison. Not to mention that a soiled reputation would make for a miserable life, no matter what she believed now.

She stepped into his embrace. He savored her warmth as she rested her forehead in the hollow of his neck. "Let's have a contract drawn up by your solicitor. We can do that without your parents' permission, can't we?"

Oh, how he wished he could say yes.

"No. Not now, anyway. Father says he will write me out of his will entirely, leaving me penniless. I would be entirely unable to support you as a husband should."

"I don't need money. I've always been poor, living on charity."

"I haven't. I don't fear hard work, but I haven't the faintest idea of how to go about living in such a manner. I could never be happy knowing that you have needs I cannot provide for. You deserve the best of everything. You deserve to be happy."

"*You* are what will make me happy," Rose said quietly.

"And you me," Oliver said through a tightening throat.

"I can show you how to find work and live modestly," Rose said, her face showing a desperate hope. "Remember, I've taught you how to sew on buttons and even how to chop onions without crying. We can make our way through any manner of challenges, so long as we are together." Her voice broke on the last word, as if she was trying to keep back tears.

"I pray you're right." Oliver could scarcely bear seeing the grief in her face. If he thought for a moment that eloping would solve everything, make her happy for more than the short term, he would have hired a coach and ridden to Scotland with Rose right then and there. "I came down to tell you goodbye, that we could never be together because my parents insist we cannot. But now . . ."

After a moment wherein he didn't continue, she prompted, "Now?"

"I cannot accept that." Seeing her had only inflamed his love hotter than ever, driven away the errand he'd thought he would complete. He could *not* say goodbye to her tonight if it meant forever.

"Then what are we to do?"

"I don't know," Oliver admitted. "Not yet. But I'll think of something."

"I'm sure to leave London any day now, and heaven only knows where I'll end up."

He nodded soberly, thinking but finding no solution to their troubles. "Will the hospital keep a record of where you go?"

"I imagine so."

"Then I'll find out where you have been employed and write you letters, daily if possible."

"And I'll write you."

"But not to this address," Oliver said quickly. "I'll make an arrangement with my solicitor for him to write to you, and you to write to his office." That way, he'd be sure to get her letters, and they'd avoid any gossips about two young people corresponding.

"Wise plan." The fact that she didn't ask why using the solicitor was necessary spoke volumes; they both understood the situation they were in.

"Somehow, we'll find a way," Oliver promised. "I don't know how, but we will. Until then, we wait." He drew Rose into his embrace and held her close, as if he might lose her at any moment.

She buried her face into his shoulder and clung to him. "I pray you're right."

I am, he thought. *I must be.*

Three

THOUGH ROSE HAD lived at the Foundling Hospital since infancy and had never known another home, packing her belongings into the trunk provided by the hospital would not take long. She owned precious few things. Most of what she used day to day belonged to the hospital and would remain behind when she left for the Continent in a few days. A Mr. and Mrs. Dover had decided to hire her, and she would be leaving within the week.

They'd come to the hospital to observe her teaching reading and basic mathematics to the young girls just starting their studies, only five or six years of age. Rose enjoyed teaching, especially when her students' faces brightened after sudden understanding, whether it was how to subtract numbers or successfully reading a sentence fluently for the first time. She taught daily now that Miss Tandy, the full-time girls' teacher, had fallen ill of pneumonia. Miss Tandy was staying with her sister's family in a cottage near the seashore, where they had access to fresh air and a doctor who visited regularly.

Miss Tandy had long-since been considered an old maid, but she didn't have the same worrisome future that young women in Rose's position had. She wasn't a foundling; she had family. If she never recovered from her illness and found herself unable to work, she wouldn't have to fear the workhouse. Her sister and brother-in-law could take her in. Miss Tandy's pride over being independent had kept her teaching well into her sixties, and she'd declared every intention of returning to the foundling girls' schoolroom.

Headmistress Holdaway and Headmaster Finnegan both seemed loath to find a new teacher, so they'd pulled Rose from her duties in the kitchen to teach until Miss Tandy returned. The decision made sense; Rose had had the highest marks of any girls her age. She'd helped Miss Tandy in the classroom before her graduation to the kitchen, so the older woman herself had recommended Rose as an interim teacher.

She harbored a secret wish that Miss Tandy wouldn't return—not wishing the woman ill, certainly, but hoping she'd enjoy the time away and decide to retire in the country-side. That might mean that *she* could stay on as a teacher. She'd still be close to Oliver.

Plus, she wouldn't have to leave London. The city had its problems—it was crowded, with dirty, winding streets, some of which smelled terrible, and it was plenty big enough to get lost in. But London was her home—the only home she'd ever known. The thought of leaving for a place she'd never laid eyes on brought on a nervous uneasiness. She suspected that when she'd felt similar things as a child, she could have been comforted by a parent's kind words and embrace. More things she'd never had. Perhaps that was why the unknown worried her so.

Many a time, she'd heard people giving rapturous speeches about how beautiful the countryside was, green with trees and foliage. Sometimes she'd felt a thrill in her chest at the idea of visiting such a place, though the thrill felt more like a chance to go home, as if she'd been to the country before. One of the many mysteries of her life. She felt certain she'd seen a land of greenery as a babe, but the memory hovered just out of reach.

Even so, she could hardly imagine such a landscape existing in the real world, though she'd seen evidence of one in a painting at another townhouse she'd been hired at. The first time she'd worked there, she'd stood before the painting for several minutes, taking in every detail, every brush stroke, from the silver-blue lake to the spire-like pines of varying shades of dark green, punctuated by clusters of white birch trees, their trunks bearing black slashes across their bark. If she could have walked straight into *that* landscape, she'd find contentment. Happiness, even. She was sure of it.

As she'd moved away from the painting to bring a tray downstairs, she imagined what walking through that forest would be like. A maid who worked at the house came down the stairs carrying a tin pail and noted Rose's interest in the piece.

"Pretty, isn't it?" the girl had said. "I understand it's a real place."

"Is it?" Rose asked. "Do you know where? I'd love to visit such a place one day."

"Oh, far away, if I understand correctly," the girl had said. She carried a pail of cinders, and her hands and cheeks had smears of gray on them.

"How far away is it? Scotland? Ireland? Germany?" Rose asked, looking at the painting again, feeling as if she could reach out and peel off some of the birch bark, bring it to her nose, and inhale the scent. What *did* birch smell like? She felt as if she should know.

"I'm not certain," the girl said, moving toward the stairs. "Somewhere north, I heard. Is Germany north?" She nodded to the painting. "Did you notice the reindeer in the corner? I didn't for weeks. They blend right in." Without waiting for a response, the girl trotted downstairs, leaving Rose alone in the entry.

She had needed to return to the kitchen to finish the work she'd been hired to do, but she felt compelled to spot the reindeer first. Sure enough, there they were: a small family— what looked like a male, a female, and a baby. What were the proper terms for them? She didn't know. As Rose admired the painting, she realized one thing: England *had* no reindeer. It was somewhere else.

Back in her room, packing her trunk, Rose wished that the Dovers had left a likeness of their estate so she'd have had some indication of where she would be living. How long would that part of her life be? She was being hired as a maid, but what all would her duties include?

If her new employers lived in the country, they might own enough land—or be near enough land—for long walks. She hoped she'd have time for such strolls. If the fates truly smiled on her, the Dover property would be near a lake not unlike the one in the painting, surrounded by pine and birch. There would be no reindeer, but perhaps there would be a path she could follow or a fallen log near the shore where she could sit and read.

Rose had put her books into the trunk first, figuring that as they were heavy and flat, they would provide a good base for anything else that needed packing, and she could be sure to spread out their weight. She'd added her best dress, which had been donated to the hospital after a lady had tired of it. The dress was quite worn in spots, with silk the color of golden scones straight from the oven. It was the finest thing she owned. It didn't fit perfectly, as it had been made for someone taller and with more of a bosom than Rose possessed, but she loved it anyway.

She placed pieces of large tissue atop the dress, then packed the rest of her clothing, which turned out to take even less room than she'd imagined. Over the years, the uniforms she'd outgrown had been handed down to younger orphan girls. In some cases, the uniforms had been passed along to several girls before they reached Rose, so that by the time she outgrew them, they were too ragged to be passed along to anyone younger. Those uniforms had been cut into cleaning rags.

With her books and minimal clothing packed, Rose looked about, trying to determine what else to pack. Until she left with the Dovers, she'd be staying in the faculty dorm to make room for some new arrivals, so while she wasn't leaving quite yet, she was packing up her life at the hospital all the same.

She had a pretty hair comb, which had been a Christmas gift from Oliver that she'd never dared wear at the hospital for fear of being accused of stealing. She still had the stiff paper box it came in, which she slipped under the yellow gown. What else?

She glanced at the trunk, still only half full, wondering if her life was really so empty as all that. If she were to pass away right then, what would be left to remember her by? Oliver's comb and a few books—most of which were looked upon with disapproval by Mistress Holdaway and Mr. Finnegan. When they'd asked her to teach temporarily in Miss Tandy's place, they'd made Rose promise not to teach such "worldly" texts as the novels she kept in her room. She'd been surprised to learn that they were aware of her books, though in hindsight, she shouldn't have been. She should have assumed that the headmaster and headmistress would know—and disapprove—of books that were not the Bible or the approved primers. After all, when she'd been young and slept in a ward lined with beds, nothing she did or possessed had been secret to anyone, least of all to Finnegan and Holdaway.

Her small collection had mostly come her way as gifts

from kind women who'd employed her for a day or two, and a few from used bookshops.

Rose might have been an adult now, but she was still—and ever would be—a foundling. And foundlings didn't deserve respect or privacy.

A patter of footsteps sounded in the corridor. Rose turned just as the owner appeared—little brown-haired Abigail, estimated to be about six years old, though as with so many foundlings, no one knew her precise birth date. Now she stood in Rose's doorway, cheeks flushed and eyes bright with exertion. She didn't speak at first, trying to catch her breath.

"Abigail." Rose hurried to the child. "Is something wrong?"

The girl shook her head and grinned, but still breathed too heavily to speak.

"Are you well?"

Abigail nodded, then managed through heavy breaths, "I'm fine. Mistress Holdaway sent me to fetch you. You're to go to her office at once."

Without meaning to, Rose glanced past the girl into the hallway, her heart sputtering to a faster pace. "Whatever for?"

"Don't know," Abigail said, still breathing heavily. "But she had an envelope she kept tapping against her hand." She demonstrated, using one hand to mime the envelope's edge being brought again and again against the opposite palm. "She said it's urgent."

Heavens. Rose fought back the press of panic on her chest. *Oliver's parents might be causing trouble.*

After last night's confrontation, and their refusal for their son to join his life with that of a mere foundling servant girl's, who knew what they would do. They might try to tarnish her name and prevent her from obtaining an honest job. If she couldn't work, she'd still have to leave the hospital at the end of the summer; she was too old stay as a resident. If she hadn't been such a help for replacing Miss Tandy, she would have been expected to leave months ago.

Where could she turn? She *needed* an employer. She lived here because she had no family. She literally had no one, not even the one person outside these walls who held her heart in their hands—Oliver.

"Well?" Abigail said.

"I'm coming," Rose answered. "Of course. Right away." She lifted her skirts with one hand and reached for Abigail's with the other as they half-walked, half-ran to the headmistress's office. The whole way, Rose did her utmost to rein in her fears.

Something of her nerves must have leaked out, however, because as they reached the office door and Rose knocked, little Abigail turned to her, squeezed Rose's hand between both of her little soft ones, and said, as she'd heard Rose say multiple times, "Everything will be just fine."

Rose leaned over and pressed a kiss to the crown of Abigail's little head. "I'm sure you're right," she said. "Thank you." She turned the door handle and stepped inside. Her knees felt about as sturdy as cold gravy, wobbly and not solid at all.

Everything will be just fine. She repeated the sentiment more than once as she entered, closed the door behind her, and found a seat across from Mistress Holdaway.

Oliver and I will find a way. As he said, somehow, someday.

Four

MISTRESS HOLDAWAY TOOK a seat at her mahogany desk and tapped the end of the envelope against the blotter. She looked from the envelope at Rose, peering over her spectacles. "Thank you for coming to speak with me so promptly."

"Of course." Rose sat with her hands clasped in her lap, ready to jump out of her skin the longer she had to wait to learn the contents of that letter. Surely, it held vital information about her future.

What if her employer was a businessman in India? What if the Dovers took her to Australia or America? Options she hadn't considered suddenly multiplied and bounced around like marbles poured from a bag, hitting the ground, clattering, hitting one another and scattering about.

"We find ourselves in an interesting predicament," Mistress Holdaway said.

That didn't sound good. Rose's stomach tightened as she waited for more information, like a prisoner before sentencing. "Oh?"

"This letter contains—" Mistress Holdaway cut off, as if debating how to begin.

"Oh?" Rose said again. She had to work at not showing any obvious reaction or emotion, though she wanted to beg the woman to keep speaking.

Once more, the envelope tapped on the blotter. "You are a good teacher, Miss Sayer."

"Thank you," Rose said, genuinely surprised by the compliment.

Mistress Holdaway let out a heavy breath that was part sigh, part resignation. She nodded toward the envelope. "This letter contains Miss Tandy's official resignation. Though her health has improved considerably, her physician recommends she not return to the city, what with foul miasma in the air and all. She's decided to retire with relatives."

A zip of excitement went through Rose, but she made certain to keep her expression and tone somewhat restrained. "She has earned a pleasant retirement." Despite her efforts, Rose heard excitement in her voice. How could she not be thrilled after being told she was a good teacher, and that the current teacher was officially retiring? That could mean only one thing.

Yet Mistress Holdaway's grim expression seemed far too somber for happy news. "As much as Headmaster Finnegan and I would like to take you on full-time as the primary-level teacher—and we do—a complication to that end has arisen." Whatever had made the always-serious Mistress Holdaway look even more severe than usual was about to come out.

"What might that complication be?" Rose asked, her voice catching. Had her throat simply dried out all of a sudden?

A knock sounded on the office door. Mistress Holdaway called, "Enter."

The door opened to reveal Headmaster Finnegan. He stepped inside, looked from one woman to the other and nodded. "Oh, good. Glad to see you both here already."

The headmistress gestured toward Rose. "I've explained about Miss Tandy's resignation, but nothing more."

"Very good." Mr. Finnegan reached for the back of a chair against a wall, picked it up by the top, and carried it so he would be sitting at the side of the desk, facing Rose. Two administrators sat against one overgrown foundling, and Rose felt every inch the unremarkable, powerless orphan she was.

"Have you finished discussing the matter with them?" Mistress Holdaway asked.

"I have," Mr. Finnegan said. "They are waiting in the front lobby."

"To what and to whom are you referring?" Rose asked, sure she'd explode if she wasn't told more soon.

"Shall I?" Mr. Finnegan asked. Mistress Holdaway nodded, so he turned to face Rose full on and—at long last—began his explanation. "We have received complaints from families you have worked for."

"What? From whom?" Rose asked, too surprised to be indignant. She'd always worked hard and had never received anything but praise and positive reports. She often arrived early and stayed late and performed more than her hired duties.

Mistress Holdaway tilted her head to one side and then the other. "I suppose it would be more accurate to say that we have received multiple complaints from *one* family."

The Witheys, of course. She'd done excellent work for them. She'd worked hard every time she'd been called there, doing her best, and leaving the kitchen cleaner than when she'd arrived. They could not possibly complain about her performance. But they could complain of one thing: their son's affection for her.

"I suspect you know which family we speak of." Mr. Finnegan raised his eyebrows in question.

No use trying to deny her understanding. Rose nodded, and the simple action seemed to unplug the reservoir of tears behind her eyes. Several trickled down her cheeks, and she swiped them away with the back of her hand. This meeting was simply *not* the time to be showing such weakness.

Mistress Holdaway set the letter on the desk, placed her spectacles atop them, and then gave a piercing, unsettling stare all too similar to the one Rose had endured as a young girl. Any number of women faculty possessed the stare that often meant punishment: a missed meal if one was lucky; if unlucky, a whipping, chores about the hospital that no soul wanted to do, or worse. Rose was too old for such things now, but the look still made her heart pound with anxiety.

"As you may or may not know," Mistress Holdaway went on, "the hospital is always in need of funding. For the last few years, that funding has been harder to come by. We are actively seeking new patrons, including artists willing to show their work in our gallery, singers and symphonies to perform in the concert hall—many of the things that have helped cover operating costs throughout the years, ever since Handel himself spent months performing here last century."

Mr. Finnegan spoke next, picking up the thread as if the two had a planned script they were reading from. "To that end, the Withey family has offered an endowment that will cover *all* operating costs for an entire year."

"A year?" Rose asked, stunned. The Withey family had money, but did they have *that* much? Or were they so desperate to secure their son's future that they'd risk their entire financial reserve to get rid of her?

"If we find a few additional new patrons, and if we manage to reduce operating costs in a few areas, we might be able to stretch that money for two or even three years," Mistress Holdaway added.

"The Withey endowment will allow us to accept one hundred more foundlings than usual over the next year."

Finnegan looked particularly pleased at that, and he tilted his head in Rose's direction, as if he knew she'd feel for the suffering young children they could help. Of course, she did.

The administrators had every reason to do anything in their power to secure the Withey endowment, not only for the current foundlings and their food, clothing, housing, medical care, and education, but also for new foundlings who could be taken in with the added funding—children who might otherwise be turned away.

"Such a gift would be a boon to the hospital and the foundlings," Rose said evenly, though her voice felt strangled as her throat continued to tighten with worry. The reality they'd been hinting at—the "complication" Mistress Holdaway had referred to—was beginning to take shape, and Rose did not think she could bear hearing the specifics of how the Witheys planned to ensure that their son's future would not include her. For despite Oliver's insistence that they would find a way, she knew all too well, as a foundling, that with money came power. His parents would be able to do many things that the two of them would be powerless to overcome.

Mistress Holdaway sighed and added her own words to eliminate any sense of resistance Rose might have felt at the idea of accepting the Withey money. "It would be such a shame to have to turn away more children next year," she said. "Have you ever been present at one of the drawings?"

Rose looked up into the woman's face, wishing she knew how to stop the direction of the conversation. "I haven't," she said. "But I've heard about them."

"I find it remarkable, really, how little some of our traditions have changed since our founder's days."

Please stop, Rose wanted to cry, but that would have been impudent, and with the Witheys as her enemies, she needed allies. Mistress Holdaway and Mr. Finnegan might not have precisely been allies, but she didn't want to make enemies of them, either.

Mr. Finnegan leaned an elbow on the edge of the desk. "Thomas Coram's idea was rather brilliant, though nothing could make leaving a child with us easy for a mother. A lottery system was certainly as fair as he could come up with, and no one has improved upon it yet."

"Seeing a mother put her hand into the bag is heart-breaking," Mistress Holdaway said.

"Oh, but seeing her face go pale as she pulled her hand out to reveal a white or black ball—" Mr. Finnegan clucked his tongue. "Pure agony, no matter the color, I must say."

Rose had always pictured the bag as red velvet with a drawstring, though she'd never seen it. On the appointed lottery days, one by one, mothers queued up and put a hand into the bag and withdrew a ball. A white ball meant her child would be accepted into the hospital and cared for under a new name, their history erased unless a parent returned to collect them at a later date by identifying a token left and sealed with the file. Sometimes it was a single token; other times, a twin to one the parent kept with them.

As all the foundlings did, Rose had often wondered about her token. She'd heard of mothers leaving coins with holes punched into them, earrings, plaited threads with beads on them, and other trinkets, sometimes with messages or initials. She'd also wondered what her name had been before the hospital took her from the arms of her mother's servant and erased her past.

Mothers who drew white balls had the most bittersweet pain—relief that their child would live and hopefully have a future, with some kind of education, but grief that they'd likely never see their child again. On the other hand, withdrawing a black ball meant the child would not be taken into the hospital. Considering the fact that mothers did not bring their children here unless they were desperate, a black ball could mean abandonment, starvation, or disease for their child.

London had far too many foundlings for any one institution to care for; Rose was one of the fortunate ones to have gotten in so long ago. How could she, of all people, protest the opportunity to help more children in need?

She cleared her throat and tried to speak with calmness and strength, though she felt neither. "May I presume that Mr. and Mistress Withey have not offered this most generous gift without conditions?" She wanted to say *strings attached*, but *conditions* sounded more proper. Though she felt quite certain she already she knew what they wanted, and that it was one thing and one thing only: eliminating Rose from their son's life.

"That is correct," Mistress Holdaway said. "If only half of what the Witheys have told us about your behavior toward their son is true, you have conducted yourself in a most inappropriate manner."

Every word of the English language seemed to have fled Rose's mind, but the overriding feeling of indignation grew stronger within her chest. She'd done nothing wrong, and neither had Oliver. He'd come downstairs into the servants' area of his own accord, and had for years. His parents had to have known about it long ago. Yes, the two of them had engaged in conversation. He'd voluntarily washed dishes and did other minor chores, though no one had asked him to do those things, and Mrs. Phelps had certainly tried to dissuade him.

Yes, she and Oliver had grown close, first as friends, and in recent months, much more. Yes, they'd shared a few kisses. They'd gone on moonlit walks, but always in public areas.

The only thing they'd done wrong was in the eyes of society: They were of different classes, and they'd had the audacity to befriend each other and, more recently, to fall in love. Oliver's family was part of the *ton*. She was an orphan, with no name, no one to recommend her, and no dowry.

"Mr. and Mrs. Withey demand that you cut off all ties with their son immediately." Mistress Holdaway punctuated the statement by firmly striking the desk blotter with the side of her hand.

"Am—am I to be in the employ of the Dover family, then?"

"Possibly," Mistress Holdaway said, sitting back in her chair.

Mr. Finnegan leaned back, too, and eyed Rose, steepling his fingers. "The Witheys certainly want you employed by someone who will take you far from London. The Dovers are moving to the Continent, so obviously, that would be an ideal situation, but we have Miss Tandy's resignation to account for, and that puts us into somewhat of a bind." He straightened and leaned toward Rose, as if about to impart words she would be happier to hear than everything that had been thrust at her so far. "I suggested another possibility."

Rose turned to him as if he'd saved her from falling overboard a ship. "And what is that?"

"Instead of going to the Continent with the Dover family," Mr. Finnegan said, "you replace Miss Tandy here at the hospital—with the promise that you cut off all ties with the younger Mr. Withey. Their donation will be given in three parts: one as soon as the agreement is signed by all parties, another in six months, and the final, largest, payment—"

"A full half of the total," Mistress Holdaway interjected.

"Yes, half of the total at the end of a year," Mr. Finnegan finished.

Mistress Holdaway picked up the thread. "If they learn, at any time during the year, that you've been in contact with their son, their gift will be revoked in its entirety, and you'll be sent to work as a domestic servant in India."

Rose would be able to stay as an employee at the hospital. For the tiniest flicker of a moment, relief made her feel as if she were flying, but that sensation was followed quickly by the sense of plummeting to the earth and hitting the ground with a thud of despair. "Do I understand," she said, trying to sort out the many details that were flying at her like arrows toward a mark, "that I may stay as a teacher, but only if I never see Oliver—that is, Mr. Withey—again?"

"That is correct," Mistress Holdaway said, looking pleased. "You are not to see him, speak to him, write to him, or communicate with him in any way whatsoever." She tilted her chin down, as if still looking over her spectacles, which were on the desk. "Are you capable of making such a promise?"

Not communicate with Oliver for a year. One year. Twelve months.

What should she do? What *could* she do? Not even seeing Oliver when he lived so nearby would be a type of death. What would happen if she was upstairs and happened to see him on the street through the window? Would his parents withdraw their money then? Would going across the channel with the Dover family to France or Germany or Italy be easier? That would mean leaving Oliver behind, never having any chance of seeing even a glimpse of him. She was being presented with two equally unsatisfactory choices.

She held on to the fact that after one year, after the final payment, she and Oliver would be free—provided that he was not yet engaged to someone else by then. He wouldn't be. He'd wait for her, as she would wait for him.

Finnegan stood, scooting his chair back so its legs slid across the wood floor. "If you agree, we'll have a teaching contract drawn up for you that will lay out the details of your employment as well as your agreement relating to the funding of the hospital. Meanwhile, I'll go inform Mr. and Mrs. Withey that we can finalize the contract and details surrounding their most generous gift. I am eager to assure them that their fears can be put to rest." He reached for the doorknob, but before turning it, looked pointedly at Rose. "If you feel at any time that you are unable to maintain your commitment, you must tell us posthaste. We will be looking for another teacher to replace you if the need arises. Don't think for a moment that we'll allow the inconvenience of Miss Tandy's retirement to blind us into losing an endowment the size of the Withey family's."

"I understand," Rose said. Did she look as pale as she felt?

Mistress Holdaway stood, marking the end of their interview. "You can and will commit to their demands, I presume?"

Rose could almost hear a subtle but unmistakable message underlying the question: *A simple young attraction is nothing to get oneself worked up about, and matters of the hospital and your own future are far more important than a fleeting infatuation.*

"I can," she heard herself say. What else could she say? She couldn't very well put the hospital in financial straits over her own personal desires, not when it would mean fewer foundlings receiving the very aid that had kept her alive and given her both an education and a chance for a future.

This won't be forever, she thought. *I'll be able to stay in my home.* Oliver would find a way out of this tangled mess, even if it took a year.

Mr. Finnegan left to give the Witheys a favorable report.

Mistress Holdaway told Rose that her trunk would be moved to faculty housing, then dismissed her. Through it all, Rose felt apart from the world around, as if she were observing someone else instead of experiencing the moment herself, hearing voices at a distance instead of in her presence.

She prayed that they would be together in a year, when the funding came through. That nothing would happen before then to keep Oliver permanently from her life. Would he be able to withstand the pressures of his family and society without seeing her for a full year? What if, in eleven months, his parents convinced him that his feelings were nothing but a passing fancy, and they attached him to some young lady with an engagement contract?

She walked back to her room in a haze that, with every step, darkened from gray toward black. She grasped for a pinprick of light, of hope, but the only bit of hope she could grasp was in remembering Oliver's declaration of love.

He'll wait for me.

Five

OLIVER HAD SPENT a most miserable time the last few days. Could he truly have endured only three days since he'd last bid Rose goodbye? He could still picture her as she'd walked into the dark night and climbed the steps from the servants' courtyard to the street, then disappeared from view as she hurried back to the Foundling Hospital.

He stood in the drawing room, staring onto the street below in the direction that Rose had gone. Apparently, his parents had seen him and Rose outside together enough times to guess at the truth. He should have been more careful. He'd since learned that they'd watched him and Rose many a time without either of them being aware. He'd been foolish to think for a moment that his mother, especially, wouldn't learn about everything happening within her own household, down to what her son did in the kitchen.

"Oh, please, stop moping." Mrs. Withey's frustrated tone grated on Oliver's nerves as she entered the drawing room, swooping through the doorway as if making an entrance on a stage.

Oliver glanced at her, but then turned his attention back to the window. "Are you and Father leaving for the concert soon?"

"Yes, but not alone."

"What?"

"*You*, my dear son, will be coming with us." She smiled, as if waiting for an expression of his undying gratitude. "We happen to have *six* tickets to tonight's event."

"Six?" What did they have use for so many tickets?

"Yes. You see . . ." As his mother's voice trailed off, Oliver waited for her to complete the thought. She and Father were up to some mischief, he was certain. He knew that glint in her eye, that curl of her lips.

"Who is attending?" he prompted when she didn't continue.

"You will be escorting Miss Priscilla Morgan."

Oliver's stomach tightened. "Mother, you didn't—"

"And her parents will have the other two tickets. They'll all be here soon, and the six of us will have a delightful stroll walking to the concert." His mother sat on a velvet chair and folded her hands together, propping them demurely on her knees. "Miss Morgan is *quite* eligible, with a sizable dowry."

"I see." Oliver turned back to the window to buy himself a few moments to cool his sudden anger. His parents were hoping to find him a match with some well-to-do young woman whose biggest point of praise was money? His mother looked pleased as punch, which meant that the lady's family was likely important. Morgan was such a common name, but even so, no young woman's face came to mind.

His parents had just set his plans for a life with Rose afire, and without any time for him to mourn or come to terms with what had happened, they expected him to welcome into his heart a new woman whom he'd never met? Did his parents know him at all?

No, he thought sadly. *They truly do not.*

He took a step toward her, hand raised as he tried to object. "Mother, I—"

"No, no, no." She shook her head and raised a hand as

well to counter his objection. Rising from her seat, she lifted her chin. "You *are* going to the concert this evening, and you *will* ensure that Miss Morgan has a pleasant time. Your father and I will be watching, and so will her parents."

Better to acquiesce on a small point in hopes of claiming time to conjure a strategy for winning the war. "Very well, I shall go," Oliver said. "You may be assured that I will be a perfect gentleman."

"I would expect nothing less." His mother stepped closer, went slightly onto her toes, and pressed a quick peck to his cheek. "You'll get that silly kitchen girl out of your head in no time. You'll see."

She spun about and left before Oliver could form a reply that was accurate but not disrespectful. Speaking the truth to his parents, and doing so without showing anger or impertinence, was becoming harder by the day.

From the staircase, his mother called, "They arrive any minute, so I suggest you hurry to put on something suitable."

"Shouldn't we order a carriage? We'll be late to any concert farther into town."

His mother's shoes tapped back up a few steps, and her excited face peered through the spindles at him. "Oh, did I not mention that the concert is at the Foundling Hospital? Harriett Foote is performing in the same hall that Handel had his concerts in when the hospital was new." She waved her hand from the wrist. "Hurry up now, darling. You haven't much time."

He wasn't entirely sure, but he thought that a flicker of victory crossed his mother's face before she disappeared down the stairs. No doubt she would stand watch and make absolutely certain that she would be the one to welcome Miss Morgan into the house to control first impressions.

Must she twist the knife? His parents could surely have found a concert, play, or other event for him and Miss Morgan to attend instead of sending him to the very place that meant a reminder of Rose.

With dread pulling at him, Oliver left the drawing room and went upstairs to change into his white tie and tails. As he dressed, he couldn't help but think that if his mother realized that most men of his age had valets to help with such matters, she would be horrified at the oversight. He preferred to care for himself. He liked his privacy and was loath to give it up, even to someone who was purportedly trustworthy, like a valet.

He leaned closer to the standing mirror to even out the bow tie, wishing that he could attend the concert with Rose. For just a moment, he allowed himself to imagine picking her up from her quarters, Rose dressed in a beautiful gown of taffeta—he wasn't entirely sure what taffeta was, but Rose had mentioned how pretty it was—her hand through the crook of his elbow. The two of them walking to the concert hall. Listening to the performance. Applauding together. Afterward, enjoying a walk together in the crisp evening after the sweltering press of the concert hall. Returning her to her door and kissing her by the light of the moon. Parting ways for but a short spell, as they would soon be married, and then he would never have to say goodbye at night.

The sudden sound of a bell made his flight of fancy evaporate, returning Oliver to the dreary present reality with an emotional thud.

He heard the front door open, followed by Mr. Arnold greeting the guests and ushering them inside. His mother's voice came next as she fawned over the Morgans. He took a deep breath and reminded himself that Miss Morgan was innocent in the matter, and as such, she deserved to have a pleasant evening no matter what devious plans their parents had concocted.

But this evening's concert specifically had to be his

mother's idea—a particularly cruel brand of torture. She had to know that sending Oliver to the Foundling Hospital, where Rose had spent virtually her entire life, being near but unable to see her at all, would be agony. He'd have to pretend to be happy about it while not knowing if Rose still lived there or had been sent away. The entire charade felt like a way for his parents to mock him and emphasize that *they* were in control of his life and future, no matter what he personally desired.

Truthfully, Oliver did not know if he was made of tough enough mettle to be Miss Morgan's companion for the evening in a manner that his parents would approve of. He would certainly try to be pleasant and amiable, to make conversation and be attentive. He would do those things not for his parents' sake, but because the man Rose believed in and loved was the man he aspired to become, and *that* man was nothing if not a complete gentleman.

With a deep breath, he left his quarters carrying his hat in his hand and headed down the stairs to meet his companion for the evening. He knew he looked the part of the young gentleman that his mother expected of him. He'd made sure to smooth his hair just so. He wore newly polished boots and his fanciest cravat—one he could not abide, for he felt like an oaf wearing the poof of lace, but his mother believed it was the most fashionable thing a man could wear, so he wore it to please her.

Winning the approval of either of his parents toward Rose would be a most difficult, if not impossible, challenge, but he was determined to do his best. And that evening, his best meant wearing the flamboyant pink cravat he so despised.

"Miss Morgan, I presume," he said as he took the last stair to the main floor. He crossed to the pretty young woman standing in the entryway. He took her extended hand, half-bowed toward her. "A pleasure to meet you."

"The pleasure is mutual," Miss Morgan said with a slight curtsy.

He greeted her parents next, then straightened and gave his mother a peck on the cheek. "Good evening, Mama."

"We shall have a delightful time at the concert," his mother said.

She called for her husband, Mr. Arnold opened the door for the party, and they went out, two by two. First the Morgans, then Oliver and Miss Morgan, and finally, his parents behind them, his mother nearly bursting with satisfaction over what she no doubt viewed as a successful coup.

Let her think as much, Oliver thought as he escorted Miss Morgan out the door and along the street. If his mother incorrectly believed that his affections had found a new object, by all means, he'd let the ruse continue. No reason to dissuade her from such an erroneous inference while he searched for how to clear a path for him and Rose to marry that allowed him to care for her properly.

Miss Morgan's voice pierced his musings. "You are ever so kind to take me to the concert this evening. I know it was an unexpected obligation on your part."

"Oh, I'm quite happy to—" Oliver's voice cut off as he fully digested her words.

She glanced over and clearly noted that he'd been taken aback, but she smiled, amused. He could make neither heads nor tails of her reaction. Fortunately, she continued, still smiling. "The concert was sprung upon me by my parents in a manner I suspect your parents did to you."

"I . . . see . . ." he said, though he didn't. It seemed like the right thing to say in the moment. Their feet made rhythmic clicks and clops along the pavement for a few moments, during which time he did his utmost to rally and determine what he was to say or do. Had he offended Miss Morgan after all?

She didn't look offended, and indeed, she'd apparently made sure to make her comment after a big enough gap existed between them and her parents for them to not be overheard. Oliver glanced over his shoulder at his parents, who were keeping their distance, no doubt hoping for Cupid to be at work.

"You see," Miss Morgan said, "my maid has let me know a bit about what has been discussed amongst my parents and yours, and I believe you and I are in similar circumstances."

At that, Oliver tilted his head in surprise. He looked over his shoulder again, at his family's townhouse, where his parents watched them. When she noticed his look, she waved, then clapped her hands together as if she had something to celebrate. "You must forgive my ignorance. I am uncertain about what you refer to."

"How long is the walk to the concert hall?"

Not the response he'd expected at all. "Five or ten minutes, perhaps. Not long."

"Then I'll offer you the most important of details and spare you the rest of the story."

"I'm intrigued."

She smiled broader at that. "You see, I've had two Seasons, so naturally, my parents are eager for me to marry, but not to just anyone."

"Understandably," Oliver replied.

"I feel as though I have found my match—a man I met my first Season, in fact. He's intelligent, kind, handsome—"

"Careful, or I may begin to feel envious," Oliver said dryly.

Miss Morgan chuckled, for which he was grateful; she knew he was teasing. She clasped her free hand to the one on his arm. "I understand that you, too, have found a great love of which your parents do not approve."

Oliver didn't mean to, but he slowed his step out of pure surprise and sudden emotion. Miss Morgan stopped entirely and looked straight at him. "So my maid Alice says. Is she correct?"

So much for trying to set aside his troubles for the evening and maintain a lighthearted air. The darned cravat was nigh unto choking him. He lowered his gaze to a nearby doorstep and tried to determine what words to say. Should he change the subject? Was Miss Morgan as trustworthy as she appeared, and a true kindred spirit, having the same trouble he and Rose did? Did his parents know that Miss Morgan had already given her heart to another? Was this a trap?

Miss Morgan pressed, "Is my maid correct?" Her voice held no guile, and in that moment, Oliver knew he could trust her as he would a sister.

"Yes," he answered huskily. "Yes, she is."

"That explains my parents' eagerness in arranging tonight's concert." Miss Morgan sighed, and she walked on. Oliver followed, finding her position and confession to have relieved some of his worries in the moment. He needn't worry that Miss Morgan would feel rejected when he didn't pursue a courtship after this evening.

"Our parents are hoping to forge a match between you and me," Oliver said, voicing the implication outright. "I suspected as much on my mother's part, but I had no inkling that your parents might have been planning the scheme with mine."

"Foolish of them, isn't it?" Her wobbly voice belied her lighthearted words, making Oliver slow his step to look at her.

"Miss Morgan?" he said gently, feeling tender toward her, as a brother might. "Are you well?"

She stared at the cobbled walkway as they continued,

neither wanting their parents to notice anything unusual or to come up on them if they stopped walking altogether. Even so, Miss Morgan sniffed, and Oliver removed a handkerchief from his pocket, offering it to her surreptitiously. She took it and dabbed her eyes.

"I love him so," she said quietly. "But they are trying to keep us apart." She held the cloth to her nose and wiped a few more tears.

"I understand completely," Oliver said, wishing that neither of them were experiencing such heartbreak.

In time, they lapsed into the silence of camaraderie. He guided her to the Foundling Hospital, but when they turned a corner and he laid eyes on it, the sight nearly stopped his heart. He hadn't realized that his feet had actually stopped, too, until Miss Morgan spoke again.

"Does she work in there? The woman you love?" She clearly recognized the pain on his face and knew it must be connected to his own dear love.

He was mystified at how Miss Morgan had divined so much, but Oliver was grateful for her insight, for someone who intimately understood what he was enduring. "She works here for now, but she was also reared here," he said. He looked back and noted his parents gaining on them. "She was left as a foundling when but a babe. Soon, she will be employed as a domestic servant by some wealthy family or another. We plan to correspond with letters until we can find a way to be together, but . . ." He shook his head and sighed.

"I understand," Miss Morgan said. "Such matters are complicated and are of far more significance in relation to one's heart than the previous generation seems to believe. A good match isn't only about contracts and dowries, position and influence . . . is it?"

Oliver placed a grateful hand over Miss Morgan's. "Indeed, it is not."

Six

ROSE UNPACKED HER meager trunk and got her belongings settled into their places in her new quarters—a place that felt strange to consider her home after being off limits to students for her entire life. No sooner had she closed a drawer than a knock sounded on her door. Having a door at all felt like a luxury—she'd had one in her most recent room, but that had been only for the last few months, and she'd shared that room with three other young women about to be sent out into the world as she was.

But now she had her own room, with nothing but her belongings, a bed to herself, and a door that offered privacy. The idea that someone would knock rather than walk in because they were more important than a mere foundling was new to her, and it brought both a smile to her face and a lightness to her step as she crossed to the door to answer.

She opened it without any idea of who might be on the other side, but assuming she'd find another teacher or servant. While she did find a black dress, a color the servants wore daily, it didn't adorn a maid or teacher.

"Mistress Holdaway," Rose said. Had she done something wrong already? She hurriedly thought through her actions since the conference in the headmistress's office and could not fathom what she could have done to merit discipline.

Instead of issuing a punishment, Mistress Holdaway spoke evenly as she relayed her message, revealing no negative emotions at all, and perhaps, if Rose guessed correctly, a cheerful mood—at least, as cheerful as the headmistress ever managed. "You are aware of tonight's concert?" she asked.

"Yes, of course," Rose said with a dip of respect, her gaze lowered. No one within several miles' distance or beyond was ignorant of the ongoing concerts that raised money for the hospital and increased the visibility of artists of all kinds.

"As I am sure you are also aware, Betty is typically the one who manages these types of events, along with the help of some of the staff, but she is shorthanded today, owing to Susie taking to her bed over a cough or some such."

"And you'd like me to help somehow?" Rose guessed. "I'd be happy to be at the ticketing table."

"No, no, no." Mistress Holdaway shook her head. "I need you to welcome guests at the door and help them find their seats."

Rose's brows drew together. "You're asking me to be an usher?" Wasn't that usually something a man did?

"Are you refusing the request? The first duty asked of you as a member of the faculty, and you say no?"

"Not at all," Rose said hurriedly. "I'm happy to help in any way you need."

Mistress Holdaway's mouth curled to one side in an odd smile that sent an uneasy feeling down the back of Rose's neck. "Very good. Wear your best dress and report at the concert hall promptly at seven o'clock."

"Yes, ma'am," Rose said with another curtsied bob of the knees.

The headmistress spun about and walked away. Rose watched her go, grateful that she wasn't in trouble for anything. She closed the door to her room and went to her wardrobe, which she opened and looked over. Such a meager selection, and her best dress wasn't nearly fine enough for a concert such as the ones hosted at the hospital. She'd look so very much out of place. She might even get pitying stares.

No wonder the headmistress had assumed Rose would decline. But there was nothing for it, so she put her hair up in the finest twist she knew how, used the curling tongs Sally, a maid, offered to lend her, and finished off the look with a length of yellow ribbon. She wore her yellow dress, which was several seasons old. If one looked carefully, the dress certainly showed its age, especially around the hem and cuffs, but she still liked it.

She gazed into the looking glass, knowing that she still didn't look like a wealthy or noble lady, but also with the realization that her reflection did hold a certain something she wasn't accustomed to seeing in herself—an *almost* prettiness. She would never mistake herself as truly beautiful, but tonight, she felt feminine and somewhat attractive. She pinched her cheeks to give them a little color, then left for the concert hall early. She was determined to do her duties as an usher in a manner beyond criticism.

She entered the grand foyer of the hospital, where she waited at the base of the grand staircase leading to the balcony of the concert hall. The wood was dark, and the staircase had a deep-green carpet climbing its length. Mistress Holdaway was already there, as was Betty, who looked eager to welcome Rose and send the headmistress on her way.

"I hear you are to help us this evening," Betty said with a smile. She approached Rose, who merely nodded as the other girl drew her toward the main concert hall doors, where, presumably, Rose would welcome audience members as they arrived. A stack of papers on a table beside the door listed the order of performances in the concert. "You'll give out these programs as attendees arrive, usually one per couple, but sometimes, both the man and the woman want one, and, of course, you'll find individuals attending alone and odd-numbered groups as well. You'll look at each ticket and direct the holders to their seats."

Rose was about to protest that she didn't know the layout of the concert hall—she hadn't ever been able to attend a concert, nor even walk into the auditorium. But Betty was ready for that concern before it was voiced.

"You may want to go inside first to familiarize yourself with how the seating is arranged."

"That would be good," Rose said in agreement. "Thank you."

Mistress Holdaway had followed them and listened to every word. She pulled a watch out of her pocket and looked at it. "Be sure to make it quick," she said. "Betty, I assume you'll work the balcony?"

"I certainly can, if that's what you'd like."

"I insist upon it."

"Very well," Betty said, sounding somewhat perplexed. "I will be sure the balcony area is taken care of, and Rose will be on the main floor."

"Good." With that, the headmistress spun about, her dark skirts skimming the wood floor, and she left.

With her ominous presence gone, Betty caught eyes with Rose and made an expression of exasperation, which nearly sent Rose into a fit of laughter, one she had to hold back by covering her mouth with her hand.

Betty turned to the double doors of the concert hall and pulled them open, but as she did so, she spoke over her shoulder to Rose. "One never knows what strange moods or demands will possess certain people." She tossed a glance in the direction Mistress Holdaway had gone, and the two women shared a silent laugh.

But as the door opened fully, and the size and grandeur of the concert hall became visible, Rose nearly gasped. She'd never seen anything so luxurious, so ornate, so . . . other-worldly. It looked like something from a fairy tale. Was this how the rich lived? She stepped inside and looked around, mouth slightly agape at the sheer size and elegance of the hall. Hundreds of people, if not a thousand or more, could easily fit inside, sitting on padded seats with wooden armrests carved on the sides with elegant designs.

The walls also had wooden sections that looked almost like columns with carvings along the tops and sometimes framing areas like the door across the way. Much of the decor was painted in gold, and the stage was framed by more wooden molding, with gold that only made the deep-red velvet of the curtain seem lusher and more expensive than it would have otherwise. Golden chandeliers hung from the ceiling, already lit with electric bulbs.

"I'm terribly underdressed," Rose managed in but a whisper. The words sounded silly even to her own ears, but that's how she felt. Completely out of place, though she wore her best dress and had spent extra time on her hair. Even the ribbon felt common and like something a country girl would have thought pretty.

"No one expects the help to wear anything fancy," Betty said, walking farther inside to show Rose around. But Betty's own clothing belied her words—she wore a gown that looked both pale blue and silver all at once. It looked made for her, unlike Rose's secondhand gown. Betty even wore matching slippers, and had a necklace and comb that complemented the ensemble.

Rose had to wonder where Betty had gotten her gown. After all, she, too, was a product of the hospital. Perhaps Mistress Holdaway had bought it so Betty would look the part as she worked concert after concert. But if that were the case, and the headmistress was even a bit concerned with how the ushers were dressed, why would she insist that Rose be at the main door, and Betty, in her pretty silver-blue gown, be upstairs, where fewer people would see her?

She likely wants me to feel inferior and humiliated.

Rose pushed such thoughts from her mind. Any prettiness that she'd felt earlier was sucked out of the room. She listened to Betty's instructions, grateful that the headmistress had taken her leave, and determined to do the best job she could. After tonight, however, she'd never again wish to work one of the concerts.

Soon she was able to distract herself, however, for ticket holders began to arrive. For nearly an hour, she greeted guests as they showed their tickets. She directed them to their seats and wished them an enjoyable evening. All seemed to be going well, and she'd begun to feel comfortable and confident in her duties. That was, until a voice—more of a sound—pierced the air and drew Rose's attention.

Tommy, a young foundling boy of about six, had been assigned to hold the programs beside her. She leaned down to him. "Did you hear that?"

"It's very loud in here," the boy said solemnly.

"Yes, it is," Rose said, straightening. "But I could have sworn I heard something besides the milling of the people."

He held out the next program from his stack, and she took it. "Thank you, Tommy," she said, and turned to the next ticket holders in line. A gentleman with a thin, gray mustache held out two tickets for her, but Rose hadn't comprehended the writing on them before she heard the sound again—the sound of someone crying, or calling for help; Rose couldn't be sure *what* she heard, only that she *had* heard someone. She lifted her gaze and looked about, past the long, winding line that went out the door onto the street.

If a young mother was outside, needing to find shelter for her child, she might not be noticed until after the concert, or even until morning. A night outdoors could be dangerous for mother and child in both safety as well as health.

"I'll be back in a moment," she told Tommy, giving the program back to him. "You take the tickets."

He gave her a look of confusion mixed with fear at the sudden responsibility, but she bent her knees and cupped his cheek in her hand. "You are a gentleman and a very mature boy." She winked. "You can do this, I'm sure. And I'll be back before you know it. Promise. Understand?"

He nodded mutely.

"You can do this, right?" she said, adopting a bit of her schoolteacher tone.

He nodded again.

"Good." She rubbed a hand through the side of his already disheveled, ginger-colored hair and hurried through the snaking crowd to find the source of the voice.

When Rose reached the outer doors without hearing the cry again, she doubted her hearing and wondered if she'd imagined the whole thing. But as she pushed the wood door fully open and stepped into the chilling evening air, she heard it again. Rose looked about for a young mother but found none who weren't already queued up with tickets and elegant gowns.

She walked the perimeter of the front courtyard, determined to find the feminine voice who was crying. At last, she reached a bench on which an elderly woman was seated and hunched over, her shoulders shaking as she cried. Could this be the voice Rose had heard? Whoever this woman was, she was far too aged to be an unwed mother looking for a place to leave her child.

Rose stood a few steps away, unsure. The woman's sobs

couldn't have carried all the way into the concert hall, could they? She pushed the questions of *how* away and sat beside the woman. "May I help you with something? Do you need food or shelter?" Even as she spoke, she doubted that the woman needed anything of the sort. Her clothes were clean, and while not expensive, they were in good repair. Her cheeks weren't sunken with hunger, and they had a healthy pink hue. The woman even wore what looked like a warm wool shawl to keep out the worst of the cold.

"I hope you can help me," the woman said, her voice twisting in pain. "But I fear my soul is damned."

Alarmed, Rose put a hand on the woman's shoulder. "Shall I call a priest for you?" In answer, the woman shook her head, so Rose asked, "A doctor, then?"

Again, the woman shook her head. "I will die soon, and no doctor in the world can save me. That's not why I'm here." She turned slightly and looked up at Rose as if about to say more, but she sucked in a breath. "Oh, gracious heavens." A hand pressed to her breastbone, as if her chest needed support to breathe. The woman had probably lost a bit of her sanity. Rose took pity on her.

"Come inside. I can find you a warm place to sleep for the night, and tomorrow, we'll find a more permanent place for you to go." Though heaven only knew if that would be possible; the city was packed with residents as it was.

Rose tried to aid the woman in standing, but she pulled away and asked, "What is your name? Please tell me."

"Rose," she answered. "Rose Sayer."

She'd always wondered what her birth name had been. *Rose Sayer* was a name given to her by someone at the hospital. All children were renamed when they arrived, to protect the privacy of both family and child. Only if a parent returned to claim a child was the record unsealed, the token—

which had to be correctly identified by the parent—discovered, and the child's birth name and history revealed. That almost never happened.

"Rose," the woman repeated. "And how old are you, Rose?"

"Nearly twenty. I was brought to the Foundling Hospital in the autumn of 1863."

"It *is* you. I knew it when I saw your face." The woman looked at her again, her face framed by white hair. "I asked the woman who met with me to call you Rose."

"Are you . . . are you my mother?" Rose asked, feeling gooseflesh rise on her arms and the back of her neck. As if her blood suddenly turned to cold water, she shivered.

Every foundling dreamed of such an event, and Rose was no exception. For most of her life, she'd clung to the distant, nearly impossible hope that perhaps, against all odds, she would be one of the few lucky ones. Most mothers who brought their children here were very young—much younger than this woman was.

"I am no relation to you," the woman said with a shake of her head. "But . . ."

Rose's heart fluttered with hope.

"I—I knew your mother. In fact, I knew both of your parents." She pressed her lips together, the wrinkles on her face deepening with a pain so intense that Rose stood quickly, ready to run inside for the physician.

"Is it your heart? Are you faint?" she asked.

"No, nothing like that," the woman said. "Memories and guilt hurt more than any physical ailment. Please sit. I need to speak these words at long last."

For a moment, Rose stood there, trying to decide what the best course of action would be. She finally sat again, this time closer to the woman, who took Rose's hands and held them between her own.

"I brought you here after—" She shook her head firmly and lowered her chin. "Lord, I can't say it," she whispered, as if in a prayer.

The flutter of hope increased inside Rose's chest. This woman knew who she was and where she'd come from. "I know nothing of my past. Please. Tell me what you know about me."

"Rose!" a stern voice called from the door. Mistress Holdaway.

"Oh, no." Rose had abandoned her post, and no excuse would be sufficient to escape her wrath. "Coming!" she called, and then took the strange woman's hands in hers. "I must go now, but I want to speak to you again. I must."

"Rose! Return at once!"

"Yes, Mistress Holdaway!" Once more, she turned to the woman and spoke quickly. "I don't know how much longer I will be at the hospital. Can you come back here, to this same spot, tomorrow morning?" When the woman seemed to falter, Rose begged. "Please. You came for a reason—to find me?"

She nodded.

"Please come back. I—I need to know before . . ." She shrugged helplessly, not knowing what her future would hold. She'd be here in the morning. She felt confident of that much, but beyond that . . .

"I'll come," the woman said, standing. "I'll be here at nine o'clock, and if I don't see you in five minutes, I will leave." She held out a hand. "Here. Something that once belonged to your father."

Rose held out her hands, and the woman dropped a small object into her palms before shuffling away and disappearing into the darkness of the city streets. From the door, she heard Mistress Holdaway clearing her throat impatiently, so Rose hurried back inside, muttering apologies. She shoved the small object into her pocket—smaller than her little finger, smooth, hard—without looking at it. She wouldn't risk Mistress Holdaway seizing it. Better to look at it tonight when she was alone in her own quarters.

Mistress Holdaway took Rose by the arm—grasping it so tightly it hurt—and marched her back to the front of the line. "You will finish your duties." She departed, leaving Rose breathing heavily, her heart pounding. Whatever happened, she needed to meet with that woman again in the morning.

As Rose returned to her duties taking tickets and directing guests, she could hardly think straight. She stammered and dropped a set of tickets belonging to an elderly couple. "I'm so sorry," she said. "Please forgive me. I'm all thumbs today."

"It's quite all right," said the wife, who appeared to be about the age of the woman outside. What quirks of fate had given one woman a life of comfort and luxury, and the other a life of, if not poverty, then of at least simple means, and some kind of deep-seated pain?

"Thank you," Rose said to the woman and her husband, smiling. "Your seats are to the right and two rows back."

The woman squeezed Rose's hand in a kind gesture as she passed. Rose smiled at the woman, then looked up to greet the next guests in line.

There, standing before her, was Oliver Withey.

Seven

AT FIRST, ROSE barely noticed the fact that a beautiful woman was on his arm. All she could see, even as her breath caught, was that her dear Oliver stood before her, looking more handsome than ever. Oliver, whom she was not allowed to see or speak to for a year.

Rose's mouth and throat dried right up, and she might as well have forgotten how to speak, so intense was the shock, combined with yearning to be held in his arms one more time.

She nodded at Oliver as if she didn't know him, then acknowledged his companion and deliberately spoke to her so no one would be able to say she'd spoken to Oliver when she was strictly prohibited from doing so. "Let's see your tickets, and I'll—" She had to force herself to take a breath and unlock her knees. "I'll help you find your seats." She held out a hand for the tickets, which Oliver offered. Her hand visibly trembled, so she clasped it in the other and merely *looked* at the tickets.

"Oh, yes," she said, looking at the lady once more. "You're in the fourth row of the middle section. Very good seats." She gestured toward the correct area of the hall.

"Thank you," the young woman said with a genuine smile. She stepped past, bringing Oliver along. He took a small step, but then paused and stood beside Rose for a moment, so near, yet neither of them able to breach the chasm of his parents' creation.

His scent—sandalwood and spice—filled her heart and made her stomach flip in the old familiar, delicious manner that now was accompanied by pain. She couldn't help but note his jaw working, as if he was trying to solve a conundrum, decide what to do or say. At the same time, the bittersweet agony of having him near wasn't something she wanted to lose. She hadn't seen him in days, and she'd likely not see him again for twelve months.

She could hardly bear to have him this near for a moment longer, so she ended the encounter by stepping behind him and addressing the next guests in line—Oliver's parents. That broke the spell for both Rose and, apparently, Oliver, who stepped purposely into the hall and was soon lost to the crowd.

Despite herself, after helping his parents find their seats—all while pretending they were nothing more than another couple—Rose's gaze wandered to Oliver and his companion waiting in the aisle to reach their seats. As if he could feel the weight of her gaze, Oliver looked over at her. When their eyes met, he smiled at her, warming her down to her toes.

He mouthed, *love you.* Then he was caught into the throng once more and lost to her sight. Rose was filled with such warmth and happiness that she felt as if she could subsist on nothing but that feeling for a week. Oliver's love would nourish her.

"Miss Sayer!" Mistress Holdaway's shrill tone pierced the air, and a cold chill went over Rose like a bucket of cold water.

Oh, no. No, no, no.

"Did I just see you *speaking* to Mr. Withey?"

"No," Rose said. "I said nothing to him. I spoke to his lady companion, and even then merely directed them to their—"

"A likely story." Mistress Holdaway ushered Dora, a hospital maid conveniently waiting at her elbow, forward. "You take Miss Sayer's place," she told the maid, who looked terrified and even more out of place than Rose had felt. Poor Dora wore her regular black dress with a white collar. At least Rose had been able to dress in something else.

"Miss Sayer," Mistress Holdaway went on, looking oddly victorious, "you will come to my office, where we will discuss your future."

Rose looked frantically at Dora, then at the last spot she'd seen Oliver inside the hall, then at the headmistress. What could she have done to avoid violating the terms of her contract? What could she do now to avoid being sent away to who knew where, away from Oliver?

"Rose," Mistress Holdaway snapped, no longer using the more respectful *Miss Sayer*. "I said, *come*." She whirled about and strode away, clearly expecting Rose to follow.

She did, but had to nearly run to keep up in a dress and slippers not meant for such activity. "Mistress Holdaway," Rose called when they'd reached a shadowy corridor away from the concert hall and out of earshot of the throng of guests waiting to enter. "I didn't know Mr. Withey was coming tonight. Please, you must believe me. I did only what you asked of me."

The woman stopped as if on a hinge, spinning about to face Rose. "What you did was violate our agreement."

"What should I have done, snubbed a concert guest? Offended him?" Rose's question was sincere. *What* could she have possibly done differently? She'd been given an assignment, one that she was clearly unable to fulfill without the risk of seeing or having to speak with Oliver. No one could reasonably expect such a thing or would view tonight's brief encounter as a violation of her contract. She'd done nothing untoward, nothing intentional.

"You impudent child," Mistress Holdaway said, venom dripping from her voice. "How *dare* you speak to me in such a fashion?" She turned on her heel and marched the rest of the way to her office.

Rose followed, frustration and hurt burning through her chest. Barring her leaving London—perhaps England—how could Mistress Holdaway, Mr. Finnegan, or the Witheys expect a guarantee that she'd never see Oliver under any circumstances, even accidental ones?

That's when a realization struck Rose with the force of a blow. Her steps came up short, and her hand went to her middle as a sinking feeling twisted inside her. Tonight's "violation" of her agreement was no accident. The Witheys, coordinating with Mistress Holdaway, had ensured that she and Oliver would come into contact that very night—forcing a violation of the contract to happen.

Now all parties who wanted to be rid of her could justify sending her away to India. Mistress Holdaway and Mr. Finnegan would be certain that the hospital would receive the full donation, and the Witheys would ensure that she and Oliver would be separated by an ocean and a continent.

A simple, devious plan to keep them apart.

Rose stood in the middle of the corridor, refusing to continue to the headmistress's office, where, no doubt, a lecture fit for a six-year-old foundling would take place. But Rose was a woman now, and a member of the faculty, if only just. She'd never let the idea of outright disobedience or rebellion enter her head, not for her entire life. The fear of punishment had always been plenty to dissuade the slightest thought of misbehaving. All that had changed tonight.

What could Mistress Holdaway—or anyone else, for that matter—do to hurt her more now? She was about to be sent away against her will. She couldn't refuse unless she wanted to doom herself to a life in the workhouse, and unless she wanted to live with the guilt of knowing that dozens of foundlings who could have been helped were not because of her.

When her footsteps didn't continue, Mistress Holdaway turned about impatiently. "Rose, come." In words and tone, she might as well have been giving the command to a dog.

"No," Rose said. "I am retiring to my quarters. Good night." She bobbed a slight curtsy, making sure to keep her face still and calm, then turned down another hall, one from which she could reach the other side of the hospital. She wanted to run, to cry, to scream, but she schooled everything about herself, walking with a straight posture and her head up and chin high, making sure her steps were even and unhurried.

Behind her, Mistress Holdaway called, "I expect to see you in my office first thing in the morning."

Rose's steps slowed, and she turned around deliberately, determined to maintain some control over the situation and to ensure along the way that she could meet with the old woman in the morning as well. "I'll report to your office at ten o'clock."

"Nine."

"I'll be there at nine-thirty." Rose turned on her heel and walked off, head high, hoping her trembling joints weren't visible at a distance, hoping that thirty minutes would be sufficient time to speak with the old woman, if she appeared at all. What if she came late, and Rose wasn't able to talk with her after all? Rose would never know about her past or her parents—where she came from or who she was.

Even with such a tumult of emotions inside her, Rose didn't dare walk faster, not even after turning a corner, where she couldn't be seen from the office hallway. She did, however, allow herself to breathe a little deeper, and tears built up behind her eyes, threatening to fall. She covered her mouth with one hand to muffle any cries that might escape.

Rose lowered her hand and returned to her attitude of calm confidence, now slipping a hand into her skirt pocket, where she could rub her room key between her forefinger and thumb, a movement that she found soothing. Her fingers first touched something else in her pocket—a hard object smaller than her key, not of metal: the button, or whatever it was, that the old woman had given her. Rose wrapped her fingers about the shape: asymmetrical and entirely smooth.

What was it made of, ivory? Bone? Some type of pale, polished wood?

When she reached her room, she released the object long enough to withdraw the key and let herself into her room. Once inside, she closed and locked the door, then lit a lamp. By the warm, golden light, Rose inspected the object. The two holes that went all the way through in the center seemed to confirm that this was indeed a button.

What was it made of, though? What was its origin? Studying it only brought more questions to mind.

She retired to bed shortly after, exhausted in both body and spirit. In her nightclothes, with her hair taken down and then plaited into a long braid, she lay her head on her pillow, drew up her covers, and reached to the night table to extinguish the lamp. Her eyes landed on the button once more. And for a reason even she could not explain, she picked it up and clutched it in her palm as she fell asleep, holding it close, as if it were a talisman that might solve her troubles and bring Oliver back into her life for good.

Eight

AFTER THE CONCERT, Oliver looked for Rose but didn't find her. She'd likely been given another assignment, or he'd simply missed her due to the throng. Not that he would have been able to manage an opportunity to speak to her with two sets of parents hovering, but he'd hoped to at least catch her eye. Send her a message of love and strength across the room.

The evening's performances were lovely. Thanks to having an understanding companion like Miss Morgan, who wasn't looking to be courted by him, and the brief encounter with Rose, he enjoyed the evening far more than he'd anticipated.

He and Miss Morgan walked back to the Withey townhouse as before, with his parents ahead of them and her parents behind them, trailing enough of a distance away to allow for quiet conversation without them hearing, but close enough to provide proper chaperoning. The streetlamps were glowing, and a cold nip had entered the nighttime air.

When they'd escaped the immediate press of the crowd leaving the concert hall, and he was certain that their parents were far enough away to not hear, he returned their conversation to where they'd left off, grateful he'd found an ally, if in an unlikely place.

"Tell me about the gentleman who has captured your heart."

The request landed as he'd hoped, for her eyes lit up, and her lips curved into a thoughtful smile. "He's wonderful," Miss Morgan said. "And I don't say that as some silly young girl who has nothing but cotton in her head and who is taken by every handsome face she sees."

"Though he *is* handsome, I assume?"

"Most definitely," she said. "Very handsome."

"What does he do?"

"He's a . . . well, he's a businessman, of sorts."

"In a respectable occupation?" Oliver said. "Your parents shouldn't object too strongly to that unless he's a smuggler or something equally knavish." He expected a chuckle, but she let out a heavy breath.

"They'd prefer he have no occupation."

Naturally, though after two Seasons, they'd clearly given up hope for their daughter even marrying old money, settling for Oliver and the new Withey fortune.

"Under the circumstances of having a *stubborn* daughter—or so they call me—they'd prefer, many times over, a man with new money to one with a lowly occupation."

Oliver murmured in understanding. He knew the customs and attitudes of the wealthy, but that didn't mean he'd adopted them or truly understood families who'd had land and wealth for generations. If her parents had pinned their hopes on him, a man with money newer than his favorite coat, they must be desperate for her to wed.

"What is his profession, then? A solicitor? Physician?"

"Nothing nearly as grand as that," Miss Morgan said, her tone growing sadder by the word. "He's a simple . . . baker. He owns his own bakery in Chelsea."

Which explained how a young lady from a family of means had met the man in the first place. A baker, even one who owned his own shop, would be a significant step down.

The Morgan family had been landed gentry for centuries, so calling Miss Morgan's love a *step down* didn't capture the distance, which could better be described as the Morgans living high atop a mountain, and the only way to reach the place in society where bakers existed was to jump off the edge of a cliff. Her parents likely viewed a marriage between their daughter and such a man as little better than actually jumping off a cliff.

"We're in similar positions, you and I," Oliver said, "though to be honest, I'm surprised your parents approve of me and my family." She nodded at that, and he was glad he didn't have to verbalize the details.

"Two Seasons, two rejected proposals—I'm hopeless in their eyes. They're more than a little worried about my future, and they've decided that instead of seeking the hand of an MP or a gentleman with a title, I'd be better served to simply find a way to be settled at least somewhat respectably and comfortably."

"And my family is *somewhat* respectable, at least when my mother isn't having one of her fits." He laughed lightly, and she joined in.

"It's all so silly, isn't it?" Miss Morgan said. "Why should it matter *when* a man and his family got money? Who's to say that the wealthy whose family lines trace back to William the Conqueror weren't simply lucky rather than inherently superior? The nobility gained their status from sheer luck, being born into the right family at the right time."

"Careful, or people will start to think you're sounding like an American, with their foolish ideas of equality."

She glanced up at him, a glint in her eye that spread to her smile until she erupted in laughter. "Those Americans may be on to something, at that."

They walked for a few steps, enjoying the fresh evening

air, which was far nicer this night than it sometimes was; the winds must have been blowing toward the Thames and sending away the foul air toward the river rather than blowing toward them and bringing the stench with it.

"My parents need no additional reason to object to my heart, but they do have one complaint that is just as insurmountable as his occupation."

"*Is* he a smuggler, then? A pirate? A criminal?" Oliver laughed at his own joke.

"In my parents' eyes, he might as well be. You see, he is recently come to London."

"Is he French?" Some English had a long memory of the wars between the countries and had fostered a lingering prejudice.

Miss Morgan gave him a pointed look. "His name is Jon *O'Leary.*"

"I see."

"They speak of my love as if he is a stray dog."

"That's *slightly* better than some of the descriptions of I've heard from locals about the Irish."

"My father adds *rabid.*"

"I stand corrected." Oliver shook his head. "And I am so sorry."

They neared the Withey home, slowing their pace a bit. His parents already awaited the rest of the group on the steps, and Miss Morgan's parents would soon catch up from behind. Miss Morgan's hand tightened slightly on his arm; Oliver sensed that she was as eager to go inside for an evening with their parents as he was, which was not at all.

"Why should one's birth be such an important element in matching young people?" Miss Morgan said suddenly—and quietly. "Why can't we decide for ourselves who we want to spend our lives with?"

Oliver's parents faced the door and climbed the steps. The door opened as if on cue, revealing Mr. Arnold to greet the three couples. Oliver and Miss Morgan stood at the base of the stairs to allow their parents to enter first. The Morgans passed by, and Mr. Arnold gestured toward the staircase inside. "Mrs. Taylor will lead you to the drawing room," he said, bowing slightly.

Mr. and Mrs. Withey stood on the bottom step and moved to enter next. As Oliver's mother moved to go inside, she paused and leaned close, whispering into his ear. "You saw Rose for the last time tonight."

"I—what?" he said in alarm.

His mother gave him a smug look of victory. After leaving her coat and hat with Mr. Arnold, she followed the Morgans up to the drawing room. Oliver and Miss Morgan hung back for a moment, and only after Mr. Arnold cleared his throat did they go inside, where the butler took their things, including Miss Morgan's wrap. The two of them walked to the base of the wooden staircase, where they eyed each other in uneasy silence.

Oliver leaned in to speak, not wanting anyone in the drawing room upstairs to hear, and knowing how well sound traveled in the townhouse. "Did you hear what my mother said outside?"

Miss Morgan shook her head, brows drawn together. "What?" she whispered.

"She'll send Rose away because I saw her tonight."

"No," Miss Morgan replied with dismay. "But it wasn't intentional. You didn't plan to see her. Surely, she must see that—"

"*She* planned the meeting, somehow, and now she, my father, and the hospital will use tonight's events as an excuse to send her away where I'll be unable to find her."

Miss Morgan reached for his arm and held it firmly. "We *can't* let that happen."

"We?" Oliver repeated.

"I'll do whatever I can to ensure that you get to be with Rose. First thing in the morning, I will take a carriage to the Foundling Hospital and speak with the headmistress. I'll pretend to be looking for a servant and ask about hiring Rose specifically. I can say that I saw her at the concert and am interested in engaging her services."

"You'd do that?" Oliver asked, stunned.

"Do you think that would work?" Miss Morgan said, not answering his question. "They might very well send her elsewhere, anyway, especially if a contract is already signed, but I might be able to learn who has hired her and where she's going."

Oliver's eyes stung at the corners—here was a woman who understood him and wanted to help. His one friend in this whole mess. "Thank you," he said, his voice suddenly husky. "I don't know that I can return the favor regarding you and Jon, but I'll try."

"I suppose we must we go upstairs," Miss Morgan said. She looked at him. "Could we stay downstairs and sit in the dining room for a chat with the curtain open and a servant or two in the room for propriety? We could use the time to work out our plans for tomorrow and beyond."

"As tempting as that sounds, we'd better go up." He didn't list the reasons, but they included the fact that he didn't trust any of the servants to keep his secrets, only those of his parents. Mr. Arnold, Mrs. Taylor, or even Sally might well relay every word to his mother at the first opportunity.

Miss Morgan leaned in and grinned, still whispering. "We may well find out more information upstairs, especially if we put on a show of being desperately interested in each other."

Oliver smiled back at that. His mother would be liable to chatter on about all kinds of things if she thought he and Miss Morgan were absorbed in flirtation. Mrs. Withey hadn't exactly been known to possess a way to stop her mouth from spilling all manner of words.

"As they say," Miss Morgan went on, "knowledge is power, and if we pretend we're powerless, we may well end up with the upper hand."

Oliver held out his elbow to her, and she took it once more. "I like the way you think."

"I feel as if we're partners in crime," Miss Morgan said under her breath as they took the first step.

"Oh, I suspect that by the time this is all over, we will be partners in preventing one."

Nine

SUNLIGHT BROKE THROUGH Rose's small window, filtering through the yellowish-gray film of coal smoke that coated the glass. She'd been awake for some time already, her nerves too frayed over the coming morning and how it would utterly change her life. Likely for worse—though she hoped for the better, she couldn't imagine how that might happen.

With a thin wrap around her shoulders, she peered through her window—*her* window. It hadn't a particularly nice view. The vantage let her see lines of narrow chimneys, seemingly stacked row upon row as the buildings extended into the distance. But it was the first view of any sort she'd been able to call her own. For how much longer? Likely for only a matter of days. What would her view be like next time she had her own window?

She glanced at the clock on her dresser and determined that she'd waited long enough to ready herself for the day. As she did, she felt as if she were donning armor in preparation for a battle, the type of which she had only the vaguest ideas about.

Ten minutes before nine, having skipped breakfast altogether due to a nervous stomach, she arrived at the spot where she'd met the old woman the night before.

Would that I could make myself invisible to those at the hospital, she thought, hoping she wouldn't be seen by Mistress

296

Holdaway, Mr. Finnegan, or anyone else who might mention her whereabouts to either of them. As soon as the mysterious woman appeared, Rose would take her elsewhere, so with any luck, they wouldn't be spotted by anyone.

When Rose arrived at the bench, the church bell hadn't rung yet, which meant the hour had not yet arrived. The woman was nowhere to be seen, so Rose sat on the bench as she had the night before and tried to be patient. After what felt like an eternity, the heavy brass *dong-dong* came from the chapel bell. Each of the nine tolls made her jumpy. She looked about, as if the sound would summon the elderly woman by some kind of magic.

But by the last toll, there was still no sign of her. Had she been a figment of Rose's imagination? What if the woman had been right about the end of her life coming soon, and she'd expired during the night? What if she'd fallen and hurt herself?

Will I never know who I am and where I came from?

Rose willed herself to wait, praying with her whole soul that the woman would appear, all the while clutching the strange, cream-colored button enclosed inside her fist.

A sound behind her made Rose flinch and look over her shoulder, her stomach jumping into her throat, fearing that Mistress Holdaway had found her. But it was only a young boy who ran along the courtyard in pursuit of a ball. She took a breath of relief and turned around, only to see the old woman approaching, taking slow steps with a cane.

"You came," she said.

The old woman nodded, saying nothing at first. As she drew closer, Rose noted her limbs shaking, so she hopped to her feet and helped the kind woman to the bench. Once seated, the woman gave her a smile. "Thank you, sweet girl."

"My pleasure," Rose said, retaking her seat. A thousand

questions seemed ready to burst from her, but she held back, sensing that her new friend needed a chance to rest and catch her breath before unloading her burden.

Please, Rose prayed, *let her tell me all before we're interrupted.*

As she waited, her fingers played with the button, which slipped from her hand onto the cobbled courtyard. She retrieved the button and sat beside the woman, then held out the object. "What is this?" she asked. "I mean, I know it's a button of some sort, but what is it made of? I don't think it's ivory, but it's not wood, either. Does it have anything to do with who I am or where I came from?"

The woman smiled at that. "Very perceptive of you. That, my dear, is carved from a reindeer antler."

Rose's mouth opened slightly and stayed that way for a moment as surprise washed over her. "I don't under—pardon me?"

"Let's start where we should have begun last night. You introduced yourself as Rose, but I didn't tell you my name. It's Minnie. Minnie Vale."

"A pleasure to meet you, Mrs. Vale."

"Mrs. Vale was my mother, may she rest in peace. Please call me Minnie." She shrugged slightly. "I've always been a servant. Minnie suits me just fine."

"Very well . . . Minnie." Using a given name with someone so much her elder felt odd to Rose. She had a multitude of questions, though, so she brushed the lesser-important ones, such as given versus family names, to the side in favor of those that mattered most to her. "You said that you knew my parents." As soon as the words were said, Rose's mouth dried up with worry, as if she were awaiting the pronouncement of a sentence.

"Yes, I did," Minnie said. "I was your mother's maid for many years."

"Who was she? I was told she died shortly after I was born, but is she still alive? Why did she send me away?" Each question felt driven to escape her lips, the answers an inch away after she'd spent a lifetime wondering, never knowing, and a million more questions simmered beneath the surface, waiting to erupt.

"Your mother was a fine lady. She died when you were only a few weeks old. Caught pneumonia, she did." Minnie's face tightened around her eyes, and her lower lip trembled with emotion, as if the events she spoke of were still new. She shook her head, which freed a tear to tumble down her cheek. She wiped it away. "I apologize for crying."

"You loved my mother," Rose said. "Didn't you?"

"I did, very much. As if she were my own daughter."

"What was her name?"

"Eleanor. Eleanor Truelock. Her family name goes back generations, but as time went on, numbers shrank, and when your mother was born, her parents were determined that she would marry into nobility to bring the family's fortunes and status back to where they believed they belonged."

"Was she of the nobility, then?" The idea that she might carry noble blood made her heart beat faster. Such information might be enough to convince the Witheys that she was their son's equal. Perhaps. If Minnie had evidence. But being abandoned as an infant and raised in the Foundling Hospital didn't exactly a fine reputation make. A child born to a noble woman wasn't necessarily noble if she entered the world illegitimately.

"No, your mother was not nobility," Minnie said. "But the family had a large estate with many tenants."

"And my father? Was *he* noble?" Rose had a feeling the answer simply had to be no—her mother had likely fallen in love with someone her parents deemed unfit, and that man was likely her father, whoever he'd been.

Minnie made an inscrutable noise. "Was he nobility?" she said thoughtfully. "I suppose that depends on one's definition of the word."

Whatever in the world did *that* mean?

Before Rose could ask for clarification, the hospital door opened. Mistress Holdaway appeared, holding the door ajar with one arm and putting the other fist on her hip. "Rose! I believe you and I were to have a conference first thing this morning?"

Rose checked her little pocket watch, stunned to see that the minutes had ticked by shockingly fast; it was indeed three minutes to nine-thirty, and Mistress Holdaway was nothing if not prompt. But Rose had barely begun to learn about her past, and if she went inside now, would she be leaving the truth behind her forever? Would Minnie be alive to return another day? Would Rose herself be on a ship bound for India by morning?

"I'm coming with you," Minnie said suddenly, breaking into Rose's worried musings. The elderly woman shakily pushed herself to a standing position. "Let's go inside. I have a word or two to say to Flora."

Rose felt her eyes go wide. "You know Mistress Holdaway?"

"She is the one who took you when I brought you to the hospital. She knows . . . well, she knows more than almost anyone. She looks very much as she did near twenty years ago. I'd remember that nose anywhere." Her rounded back seemed to straighten with a confidence she lacked the night before. The sight gave Rose a little courage, too.

"Shall we?" Rose asked. She held out her arm so Minnie could use it for support, and the two made their way— shuffling and slowly—to the hospital door and thence to the headmistress's office.

When they entered, they found a young woman already inside. She appeared to be about Rose's age, wearing a beautiful pale-green dress that looked to be made of silk. She was familiar, though Rose couldn't quite determine why.

Mistress Holdaway gestured toward the young woman. "This is Miss Morgan. She's interested in hiring a domestic servant, and she specifically requested you."

"You came highly recommended by a friend," Miss Morgan said.

And then understanding dawned on Rose—this was Oliver's companion from the concert. Was he here now, at the hospital? Was this woman envious of Rose? What other reason could someone of Miss Morgan's caliber have to come here, of all places, to look for hired help?

This woman might be her future employer, so Rose determined to be pleasant and kind. "Where do you live, Miss Morgan?" she asked, hoping her voice sounded innocent. Anything closer than India would be welcome.

"Not far from London," she replied.

"How lovely," Rose said.

Miss Morgan didn't appear envious or irritated or anything but friendly and kind toward Rose. Her smile seemed to say that she and Rose were friends who shared a secret. Did they? Would she hire Rose, and invite Oliver to visit, so they could see each other during their year apart?

"Unfortunately," Mistress Holdaway interjected, "another family has already requested your services, and they will be paying handsomely for the opportunity—sponsoring the hospital and many poor little foundlings like you once were."

The hopes that had begun to take flight inside Rose now crashed to the ground in a heap.

"Flora, I have something that must be said." Minnie piped up.

The sound of her given name made Mistress Holdaway's head come around and mouth open slightly, like a fish. She clearly wasn't used to being spoken to in such a manner. Rose tried to hold back a smile, and she caught Miss Morgan doing the same. Their eyes met, and they both had to cover their mouths to hide their laughs.

"I brought Rose here when she was but a babe," Minnie said. She marched across the room, pulled up a chair, and plopped herself into it in a manner that seemed to say, *I am not moving until you listen to all I have to say.*

"I remember," Mistress Holdaway said. "That is not an evening I am likely to forget."

"Then you will likely remember that I believed her to be an orphan."

Believed to be? Shock flooded Rose. *Might I have family?*

"What do you mean by that?" Mistress Holdaway said, sounding aggravated. "You said you were with her mother when she passed."

"I was," Minnie said. Her eyes grew glassy. "I held her hand between my own as life left it and her fingers grew cold."

All humor had drained from Rose's body. Her mother was really dead. But what else would Minnie reveal? The past had always seemed like a translucent unreality, but now it had a few facts, structure. And she needed more.

"Why are you here?" Mistress Holdaway demanded of Minnie.

"I've come to learn that she has living family on her father's side."

Rose's heart nearly leapt from her chest. "My father is alive? Who is he? Why did—"

Minnie cut her off with a raised hand. For a feeble, sick old woman, she'd found a formidable strength in speaking a truth she'd been carrying for two decades. "I am unsure about your father, but I know you have family on his side that is yet living—and looking for you."

A hand flew to Rose's mouth. She sat back in her chair as the room seemed to spin.

"He was away, fighting during the Crimean War in Avaria, where many died. My lady and I were in a foreign land. Between us, we knew only a few words of a strange language. After she passed, everyone around me mourned the death of the babe's father. Not knowing what else to do, but believing that my lady would want her child to be raised in England with her family, I brought her back."

This time Rose interjected. "Were my English grandparents dead by then?" That would explain why Minnie had brought her here.

"They were alive and well," Minnie said sadly. "The Truelocks did not believe that you were your mother's. They believed you were mine, and that I was trying to hide my own misdeeds by sullying their daughter's memory. I should have known that was how they'd respond. After all, they'd disowned Eleanor by then. I was foolish to think that you would be better off returning to England."

Rose's mind spun with so many threads that she could hardly keep track of them, let alone of the tapestry that Minnie seemed to be weaving with them. Much of Europe had dealings in the Crimean War, so that part wasn't confusing, per se, but nothing else was making sense. "I don't understand," she said. "Where were you when my mother passed? That is to say, in what country?"

Turning away from Mistress Holdaway and fully facing Rose, Minnie told more. "Let me begin the story properly. Your mother was the apple of her father's eye. He had a plan for how he believed her life should go. Marrying a university student from a foreign land was not something he wanted nor could have imagined. But when Eleanor first saw Peter . . ." Minnie smiled softly. "She was never the same again."

"Peter," Rose repeated. "That does not sound like a foreign name."

"That's because *Peter* was simpler for the English to say. His name was really Petri."

"Where is that name from?" Rose asked, nearly begging.

"One could consider him any one of three different nationalities: Russian, Swedish, or Finnish."

"I don't understand." Three words, but they spoke volumes—volumes that Rose prayed Minnie would explain.

"The Finnish people were ruled by the Swedish for centuries, and the language is still spoken by the upper class. He spoke both, actually. Russia controls the Finnish people now. They are part of a Grand Duchy, and . . ."

When her voice trailed off, Rose nearly pounced to hear more. She could scarcely breathe. She had to stand to inhale and then move about, needing to expel some of the extra energy trying to burst from her. "I'm half Finnish?"

"Your father came from an influential Finnish house, and your father and his brother shared the inheritance."

Mistress Holdaway scoffed form her seat across the table. "A likely story."

"That is precisely what the Truelocks said when I brought Rose to them. They refused to take Rose in. At the time, I truly thought that bringing you back to England was the right thing to do. I assumed that any inheritance you might have received would go to Petri's brother because you were not a son. I've recently learned that the laws are very different over there." She shook her head with frustration at herself. "I should have suspected as much, as your parents fled to Helsinki to marry— eloping within the British realm would have been disastrous, but not there."

Rose understood that concept all too well; even when she'd suggested elopement to Oliver, she'd known that doing so would be foolish.

"At the very least, I should have considered that your Finnish family would want to care for you and know you. They knew you were born within the bonds of matrimony and were not a source of shame." Minnie lowered her gaze to her lap and swallowed. When she spoke, her voice shook. "I regret so many things. That I didn't try harder to learn the laws and language of the Grand Duchy. That I didn't leave you with your Finnish family. You must believe that at the time, I could not bear to do so after my lady's passing. But then, back in England, I wish I'd been able to care for you, but I could scarcely feed and clothe myself. When your English family rejected you, not believing that you were their blood, or that you were born legitimate, I brought you here. By then, I yearned to return you to your father's family but lacked the means. I'm so, so sorry, Rose—or rather, Ruusu."

Rose's head came around. "What?"

"That's your birth name. It means *rose*. In fact, I insisted that you be named Rose." She looked pointedly at Mistress Holdaway. "Isn't that so?"

"I wouldn't recall," the headmistress said, though whether she spoke the truth, Rose could not tell.

Minnie leaned forward. "Flora, you told me that you'd never before allowed someone to name a foundling, and you'd never allow it again. I'm sure you remember *that*."

Mistress Holdaway's left eye twitched. She folded her arms tightly and lifted her chin. Minnie pressed on. "Open her file, Flora. Let me prove to you that I am telling you the truth. Break the seal and let us all see the token."

"I can't do that without proper approval," the headmistress said, but her voice wavered slightly, and Rose marveled at the sudden paleness of her face.

"The guardian who delivered the child gives you the authority. *I* am the one who brought her here. *I* can describe the token. It is an embroidered family crest—the Brunberg family crest."

"Enough of this foolishness," the headmistress said. "Miss Vale, you admit that you are not Miss Sayer's blood relation. Therefore, you lack the authority to insist upon anything regarding her file. Miss Sayer, you are excused. I have business to discuss with Miss Morgan, and a deep apology to make to her for her having to endure this unfortunate outburst."

Minnie placed the flat of her hand on the desk with force. "I'm telling you to get the file and open the token. You will find a golden lion wielding a shield and a sword against a blue background."

The headmistress laid her clasped hands on top of the desk. "And I am telling you that you are unwelcome on these premises. I must insist you leave. Now." She turned her head and looked squarely at Rose. "Miss Sayer, you've disgraced yourself, first by breaking your word regarding Mr. Withey at the concert on the very day you promised to not see him, and you behaved abominably again this morning by creating such a scene, both outside on the grounds and now here in my office. You are no longer welcome here. I must insist that you return to your quarters at once. I will determine our next steps with what to do with you later. You will wait to be summoned."

Minnie's face had turned red with anger, and Rose sat there bewildered, unable to believe that they'd come so far yet fallen short. Mistress Holdaway could have Minnie and Rose both carried away by the constable if she wished, and neither of them had the slightest bit of influence or power to prevent it.

A chair scratched against the floor, and Miss Morgan stood suddenly. She spoke for the first time in several minutes. "I truly am shocked and appalled, but not by what I've seen and heard from Miss Vale and Miss Sayer. I am appalled by *your* behavior, Mistress Holdaway, and if you do not fetch the unopened file belonging to Rose, to be opened in this room, under the watchful eyes of all present, I will ensure that your appalling behavior is known throughout London. I will personally contact the newspapers, who, I am quite sure, will be eager for such a story. When the news spreads, the Withey family will recall their endowment, and you will have single-handedly destroyed the reputation of this august institution through your unethical and immoral leadership."

Mistress Holdaway's eyes narrowed. "You wouldn't."

"Wouldn't I?" Miss Morgan said with a tilt to her head. "I advise you not to underestimate me, not if you hope to have a comfortable retirement or any speck of reputation left after today."

If possible, the headmistress's face paled even further. "I'll go get the file." She seemed to nearly hop to her feet and scurried out the door.

Miss Morgan let out a breath of irritation and sat back down. "That woman . . ."

"Thank you," Rose said. "I've always wanted to speak my mind to her, but I've never dared."

"I was lucky to be born into a position of influence," Miss Morgan said. "Using it for the good of those who did not have the same fortune is the least I can do."

Minnie shook her head, looking impressed. "It was still a mighty fine thing to see."

"And I've learned more about myself in the last ten minutes than over the rest of my life, combined. I'm half Finnish." A realization came over Rose. She reached into her pocket and pulled out the button. "Reindeer live in Finland, don't they?"

"Yes, and you would love it there," Minnie said. "Lush forests and lakes. Berries and mushrooms you can pick and eat straight from the land."

Awe settled on Rose's shoulders. Perhaps that was why she was drawn to that painting on the wall with the forest, lake, and reindeer. It looked just as Minnie had described. The painting had called to Rose as if beckoning her home. Now she knew why.

"That button came from one of your father's coats. I believe he hunted the reindeer himself," Minnie explained as Rose turned the button in her hand, studying the shape once more. "And . . . I've learned that your father might not have died in the war."

"I'm not an orphan?"

"Possibly. I'm unsure," Minnie said. "All I know for certain is that he wasn't listed among the dead from the battle he was thought to have died in. You'll have to go find out."

Rose's eyes filled with tears, so though she tried to take in every detail of the carved antler button, she could scarcely see it. Her father's hands had formed the button. Might he still be living, and might she one day know the touch of those hands?

"Rose," Minnie said.

"Yes?" She glanced up.

"You are half Finnish, but there is more." A thick silence followed, one filled with energy as everyone present awaited the next words. "The Brunberg house is of the Finnish nobility." She licked her lips and then said, "Rose, you're a countess."

Ten

OLIVER STOOD AT the drawing room window, looking at the city street below for any sign of Miss Morgan's—victorious, he hoped—return. His gaze was locked on one side of the street. The bustle—carriages clopping both directions, people hurrying about—went unnoticed. All he cared about was spotting Miss Morgan as she returned to the townhouse with news of Rose. His very future hung in the balance. Would Miss Morgan be able to learn who'd offered to employ Rose and where they would take her? That was the most he dared think would happen, and it would be a success of a sort. He'd be able to write to Rose through his solicitor's office. An ideal situation would mean the hospital accepting Miss Morgan's offer to hire Rose as her own lady's maid. The salary to be paid by Oliver, though no one need know that.

Each tick of the grandfather clock grated on his nerves. He was already on tenterhooks, and each tick made the feeling worse. Miss Morgan had been gone nearly an hour. Even accounting for ten minutes of walking each way, the intervening time was more than enough for the conference to have been completed. Was a longer meeting a good sign for their cause, or a portent of doom?

Would that he could see into the offices at the hospital or hear what was being said and done there. Would that he knew whether he'd be able to see his beloved Rose at the Morgan household, whether exchanging letters would have to suffice, or whether—God forbid—he and Rose would be entirely cut off from each other for the span of a year, if not for life.

His mother had come into the drawing room, demanding that he stop moping about.

"I'm not moping, Mother," Oliver told her. "I'm waiting for Miss Morgan's visit."

"That is wonderful news," his mother said. "I'll tell cook to make tarts for tea." She hurried off before Oliver could mention that Rose was the one who made the family's favorite tarts.

She wasn't the only interruption. Mr. Arnold and Mrs. Taylor had each suggested he come down to the dining room for some nourishment. His stomach rolled as if he were on a ship; food would not help the situation, and his condition wouldn't resolve until he knew his and Rose's fate.

The sound of the brass knocker on the front door made him startle. Who was there? He hadn't seen Miss Morgan or Rose approach and hadn't noted anyone else approaching the townhouse, either. Oliver kept his eyes on the street but lent his ear to the entryway on the main floor, where Mr. Arnold's footfalls sounded as he went to answer the door.

A click as the door unlocked, a deep groan of the hinges as they whined open, and then someone with a high, quiet voice spoke. "I have a message for Mr. Oliver Withey." The visitor sounded like a mere child, which explained how he hadn't noticed anyone. He certainly hadn't been looking for a child.

"I'm afraid Mr. Withey is indisposed at the moment," Mr. Arnold said.

Under other circumstances, Oliver would have appreciated Mr. Arnold's attempts at giving him the privacy he'd requested. The butler, however, did not know *why* Oliver had withdrawn from the family. Something told him that the child had come from the hospital, so Oliver hurried out to the narrow staircase and nearly flew down the steps, which creaked in protest as he thundered down.

"Arnold, stop!"

The butler was closing the door on a young boy standing outside, but paused at Oliver's interjection. He looked back, clearly bemused. "Mr. Withey?"

"I'd like to receive the message this young . . . person . . . has come to deliver." He hadn't seen whether it was a boy or girl.

Looking no less confused, Mr. Arnold nodded with a slight bow. "As you wish, Mr. Withey." He opened the door and made his leave. Standing on the step outside was a young boy.

"Have you come from the Foundling Hospital?" Oliver asked anxiously.

"I have," the boy said, looking intimidated as he clutched a folded paper in his trembling hands. The boy's uniform did indeed hearken to that of a military one, as Rose had described—a tunic and pants and a shirt with a collar. Seeing one now, Oliver's heart ached. Did this boy have a future he would be able to choose? Was he fated to join the military, with no other options?

Gesturing, Oliver asked, "Is that message for me?"

The boy looked at the paper held protectively against his chest. "Are ye Mr. Withey? Mr. *Oliver* Withey? I was told to give it to none else, not to the elder Mr. Withey or to Mr. Oliver's mother or anyone else."

"Mr. Oliver Withey at your service." He made a formal bow.

The corners of the boy's mouth twitched at that; he was clearly pleased by being treated like an adult and an equal, something that almost assuredly had never happened before. In a quick motion, he held out the note. "Here. I'm to stay while you read it."

Oliver stepped outside and pulled the door closed behind him to provide privacy from the household. He sat on the top step and gestured for the boy to do the same. Time to open the note, but now *his* hands trembled slightly.

"It's important news, I suppose," the boy said. Sitting beside Oliver, he seemed even smaller and younger.

"Indeed," Oliver said. "What's your name?"

"Matthias," the boy offered. "That's my foundling name, anyway. I don't know my real one." He spoke so matter-of-factly, which made Oliver ache for the child.

"Matthias," Oliver repeated as he unfolded the note and read the words in pretty script.

All is well. Come to the hospital at once. —PM

For a moment, Oliver forgot that Miss Morgan's given name was Priscilla. PM was Priscilla Morgan. "It appears that I am going to the hospital."

"I'll show you the way," Matthias said, hopping to his feet.

"Then let's go." If they happened upon a carriage for hire as they went, all the better, but walking would be faster than waiting for a family carriage to be made ready.

They walked, then half-ran, the entire way. When they reached the hospital, Rose and Miss Morgan stood outside, the latter's maid hanging back, but an elderly woman he did not recognize was with Rose and Miss Morgan. He saw no sign of the headmaster or headmistress. The women glowed in the midmorning light, the sun glinting off their hair, their eyes sparkling with what could only be described as joy.

The news must be good, then. Relief washed through Oliver as he rushed over.

"What's happened?" he asked between breaths. He slipped Matthias a couple of coins, and the boy grinned his thanks before running back into the hospital.

"Good news, then?" came another voice—a man approaching from the other direction. Miss Morgan's face lit up, and then she whirled about and ran to meet the man. She took his arm, wrapping both of hers around it, and dragged him to the rest of the group by the elbow.

She quickly made introductions—this was indeed her beloved Jon O'Leary—then turned to her love. "Dearest, what would you think about setting up a new bakery in another country?"

Jon cocked his head. "I'd say I've done it afore, and I can do it again. What do ye have in mind, lass? Going to America?" He didn't know what the women knew or were scheming any more than Oliver did, and that fact gave the two men something in common, acknowledged by a glance and smile between them.

Rose stepped close to Oliver, and she took his arm, practically hugging it. She gazed up at him, and the sight of her love and happiness made his heart flip. "Your parents no longer have any reason to object to our union."

Oliver looked to Jon as if he might have a clue, but of course, he didn't, and indicated as much with a shrug. "I don't understand," Oliver said.

"Minnie here was lady's maid to my mother." Rose stepped to the side and opened an arm to the old woman. The two hugged. "She came and told us everything. She identified my token."

Oliver was still unsure of what was happening. Oh, how he wanted to hope. "Tell me more."

"I was *not* illegitimate. I was born to married parents who were deeply in love. They met in England, but when her family rejected the match, they fled and married elsewhere—and no, not in an elopement." She added that when Oliver's face must have registered alarm. "My parents have both passed on, so I am indeed an orphan. But . . . I have family."

"That's wonderful!"

"They live in Finland."

"In—" Oliver felt his jaw open in surprise. "How—"

"*And,*" Rose continued, her eyes sparkling with excitement, "I am a *countess.*"

"A—" Oliver nearly choked on his tongue. "Goodness!"

"I am of the noble house of Brunberg. They have been looking for me for many years. And now, thanks to Minnie, they've found me." She stepped closer and placed her hands on his chest. He pressed a hand atop hers. "Oliver, I have a name, and a title, and money waiting for me." She slipped her hand into her pocket and withdrew a piece of embroidered fabric. "My token has at last been opened. I have been claimed. This is the Brunberg family crest."

With a portion of awe and reverence, Oliver took the token from her and gazed on the crest of gold and blue. "Amazing." Remembering his brief conversation with Matthias, he looked at Rose. "What is your . . . real name? Do you know?" He felt a twinge of sadness at the idea that his beloved wasn't actually named Rose.

A Rose by any other name, he thought, comforting himself with Shakespeare.

"My name is still Rose," she said. "But in Finnish, it's Ruusu."

"Ruusu," he repeated, stroking her hair. Blond hair was common in England, but hers was paler than most, a fact that now made even more sense—her Nordic father had passed along his characteristics.

Rose reached up and held his face between her hands.

314

"We can go to Helsinki, claim my title and my inheritance . . ." Her eyes glittered with excitement. "And we can *marry.*"

"Marry," Oliver repeated, the single word tasting like honey and joy in his mouth. He held her face between his hands, leaned in, and kissed her soundly right there on the street, caring nothing for their witnesses. Some things in life simply had to be celebrated in the moment, and this was one of them.

"I'm so happy for you," Miss Morgan said.

Oliver and Rose turned to see the other couple, happy together in this moment, but with a slight cloud above them. Their love did not have a bright future for them. Not yet, anyway.

"You'll come with us," Rose said, then, looking at Oliver for confirmation, "Won't they?"

"Absolutely," Oliver said.

Miss Morgan's face lit up. "Truly?"

"Do ye mean it?" O'Leary asked.

Oliver slipped an arm about Rose's waist and held her close, kissing her temple before saying, "We wouldn't dream of going without you both. After how much you helped bring us together, we can't possibly leave without offering the same happiness to you."

"Please say you'll come," Rose said. "We'll ensure that you're taken care of."

Jon O'Leary laughed, a deep, happy sound from his chest. "I suppose we'll be startin' a bakery in another land, just as ye said, love."

With a cry of happiness, Miss Morgan threw her arms about his neck, and they twirled about, laughing in celebration.

Oliver and Rose watched. He was so happy for them, and he could feel that happiness all the more for how complete was his own joy. He shifted so Rose faced him in his arms. "I hear that Finland is a beautiful place, if a bit cold and dark in wintertime."

Rose gazed into his eyes. "To stay warm, all I need is you."

So much had happened in a single morning, evoking powerful emotions, that Oliver stood there, grateful and overwhelmed. Rose searched his eyes. "Tell me what you're thinking. Our world has turned upside down in a moment."

He took her hands in his and raised them to his lips, then kissed her knuckles—ungloved, which would be scandalous for high society women, but was typical for how he knew Rose.

Rose, the girl he'd known as a servant but was a countess.

Rose, who easily outranked him and his parents.

"Rose—Ruusu—I would follow you to the ends of the earth." He kissed her knuckles again and smiled. "My Countess."

Annette Lyon is a *USA Today* bestselling author, a 6-time Best of State medalist for fiction in Utah, and a Whitney Award winner. She's had success as a professional editor and in newspaper, magazine, and technical writing, but her first love has always been fiction.

She's a cum laude graduate from BYU with a degree in English and is the author of over a dozen books, including the Whitney Award-winning *Band of Sisters*, a chocolate cookbook, and a grammar guide. She co-founded and was served as the original editor of the *Timeless Romance Anthology* series and continues to be a regular contributor to the collections.

She has received five publication awards from the League of Utah Writers, including the Silver Quill, and she's one of the four coauthors of the *Newport Ladies Book Club* series. Annette is represented by Heather Karpas at ICM Partners.

Find Annette online:
Blog: http://blog.AnnetteLyon.com
Twitter: @AnnetteLyon
Facebook: http://Facebook.com/AnnetteLyon
Instagram: https://www.instagram.com/annette.lyon/
Pinterest: http://Pinterest.com/AnnetteLyon
Newsletter: http://bit.ly/1n3I87y